SAPPHIRE

Tales of a Gemstone Traveler

M. VAN

42Links
Publishing

Cover design by
Jolua Specialized Design & Graphics Studio

Edited by
Book Helpline

ISBN: 978-90-827447-5-0

CHAPTER ONE

"Poison." The word resonated inside my head on repeat, and I couldn't quite fathom why. At the same time, guitars guided me into consciousness, and at the words "You're poison," I opened my eyes. The numbers on my alarm clock read six a.m. as I recognized the Alice Cooper song spewing from its small speaker. The old rock classic wasn't a song I wanted to wake up to. Maybe listen to in the car, but definitely not wake up too.

Relieved to hear the DJ announce the news, I rolled onto my back and stretched my limbs. I stared at the ceiling for a while, and as a new song began, I realized I hadn't heard a thing of what the news anchor had said.

A shrill beeping made me cringe, and I groaned at the second reminder to get out of bed. The annoying sound produced by my phone, which I had left on my desk before getting into bed last night, gave me a renewed appreciation for the Alice Cooper song.

With another groan, I rolled out of bed, killed the aggravating noise, and found my way to the bathroom without turning on any of the lights. Even though I'd lived in this ground-floor apartment a little over a year now, I'd only bought the bare essentials, so I wasn't in any danger of stomping my foot against some strayed object.

The tiny place wasn't anything special, but I didn't need much. That's why I hadn't thought twice before signing the lease. A simple apartment to call home in a small town called Hillside Creek just north of Seattle was just what I needed to get my act together. I just wished they'd told me beforehand that the place above mine had also been available because that might have severely influenced my decision. Unfortunately, what was done was done.

I shuffled across the hall and stopped to glance in the direction of the living room. A quick glimpse through the window revealed the first signs of dawn on the horizon. Not that I could see the horizon, just the light creeping inside from beyond the windowsill and the apartment building across the street.

Inside the bathroom, I flicked on the light and waited for my eyes to adjust. A cold shiver ran down my spine, reminding me that September would end soon and the time for turning on the heat was coming upon us again.

As I shoved a toothbrush into my mouth, I took a reluctant glance in the mirror. Rings under my gray eyes betrayed another fitful night, and I longed for the times when I managed to sleep seven hours straight. My hair stuck out on all sides, and even pulling a hand through it didn't flatten any of the short strands poking out. Not that long ago, my blond hair would've reached just below my shoulder blades, but around the same time that I'd decided to move here, I had also chosen to cut my hair short. I shrugged at myself in the mirror and figured a shower would take care of the wild mess on top of my head. Besides, if people were bothered by it, then they should probably look in a different direction.

After getting dressed, I pondered breakfast for a moment, but a quick look inside the nearly empty fridge made the decision easy. One of these days, I'd have to start buying real food, or at least some milk that could go with cereal. Making a mental note to stop at the grocery store after work, I headed out the door and made an effort to ease it shut with the slightest click of the lock before I took the steps down to the sidewalk.

I was still searching for my car when I heard a voice call my name. My eyes closed reflexively, and I let out a long sigh before I turned and looked up to see Sally Judd, commonly known as my mom and the reason why I couldn't find my car, standing on her balcony.

"Oh, Samantha," she said, sounding way too chirpy for this early hour, "I'm so glad I caught you." She said it as if she hadn't been waiting for me to step outside.

"Morning, Mom," I replied. It had taken me years of practice to manage a civil and polite tone as I spoke to my mom in moments like these. It wasn't that I didn't like to see or talk to her, but I preferred an order to things to make these early hours bearable. I'd rather keep the interaction with people to a bare minimum. I had enough coworkers and people to talk to at work, and I enjoyed my alone time whenever I could get it.

"Have you heard those sirens?" she said, waving a hand in the air. "They've been keeping me up all morning." I gazed up and listened. There weren't any sirens, and I hadn't heard anything.

"Probably your neighbor's TV," I replied. "Why were you glad to catch me?" She threw another hand in the air as if I could ever believe that she would have forgotten what she wanted to ask. She had probably lain in, waiting from the moment she'd heard me moving around in my apartment.

"Oh, do you mind leaving me the car today?" Mom asked. "I need to run some errands." The civil and polite tone that had taken me years to master left my voice as annoyance took over.

"Mom, you've had the car three times already this week, and it's Thursday," I said as I raised my arms. "And I'm dressed for work already."

"Oh, please, darling," she said with a sense of urgency that didn't even exist in her world anymore. She had fully embraced her retirement from working as a teacher about five years ago and since then had only done things she wanted to do. "I promised Patty to meet her today. We're supposed to go shopping. Do you need anything—oh and I've finished your laundry." There it was—the guilt trip. I couldn't get her to not do my laundry or wash my windows, but every time she needed me to do something or wanted something from me, she happened to mention those things. I raised my arms again but in defeat this time. It was too early to deal with this.

"I'll drop the keys in your mailbox," I said while I suppressed a growl and stomped back up the steps. Why she even bothered to return the keys at all baffled me.

"Thank you, dear," she replied, but before I could venture back inside to change, I heard her call my name again. "Oh, and Samantha, dear..."

Closing my eyes, I took a deep breath before I stepped back from underneath her balcony, so she could see me again.

"Yes, Mom." I felt somewhat pleased at keeping myself from sounding overly annoyed.

"You look like you've only slept for about an hour and you look even thinner than you did when you were a teenager. You should eat better," she said.

I glared up at her for a moment, unsure if I should feel touched by her concern or frustrated by the fact that she still berated me like a child. It wasn't even the berating that bothered me, but her words had an undertone that to my ears sounded a lot like, "Why don't you ever listen to me?"

It was that little undertone that had me going in precisely the opposite direction. I hadn't asked for her to move into the apartment above mine, and if I had known about the vacant flat, I would have surely searched for a different building to live in. This felt too much like living at home again. I was thirty-two years old for crying out loud. If I wanted to skip breakfast, I should be able to do so.

"I'm fine, Mom," I said and started for the door. "I'll see you later." Before she could reply, I slammed the door behind me and hurried to find my running gear.

With the heavy bassline of electronic dance music assaulting my ears and dictating my pace, I ran along Tranquil Lake Trail. It was only a little over two miles from my home to the Grain retirement home where I worked, and usually, I could run it under twenty minutes. I enjoyed running and often embraced the time spent inside my head as my feet thumped on the pavement, but today I wasn't feeling it. Somehow I felt anxious, although I had no reason to be.

The constant blaring of sirens that had reappeared after I'd left home and that seemed bent on waking up the surrounding neighborhood didn't help either. It turned out that Mom hadn't imagined the racket after all. I looked up as I heard another emergency vehicle approach, even though I couldn't see it from the trail. The sound raised the hairs on the back of my neck, and a shiver ran down my spine. Turning up the sound level on my phone, I forced myself to refocus. The path along Tranquil Lake was beautiful in its own right, but my mind-set didn't always allow me to see it.

Life had a tendency to overwhelm me, and retreating into the world that existed inside my head had become my refuge. It had even gotten to the point that I couldn't stand to be in the city anymore. Seattle had been my home for as long as I could remember, and it had become my place of work as well. I couldn't quite recall when it all started to fall apart. My father's untimely demise two years ago might have had something to do with it, although that had hit my mother harder than it had hit me. Having a father who preferred to drink himself to death instead of spending time with his family wasn't exactly something that would strengthen a bond.

It wasn't that I'd describe my dad as a bad guy, but selfish was undoubtedly a label that fitted him. I understood that life had dealt him a bad hand when the company he'd built with his own father had gone bankrupt. With all these big retailing companies sprouting from the ground, my dad's old-school hardware store never had a chance, but that had been over ten years ago. He'd never been able to pick himself up after that and instead had Mom and me pick up the pieces. Mom had never been able to let him go even after he turned into a mean old drunk. I just stopped caring. Besides, I'd been too busy building my own career.

It was only after the situation at work had turned itself upside down that I'd felt the need to run from everything. Even though I had moved only a little over an hour's drive north of Seattle, Hillside Creek had gradually helped me to get past these things that I so desperately wanted to forget, but today it seemed a bit harder to do that. This weird feeling had resonated inside my gut from the moment I'd woken up this morning, and even running didn't seem to diminish it. The sounds of sirens blaring didn't help either as I heard another emergency vehicle pass.

My interest piqued as I crossed the intersection that led me down the street of the place where I worked, and I removed my earplugs. Police cars, ambulances, and other emergency vehicles blocked the road. Even a hearse stood parked at the curb, and I felt my stomach drop.

Up until then, the Grain retirement home had provided me with a quiet and uneventful job that focused on administrative duties. Even though my boss might have thought she worked at an enormous corporate firm and dressed for the part, my most eventful day had been when old Miss Marshall had died. She'd been a resident for over twenty years, and her death had touched a lot of people. For me, it had meant updating the computer files and shipping the few things she'd still owned to her grandchildren. I hadn't been there that long at the time and didn't know her, so...

I slowed to a jog as I pushed through a throng of people who all seemed to be staring up. The yellow tape kept the onlookers at bay, and a few police offi-cers stood guard to prevent anyone from crossing the line. The thought of being late for work and the scolding I could expect from my boss kept me moving through the crowd.

Not having noticed any of my coworkers, I scanned the people for familiar faces, but soon the murmur of conversation around me triggered my curiosity. I glanced up the five-story-high building with its sad, gray facade and gasped as the sight of a blackened hole in the face of the building pulled me to a stop. At the same time, I felt a hand on my shoulder, but even though I flinched, I had a hard time tearing my gaze away from the structure.

"Holy shit," I exclaimed, not sure if I saw this correctly. Shaking my head, I directed my attention to the person holding me by the shoulder. I was startled by the stern look from a police officer.

"You can't go this way, ma'am," he said. Blinking, I looked back at the square hole in the wall that occupied a section of the third floor. From the size and the location of the gaping hole, it appeared as if only one of the rooms had been affected. My first thought veered toward a gas-line explosion or something, but on closer inspection, it seemed this couldn't have been an explosion. There wasn't any debris, and it looked as if the missing section of wall had been cut out with a cutting torch. Burn traces edged the rims of the cut, and in some places, I could still see it glowing red-hot. Smoke billowed up from those areas, but there didn't appear to have been a fire. Some scorch marks had blackened the surrounding bricks, but the rest of the building was untouched.

My eyes returned to the officer patiently observing

me. The tag on his chest revealed the name Klein, and the buttons of his uniform looked all shiny and new. Officer Klein kept the stern gaze as he watched me, but his baby-faced looks screamed rookie.

"Oh, I'm sorry," I said, "but I kinda have to get to work." I pointed at the building, but then I realized that was where he didn't want me to go. With a shrug, I added, "I mean, that's where I work."

He glanced over his shoulder as if he needed the confirmation of which building I would have been pointing at, but it wasn't as if there were any other buildings occupying this block. The Grain retirement home's forefront took up the entire street.

"Samantha," a shrill voice called out. I flinched at the sound that drew both the officer's and my attention. "I'm so glad you finally made it." The combination of pettiness and accusation in Trish Johansson's voice made me cringe, and I automatically checked my watch. It turned out I was still six minutes early to start my shift, and I would have been at work already if this officer hadn't stopped me or if there hadn't been a sizable chunk of the building missing. I also knew my boss wouldn't care about any of that.

She stopped and stood next to the officer on the other side of the yellow tape. Trish must have been inside the building already, and I wondered if she knew what had happened.

"Officer, thank you so much, but I can take it from here," she said as if she were his superior. To his credit, the officer didn't waver.

"Ma'am, this area is contained. I cannot let

anyone pass the line," Officer Klein said in that same polite voice that he'd offered me.

Trish looked shocked and stood aghast in the wake of the officer's refusal to grant her wishes. With any other person, I'd have imagined the look of disillusion on her face was fabricated, but in Trish's case, I knew it was real. In her pinstriped tailored jacket and matching skirt, Trish would have fit right in with the executive crowds working in fancy office buildings in the big cities. Her ginger hair, thick and long, looked immaculately styled, and I had no idea how she kept herself upright in those heels.

"This is Samantha Judd, one of my employees, and I need her assistance in containing the situation," she said in utter dismay. "You cannot expect me to assist our clients without the help of my staff."

"Ma'am—" Officer Klein started to say, but Trish was relentless.

"Officer, I appreciate everything you're doing out here," she said as she waved a hand around dismissively, "but please don't make me go back inside and get Captain Ford. I'm sure he has enough on his mind."

Officer Klein glanced at me with a raised eyebrow and shot me a look of sympathy. Then his eyes turned down as he inspected my running clothes and asked, "You work here, ma'am?"

"Unfortunately," I said underneath my breath but corrected myself as I witnessed Trish's eyes almost bulge out of their sockets. "I mean, yes, Officer, I do."

The young man grinned before he asked, "Do you carry any form of identification?"

"I am telling you who she is," Trish interjected as I reached to undo the strap around my arm that held my phone.

Officer Klein ignored her as he took the ID card that I kept inside my phone case while running. As he inspected it, he said, "The front of the building is off-limits, but we've been evacuating the residents to the south wing."

I took the card from him and slipped it back into the case.

"My office is in a separate building on the east side," I said. "Is it okay to go there? I need to change."

Officer Klein smiled as his eyes shifted over my running clothes again.

"That should be fine," he replied. "But you should probably go around." He pointed a finger in the direction that I already knew I needed to go.

"I'll check in, in a few minutes," I offered Trish. She placed her hands on her hips and gave me an urgent look.

"Hurry," she said, "and meet me in the cafeteria." I wasn't sure what she wanted me to do here. I wasn't any good with the elderly, and I doubted I'd be able to get any of my usual work done. Still, I excused myself, ignored the wink Officer Klein offered me, and jogged off.

CHAPTER TWO

A quick shower and a change of clothes would have to be enough to prepare me for whatever Trish had planned for me. The small building on the east side of the Grain that held my office and a separate area that contained a couple of servers along with a desk for Ron Hanson, our part-time tech-guy, used to be changing rooms in the old days to accommodate a swimming pool. Lack of funding had turned the swimming pool into a grassy lawn, but fortunately, the shower facilities had remained after the building had received its new purpose.

Except for the days that Trish had me running after her while she dictated her demands, I gratefully spent the remaining time alone within my fifteen-square-feet of an office. Ron only worked on Wednesdays and at times when I had to call him in for an emergency. Like last week, for instance, our WiFi crashed, and I couldn't get him here fast enough after our residents started to complain about not being able to connect to Facebook. Because today was Thursday, Ron wasn't expected to come in; I, unfortunately, wasn't that lucky.

I couldn't fathom how the nursing staff did what they did; I only knew that I wasn't cut out for it. On the other hand, whatever had happened to the front of the building seemed to be contained. It hadn't affected any other sections of the retirement home. Sure, the residents were one big pile of concerns and had questions from here to Tokyo, but the structure seemed intact, although we were still waiting for an official confirmation.

None of the essential systems had been affected. Power was still on, none of the fire extinguishers had gone off, so there was no water damage, and the kitchen was up and running. Nothing indicated that anything had happened except for the hole.

Because of the incident, all five floors in the south wing had been deemed off-limits until the fire department could inspect the building's integrity. That meant that all the residents living in that wing had been moved to the cafeteria, and while some of the staff tended to the exiled elderly, others went off in search of a way to accommodate the bedless in case these people couldn't return to their rooms by the end of the day. Unfortunately, Trish had assigned me to the cafeteria.

I would have offered money to get out of that task, but Trish had been keeping a watchful eye on me all morning. I wished that I wasn't wearing a white button-up shirt with my jeans, but under Trish's scrutiny, I stayed on task. I just hoped Mom would be able to wash out the stains.

It wasn't as if I didn't want to help these people or that I felt too good to be doing it. I didn't mind helping a little old lady go to the bathroom, even the third time within the same hour; I wouldn't have minded if only she'd just stop talking for one minute. Each time she told me about her son who was supposed to come that day, and I would have to remind her that her son came on Sunday and not Thursday; something she had told me herself. Then she'd give me a confused look and ask if I were new because she'd never seen me before. This conversation repeated itself about six times before I could even get her to the door of the bathroom, and I nearly started crying. I just wasn't cut out for this kind of work.

"Had your break yet?" Ellie asked as I handed Mr. Beeks a glass of juice. I looked up to meet Ellie's bright smile. Ellie Norris had become a legend in the almost twenty years that she had worked at the Grain, and it was easy to see why. Never in my life had I met someone so committed to taking care of people. She knew all the residents by name, and probably the names of all their closest relatives, always had a kind word for everyone, and could make anyone feel right at home—even me.

My head ached, but the sight of her brought a tentative smile to my face. Ellie always looked so put together, and not in a forced, Trish kind of way. She never wore any makeup except for the bright-red lipstick that complemented her dark, nearly flawless skin. If I hadn't known any better, I wouldn't have guessed her to be over forty-five. Instead, Ellie was nearing sixty, with coppery hair that was always styled in the latest trend. This time that meant a relatively short bob.

With a glance at the clock on the wall, I realized it was nearing 1 p.m. As if on cue, my stomach rumbled. I hadn't eaten this morning, and I figured that would probably explain my headache.

"Judging from your glazed expression and the sound coming from your stomach, I guess not," Ellie said before I could answer. "C'mon. Let's fix you something before you keel over." Almost forcefully, she took me by the arm and dragged me over to the counter that connected to the kitchen.

At five-foot-five, Ellie was about four inches shorter than me, but because of her muscular arms that I guessed had come from a lot of people lifting over the years, I knew it would be a waste of time to resist.

"Ellie, you don't have to—" I started to say, but Ellie cut me off as she called out,

"Jeff, make this girl one of those veggie sandwiches on wheat, you know, the kind you always tell is good for me. And use the special sauce."

"Coming right up," Jeff answered from behind his counter. Then as an afterthought, he said, "You should try one yourself, you know. It's good for you."

One of Ellie's eyebrows nearly rose to her hairline as she placed her hands on her well-rounded hips.

"Are you saying what I think you're saying?" she said with a note of playful defiance in her voice.

"I'm just saying," Jeff replied as he busied himself with my sandwich. Jeff had been one of Trish's hires to help bring back a healthier diet to our everyday meals. With his toothy smile and toned body, he looked like one of those fitness gurus you'd find in health infomercials, although his unnaturally tanned skin didn't look that healthy.

Trish's act might imply a concern about our residents' health, but before she'd hired him, Trish had had me do the calculations, comparing the average cost of employing Jeff and the cost of buying healthier food with the income from having a person live longer while they remained at the Grain along with some other numbers. Let's just say keeping a resident alive and living here for as long as possible turned out to be cheaper than finding new ones.

Ellie shot Jeff a knowing smile before her attention veered back to me. I could feel her eyes roam over me as if I stood in some lineup for inspection.

"You look thinner," she said with a hint of concern in her voice. "Are you eating all right?"

"With my mom living above me, how could I not eat right?" I said and forced a smile. I didn't mention the fact that I tended to decline my mom's invitations and chose a microwave dinner or takeout more often than not. As a distraction to steer her away from the topic of me, I pointed at the elderly sitting in groups around the tables in the cafeteria.

"That was something else out there this morning,"

I said. "Any ideas of what caused it yet." My distraction seemed to work as Ellie turned her attention to the folks playing board games, watching TV, or staring at a blank wall.

"Nothing yet, although I spoke to Suzanne from the night shift and she said that she'd heard a strange whooshing sound around five this morning before all the alarm bells went off." She shook her head. "It's the weirdest thing, I tell you."

I nodded in agreement as Ellie continued.

"Mr. Exter is one lucky man that he wasn't inside his room when it happened. One of the firefighters told me that there was nothing left of that room, and the stuff inside was charred dust."

"That was Max's room?" I said in surprise. Equally surprised, Ellie looked at me.

"You know Mr. Exter?" Ellie's tone suggested the absurdity of the notion. I felt my face flush because her insinuation was correct. I didn't know any of the people living here. In fact, I didn't even visit the main building unless I had to, which usually came with orders from Trish, or to pick up lunch. My office was located in a separate building, and I tried to spend as much time in there as I could. Being around too many people gave me a headache, although I did know Mr. Exter.

"Yeah," I said as I glanced across the room again. "I haven't seen him. Is he okay?"

"He was, the last time I saw him, but that was a while ago," she replied. "But if you know him, then you probably know he's not able to sit still for very long. He'll show up when it's time for dinner."

I couldn't help feeling a bit sorry for the elderly man; everything he owned must have been inside that room, and he had lost it all. The urge to find him rose, and I had an idea of where I should look. Just as I wanted to tell Ellie, I noticed someone had caught her gaze. Beth, a young intern who had joined the staff about two months ago, purposely made her way toward us.

Her petite frame slipped easily between the tables and the elderly people sitting around them. Lips set in a tight line replaced the usual perky smile, and her eyes looked troubled as they homed in on us.

"I think someone might have stolen her lipstick again," Ellie said as she leaned in and whispered near my ear. I grinned at the memory of the story that Ellie had told me a few days ago. Beth had accidentally dropped her lipstick, and Mrs. Henshaw, who had found it, had applied a generous amount before passing it around to her lady friends. Apparently, it had been some kind of expensive brand Beth had received as a gift from her boyfriend, and she had been devastated.

"This...is getting crazier by the minute," Beth said as she reached us, instantly grabbing Ellie by the arm and tugging.

"What has gotten into you, girl?" Ellie said as she resisted following Beth. Ellie wasn't someone to boss around, and that should've been one of the first things Beth had learned these past two months.

Beth relented and sounded out of breath as she said, "You won't believe...what I...just saw."

I wasn't sure if she was trying to catch her breath or raising the suspense as Beth's wide eyes darted from Ellie to me and back again. Ellie rolled her eyes at the young woman's expectant expression.

"I'm not gonna stand here guessing like an idiot, so just spill it."

"Okay, okay," Beth said and checked the room before she moved closer to us so no one would overhear. "I walked by Trish's office and heard her talking to someone. I think it might have been the police."

Beth eased back, eyebrows raised, and nodded her head emphatically.

"I think that would be standard procedure in these circumstances," I replied.

"I know that," Beth said, sounding indignant, but kept her hushed tone. "It was what they were talking about." She did that building-the-tension thing again by pausing to gage our reaction.

"If you don't want me to give Mrs. Henshaw another go at your precious lipstick, you better start talking faster," Ellie said as she crossed her arms. I wasn't sure if it was Ellie's stern look that did the trick or if Beth was unable to hold it in any longer, but the words came spilling out of her mouth in waves.

"Trish and this other person, probably a detective, because he wore a suit and all that—anyway, they were talking about this thing that was up in the room that was hit. I mean not hit, but, you know, burned and stuff."

Ellie waved her hand in a circular motion to keep Beth on track with the story.

"Right, sorry," Beth said. "At first, I feared there might have been a casualty after all, but then the way they were addressing this 'thing'"—Beth added air quotes before she continued—"it got me curious, and I went up to see for myself."

"Wait," I interjected, holding a hand up. "You went up there? Isn't that like interfering with an investigation or something?"

"Shh," Ellie said as she waved me off. "Not if no one saw her. Did anyone see you?" Beth shook her head.

"I don't think so." Beth's face had innocence plastered all over it, and I wondered if she'd even thought of the consequences if she'd been caught up there. The police might have thought she'd have something to do with the situation; she could have been arrested.

"How could no one have seen you? The place is crawling with cops and emergency personnel," I asked and almost sounded appalled.

"I have my ways," Beth replied with a wink.

Ellie nudged me with an elbow. "Let her finish, Sam."

Undeterred, Beth continued.

"Well, Mr. Exter's room is right across one of the emergency exits. So, when everything returned to relative quiet, I snuck up there and waited for the right moment. A cop was posted at the door, so I had to keep the emergency door ajar, but as soon as he turned his back, I peeked."

Beth's eyes narrowed, and she looked around the room again. Jeff hadn't returned with my sandwich, and the elderly were still sitting in the same spots. There was no reason to delay her response, but it seemed Beth enjoyed building up the tension. It worked too and felt a knot form in my stomach, and my throat felt dry. My hands had started to tremble, and I shoved them into the pockets of my jeans so no one would notice.

"And?" Ellie said as she lifted her hands in impatience.

"I saw this." Beth slid a hand into the pocket of her nurse's uniform and pulled out a phone.

"You were lucky that the security systems haven't been reset yet after the initial alarm, or else you'd have gotten yourself in a heap of trouble, opening that emergency exit," I said as my gaze shifted to Beth's phone.

Beth stabbed at a button, and with a few flicks across the screen, an image appeared, and she held the phone up for us to see. I squinted my eyes, not sure what I was looking at.

"Is that—" Ellie started to say but then tilted her head to take another look. "Did Mr. Exter have a mannequin in his room?" The question sounded absurd, although I had to admit that was what it looked like to me as well—a charred and deformed mannequin at that.

In her picture, Beth had captured the open door to Mr. Exter's room. Although partially obscured by a police officer facing away from the camera, I could clearly make out something that looked like a person pointing a bony finger at a wall. Like everything else inside the room, the figure was charred black. The only thing that wasn't covered in soot was the man-sized mark on the wall that the figure pointed at.

Even though the picture had come out a bit blurry, I had to admit the figure in the picture looked ominous, but I quickly dismissed it as being a person because some features of its anatomy seemed off. For one, its jaw looked out of proportion with teeth sticking out as if they belonged to a piranha or something, and I didn't think a human being would be able to stand upright after being scorched to death; at least, I hoped they wouldn't. Besides, there would have been something on the news by now about a casualty, and I didn't think Trish would have kept us in the dark about something like that.

"What do you think?" Beth asked. She sounded excited, as if she had just made the most profound discovery of her life. I hesitated to answer, unwilling to crush her find, but Ellie didn't seem to have a problem with that.

"That can't be a person."

"Why wouldn't it be?" Beth asked with a note of disappointment in her voice.

Ignoring her tone, I replied, "A person wouldn't be standing after something like that. Besides—"

"Besides, Trish would have informed us." Ellie finished the sentence for me and wrapped an arm around Beth's shoulder. "It's probably just some life-sized doll or something."

"But it could be something else, something unknown," Beth said as her eyes perked up. "Why else would that detective be talking to Trish?"

"Probably just a formality," I said.

"C'mon," Ellie said, tugging Beth along. "I'm gonna put you to work right here, where I can keep an eye on you and you won't be able to sneak off again."

I hoped Beth would erase the picture, because even though I doubted it to be significant, it looked nasty, like something out of a horror movie. Despite how little I knew of Beth, I had a feeling it wouldn't be long before the picture would end up on Instagram, Facebook, and Twitter.

"Here you go, Sam," Jeff said, just as I felt a shiver go down my spine. I closed my eyes for a second and took a deep breath to let the feeling pass. It wasn't just because of the picture Beth had shown us. My brain had trouble dealing with things if they didn't comply with the structure I had devised for myself. I wished I could just head back to my office and hide while all of this played out, but I had a feeling Trish would find me.

It might be that I've always been like this, but things had intensified after that one eventful night about six months before I moved here. Maybe my previous job had kept me too busy to think about it before that night, or perhaps because the events that had led up to it had been so out of character for me that it had triggered some sort of defense mechanism. The fact was that I had trouble dealing with changes in my routine, and when that happened, my body revealed some telltale signs.

Jeff moved out from behind the counter and offered me a neatly wrapped package. My hands were still shaking as I took it, and Jeff must have noticed. "You okay?"

With the perfect excuse already in mind, I smiled at him.

"Skipped breakfast."

With my neatly packed sandwich, I started down the path at the rear of the main building that would lead me to the lake. The only thing I could think of to calm my nerves was to sneak a little routine into this off-putting day. I deeply inhaled the fresh air as I walked, and I felt relieved to be outside. Out here, only birds and the soft hum of distant traffic broke the silence, and with lunch hour over, there weren't many people hanging around, sitting on the grass, or enjoying the sun.

Instead of walking to the lake itself, I veered off the path and onto a narrow trail lined with brush. A few yards in, I found myself on a different path, hidden and not well traveled. Leaves scrunched underneath my sneakers as I weaved through the trees and around bushes. From here I couldn't see the main path or the people walking on it, and I would have liked to have thought that they wouldn't be able to see me either. I found what I was looking for as I stopped at a small clearing.

In the middle of a patch of grass stood an old stone bird feeder, and to the right, there was a bench. The first time I'd wandered into this place, I had felt as if I'd found one of those secret gardens they sometimes write about in novels. Calling it a garden was far-fetched, however, with only some trees and brush cover to hide it from plain view and no flowers to speak of, but it was quiet. Still, I wasn't the only one who enjoyed coming here.

"Hey, Max," I said to the elderly man sitting on the small bench. "Want some company?" Max Exter looked up from the bird feeder with a broad smile that emphasized the creases in his wrinkled face.

"I always welcome your company," he said in a low, deep voice. Hearing him speak always reminded me of James Earl Jones. Every so often, I asked him for a Darth Vader impression, but Max insisted that he didn't know who I was talking about. I walked over and sat next to him on the bench. Dressed in sneakers, jeans, and a hoodie, Max didn't look anything like his fellow residents at the retirement home. His hair was a white mess that looked like Einstein's, and his handsome, dark face resembled an actor whose name I couldn't remember. Come to think of it; he reminded me of a lot of people.

"How are you doing?" he asked after I settled in next to him.

"Shouldn't I be asking you that?" I said, and I couldn't hide my concern. That picture Beth had taken lingered in my brain, and even though I knew that there would be a rational explanation for the strange, burned-to-a-crisp figure standing in the middle of Max's room, the thought of it made me feel queasy. Still, the fact that this man had probably lost everything he owned weighed heavier in my mind. "What happened?"

For a moment he stared at me as if he had no idea of what I was talking about, but then his eyebrows rose.

"Oh, that," he said as if it had slipped his mind, and waved a dismissive hand in the air. "I don't even understand what the fuss is about."

"Fuss?" I repeated incredulously. "A freaking chunk of the building is missing right where your room was supposed to be."

"Well, I wasn't there, so..." he said and shrugged.

"But all your stuff," I said. "Everything you owned must have been in that room." Max smiled and shook his head.

"Everything that is precious to me fits right inside this bag," he said and patted a dark-green bag that stood on the ground by his side. The bag that never seemed to be far from his side looked to be army issue and had seen better days.

I just stared at him, not sure what to say. He grinned, and his eyes lit up. Shifting on the bench, he leaned in closer and placed his hand on my knee.

"Not much is worth getting worked up about once you reach my age," he said in a conspiratorial whisper. I glanced down at his hand on my knee and noticed the age spots that made his hand look even darker in places. I smiled.

"That is nice," I said and meant it. To worry was a stupid activity in which you always seemed to fret about the things that would never happen before life hit you upside the head with something else. "Maybe you could teach me sometimes," I added. Max pulled his hand away from my knee and smiled.

"I could," he said, "but the young never listen to what the old have to say."

"I might," I replied as I faced him. I couldn't quite fathom what I saw behind those eyes, but I felt something come over me. Maybe it was because I hadn't eaten all day and my blood sugar levels had dropped, but as I stared into his dark gaze, it felt as if he could read my soul. A sensation of being sucked into a black hole caused tears to sting my eyes, and I had to blink, or else they would have spilled over. As if a spell had been broken, I managed to push the feeling aside and felt it replaced by embarrassment.

Heat rushed into my cheeks, and in an attempt to hide it, I started to fiddle with the wrapper of my neatly packed sandwich. From the corner of my eye, I noticed Max staring at me. His head slightly tilted as he studied me.

"You look a little out of sorts," he said. I tried to ignore the intensity in his eyes and shrugged. "Trish riding you hard again?"

I shrugged again and shifted my attention to our surroundings. This spot had become my go-to place to eat my lunch as soon as I had found it, which hadn't been that long after I'd started working here. On one of those lazy afternoons when the sun burned bright and the air felt hot, I'd found Max sitting here. Ever since then, we'd been sharing a meal here regularly— about a year now.

Because we had known each other for a while, Max had learned a few things about my troubles with Trish. Not that I talked much about it, but one wouldn't have to be a rocket scientist to figure that one out. Trish wasn't an easy person to work with for anyone; I just had more trouble with her than most. It turned out she knew how to pick her targets, and I often wondered if she'd been like that back in school or if she'd been the one who got bullied and it had turned her into one.

"It's just a hectic day," I said, not willing to talk about it. I wished this would be more like our usual lunches in which Max would delight me with one of his elaborate tales.

It seemed impossible, but every time we managed to meet up, he had a story or an anecdote ready to tell. Stories like how he had crashed his bicycle into an elephant's rear while he traveled across India as a young man or how he had met a guy in a pub in Ireland who, after a couple of hours chatting and drinking, had invited him for a visit to Lapland, always brought a smile to my face. Of course, the tale of his travels to Finland had followed the next day. I'd gotten to know him through his stories, and I felt sorry for him for having lost everything he owned.

"I know it's easier said than done," Max said, "but you shouldn't let her get to you."

"I won't," I replied and tried to sound nonchalant.

Max shot me a weak smile as his eyes turned toward my lap. "So that isn't why your hands are shaking?"

The heat that I had felt before returned to my cheeks as I increased my grip on the wrapped sandwiches.

Had those words come from my mother's mouth, I might have felt annoyed, but coming from Max in his warm, caring voice, I appreciated the concern. He looked at me like a grandfather might have looked with care at his grandchild, even though I had no recollection of ever experiencing it myself.

I had never told Max about my body's tendency to rebel against my wishes. We usually met within the confines of this clearing, and this place always helped to calm my nerves. I told myself Max wouldn't be interested in a story of how I'd lost my faith in a lot of things people had to offer. The truth was that I feared to dig up those memories. The way Max looked at me, though, made me feel as if he knew something was up. For a moment I wondered what it would feel like to tell someone what had happened other than the therapist, who had actually encouraged me to talk about it.

"I..." I started to say but hesitated. How was I going to explain something to someone who barely knew me when I couldn't talk to my best friend Kay or my mom about it? Besides, it wasn't as if I remembered a whole lot about it. Instead, I opted to stray from the subject. "I skipped breakfast."

Max shot me a knowing smile.

"Well, if you ever feel like talking about that," he said, "I'm a pretty good listener."

"I'll be sure to remember that, the next time I skip breakfast," I replied with a smile. Hoping to stray even further from the subject of me, I debated if I should ask him about the figure with the pointing finger, but then I wasn't even supposed to know about that. I didn't want Beth to get in trouble, so I decided to keep that to myself.

"Have you talked to the police?" I asked instead. From the corner of my eye, I noticed Max still hadn't moved. His gaze seemed fixed on me, and it started to unnerve me. Instead of fiddling with the paper, I unwrapped the package and found two sandwiches. As if the sight of the sandwiches snapped him out of his haze, Max shifted in his seat.

"I...eh," he started to say, but his—usually steady —voice betrayed him. After clearing his throat, he added, "I talked to someone, but they couldn't tell me much. I think someone's coming by tomorrow."

"Nothing much to get worked up about," I said jokingly and found the courage to look him in the eyes again.

"Exactly," he said.

"Well, I'm glad you weren't in your room when it happened," I said. It occurred to me that I hadn't even wondered where Max had been at that early hour. Knowing Max, he'd probably been on a walk or something. Like Ellie had said earlier, Max wasn't someone to sit still for a long time.

Max stared at me with the curiosity of a child, which seemed odd for a man in his eighties, and I had never witnessed any signs of Alzheimer's from him. I felt the heat rise to my cheeks again, but my hands only held the barest of tremors as I raised my offerings.

"Would you like one of these?" I asked with a shyness in my voice that I didn't recognize.

Max smiled, but instead of answering my question he said, "You have an old soul."

I looked up at him a bit shocked, not sure how to interpret that. As if he sensed my discomfort, Max smiled and nodded.

"I would love one."

CHAPTER THREE

After finishing his sandwich, Max handed me his empty wrapper as my phone rang. I fished it out of my pocket and picked it up, hearing Ellie on the other end of the line.

"Sam, you still at lunch," Ellie asked.

"I was just on my way back," I said. "Please don't tell me, Trish—"

"No," Ellie interjected, "Trish hasn't missed you yet. She's too busy giving this detective a tour of the premises." I couldn't help sighing a sigh of relief as Ellie continued. "They want to talk to Mr. Exter, so if you see him, tell him to meet them at his room."

"Actually, he's right here with me," I said and turned to look at Max. There wasn't any reaction at all on Max's face as I added, "We'll meet them there." I hung up the phone and shoved it back into my pocket.

"The police would like to talk to you and asked if you would meet them at your room."

"Well," Max said as he got to his feet, "that was to be expected." He was already moving toward the exit of the small clearing, and I followed his example. For an old man, Max still walked with a firm stride, and I had to push my legs to keep up with him and nearly stumbled onto the path that would lead up to the east wing of the main building of the retirement home. We walked side by side in silence until we reached the rear entrance, where I held the door open for him.

"Thank you," he murmured and proceeded toward the elevator.

"I half expected you to start running up the stairs," I said with a chuckle as he pressed the button to call the elevator.

Max cocked an eyebrow and looked at me as if I were an idiot. "Why on earth would I do that?"

I shook my head. "I don't know. Just a thought."

The elevator dinged, and silence returned as we rode up the few floors until we reached Max's. As the door slid open, we were greeted by Trish, a tall man dressed in a suit that had something that looked like a coffee stain on its lower right sleeve, and a uniformed officer who I recognized as Officer Klein.

"What are you doing here?" Trish said in her shrill voice as soon as the doors opened, shooting me a piercing glare.

"I..." I started to say, but I struggled for words. Trish's accusing green eyes bore into mine as she waited for my reply. I hated how she always managed to get me off balance.

"I have asked Ms. Judd to join me," Max said and unintentionally probably kept me from saying something stupid to my boss. "I am an old man living on his own, and Ms. Judd is probably the closest thing I have to a family at this point."

Taken aback by his comment, I raised an eyebrow and glared at Max. He caught my eye, and I could see a muscle twitch in his cheek. From the mischievous glint in his eyes I knew he was suppressing a grin.

"I see," the guy in the coffee-stained suit said. "Mr. Exter, my name is Detective Holden, and we would like to go through the events of what happened here last night if you don't mind?" Holden seemed to be in his mid-forties, with short, cropped hair and a freshly shaven face. He looked stern, but with a layer of charm that made him appear approachable. Max shook his head.

"Not at all."

"This is Officer Klein," Detective Holden said and gestured at the uniformed officer. Officer Klein shook Max's hand and nodded in my direction in recognition.

"It's this way," Trish said, sounding annoyed, and all but charged in the direction of Max's room. Her heels clicked on the linoleum floor as I trailed behind the rest of them. As we ventured into the south wing of the building, I could already see the yellow tape crisscrossed over Max's door, and we stopped in front of it.

"Unfortunately, we have to ask you two to stay out here," Detective Holden said to Trish and me. I just nodded and kept my head low in an attempt to avoid Trish's deathly glare that I knew would have reached her face by now. Trish wasn't the kind of person who accepted things being kept from her— especially not if it concerned what she saw as her facility.

"As the chief administrator, I can assure you—" Trish started to say, but Detective Holden cut her off.

"I appreciate your cooperation in this, and I'll make sure that you will be filled in with everything that you are required to know." He offered her his hand and slightly bowed as she took it. Using that charm of his, he added, "We would like to hear Mr. Exter's version of events without him being distracted." Then he shot her a wink that suggested Trish might be that distraction for an entirely different reason than I would have picked her for a distraction, and I had to bite the inside of my cheek to keep myself from laughing.

"I see," Trish said. A nervous smile flickered across her face, but as she turned to me, I might as well have been staring at a brick wall. "Well then, Sam, come along, and you can fill me in why you're not at work in the cafeteria."

That woman always managed to make me feel even more of a child than my mom could. Repressing a sigh, I nodded.

Officer Klein had busied himself with removing the police tape covering Max's door as Trish started to stomp off in the direction of the elevator. I was about to follow as a hand on my arm stopped me.

Flinching at the sudden contact, I instantly whirled around and looked straight into Max's dark, deep gaze. I quenched the sudden feeling of being trapped that had washed over me and stifled a yelp. With a thoughtful expression, Max's eyes shifted from my face to my arm where he held it. He released his grip and forced a smile. I couldn't decipher the look on his face, but I figured he must have thought I'd lost it. I shoved the thought aside as he started to speak.

"Could you do me a favor, Sam?" he asked, and his deep voice held a tentative note.

Detective Holden opened Max's door, and I briefly glanced at the two policemen as they stepped inside the room. A draft that, without doubt, was produced because of the section of wall that had gone missing wafted the smell of smoke up my nose. I shivered at the thought of what could have happened if Max had been in there.

Unable to contain my curiosity, I glimpsed inside the room. Beth's picture had given me an idea of the statue-like figure, but the image hadn't done it justice. Up close, it looked much more eerie. It had a skeletal frame, but resembled nothing of a human body, although it did stand on two feet and had two arms; one of which pointed at a spot on the wall that seemed untouched by whatever it had been that had struck Max's room.

Detective Holden tapped the pen to the creature's head, and the sound returned solid like stone.

"Weird, isn't it?" I heard Detective Holden say. "It has no eyes or nose."

"It reminds me of those *Alien* movies," Klein said. "What was it they called it, xeno...something, except without the long head and the tail."

My stomach churned at the sight of the strange statue as if there were more to it than just a figure. Max must have noticed, because he placed his hand on my arm again.

"Don't mind that," he said in a soft tone. "It'll all be explained." It wasn't as much the words as the way he looked at me that made me believe him, although I didn't think it would be as simple as he made it out to be.

"What was it you wanted me to do?" I asked.

Max's eyes strayed down to his feet, and he tapped his upper thigh. "It seems I've forgotten my bag. Would you be so kind to go get it for me?" he said. "I'm sure it should still be at the clearing." I remembered the green bag where it stood next to the bench.

"Sure, I'll get it right now. You want me to bring it up here?"

"No," he said, shaking his head. "Why don't you take it to the cafeteria? This might take a while."

"Okay, sure, I'll see you there."

Max patted my arm as he drew in a breath and puffed out his chest.

"Now, I have to go and entertain the kids." He shot me a smile before he turned and entered what remained of his room.

"What was that all about?" Trish asked as I met up with her at the elevator.

Not thinking anything of it, I replied, "Mr. Exter just asked me to pick up his bag that he left—"

"Not that," Trish said, sounding annoyed. "The bit about the family thing."

Blinking, I met her gaze. I had almost forgotten about that part, which had come to me as much as a surprise as it apparently had to Trish. Momentarily at a loss for words, I shrugged and shook my head.

"I don't know," I said and noticed the stammer in my voice.

"I understand residents getting attached to our nursing staff. After all, they are around them all the time," Trish said. "I do not understand our administrative employees attaching themselves to our clients, and I cannot approve such actions."

The harsh sound of Trish's voice cut through me like a knife through butter, and my heart started to hammer against my chest so fast that it became hard to breathe. Not that long ago, I would've cut her down like a tree for a remark like that. It seemed I'd lost all the stamina that came with making a tough sell or standing up against men or even women like Trish while working at a testosterone-filled office. It seemed I had left that fortitude behind along with my old job.

I stared at her, dumbfounded, feeling like an idiot for not being able to stand up to her. There was nothing wrong with the friendship I'd developed with

Max over the past year. Sure, his remark had come as a surprise, too, but what I had seen in Max's eyes had assured me he had only been half serious. Still, Trish had no right to berate me like that. Besides, there weren't any rules about having friendly relations with the residents—the retirement home's policy even encouraged it. The only thing that I could think of that Trish would be miffed about was the fact that she hadn't known about it. Trish always knew everything about anything within the Grain, and being caught by surprise always put her in a foul mood. Added to that, that something had cut a hole in her building seemed enough to make her intolerable.

The elevator dinged, and the door slid open.

"I am glad we understand each other on this matter," Trish said as she stepped inside the box, "so I expect you to keep your distance." I just stared at her as I remained standing in the hallway while the doors tentatively slid closed. Trish stabbed a button on the panel, and the doors started to open again.

"Are you coming?"

I shook my head, too stunned to move. "I'll take the stairs."

Trish huffed out a breath and crossed arms over her chest as the doors slid closed.

"I'll be expecting to see you after your little errand for Mr. Exter."

The sound of Trish's shrill but muffled voice from behind the elevator doors seemed to follow me until I reached the main entrance and stepped outside.

I closed my eyes and took a deep breath. The

relief of being outside again and the soft breeze that brushed my skin helped soothe my reeling heart, although my hands were shaking like leaves and I inwardly cursed myself for becoming such a wuss.

Trying to forget Trish and the fact that I would have to deal with her once again after retrieving Max's bag, I made my way to the clearing. Max had been right—his green bag still stood where he had left it. As I moved over to pick it up, I remembered what he'd mentioned about the bag. "Everything that is precious to me fits right inside this bag," he'd said.

Max didn't seem to be a forgetful person, despite his age. The fact that he'd said that everything that was precious to him was inside that bag made me wonder if he'd left it on purpose. He'd also told me not to bring it up to him, but to leave it in the cafeteria. *Had he thought the police would be interested in it? Why would the police be interested in an old man's bag?*

I shook the thought from my mind, grabbed the bag's strap, and jerked it up in one motion with the intention of getting back to the home as fast as possible. I wasn't going to give Trish any more ammunition today because I didn't think I could handle it. If it were up to me then I'd change into my running gear, get home, and veg out on my couch for the rest of the day. Unfortunately, the bag had a different idea as it snagged behind the bench. Off balance, I fumbled to regain my footing, and in turn, I managed to kick the bag.

My heart sunk at the idea of breaking some of the last of Max's possessions as the bag toppled over, and several items spilled to the ground. A small wooden box with its lid open lay upside down, along with a bar of chocolate and a pair of swimming goggles.

"Shit," I muttered as I knelt to pick up the bag's contents. I grabbed the chocolate bar and shoved it back into the bag, feeling relieved that nothing of value had spilled onto the ground. I wouldn't want to be the one to damage the few belongings Max still owned. The swimming goggles seemed a bit odd to carry around, but then perhaps Max enjoyed the occasional swim.

I grabbed the box and flipped it around. The inside of the box was divided into twelve square sections with a name etched above each section. To my horror, I found the contents of the sections had spilled into the grass. Twelve colorful stones had fallen from the box, and I held them out on the palm of my hand after picking them up. I wasn't afraid of damaging them, but I had no idea of where they were supposed to fit. *In which little section of the box did each of them go?*

I stared at the labels inside the box, with strange names such as sardonyx and chrysolite. My basic knowledge told me that these were precious stones or gemstones and that sapphire was usually blue and emerald green. Beyond that, I had nothing. Realizing that I'd never be able to place the stones back into the right spot and that I would have to tell Max what had happened, I wrapped my fist around the small stones.

As soon as I closed my fist, it felt as if someone had set my hand on fire, and I hissed in pain.

"Son of a..." I said and instantly dropped the gems. I frantically waved my hand as the stones tumbled back into the grass. "What the hell?"

The pain faded, and I stared at my hand. Around me, a sharp wind rustled the leaves in the trees over my head, and a cold shiver ran down my back. A strange feeling of discomfort settled in the pit of my stomach, and I shivered again. It was definitely time to get back.

Testing the stones' temperature with a tentative finger, I realized they had returned to normal. One by one, I quickly picked them up and deposited each of them randomly in one of the sections. Closing the lid, I shoved the box into Max's bag and stood. With one last glance at my hand, finding nothing wrong with it, I filed this experience under too much stress and made my way back to the retirement home.

CHAPTER FOUR

Unfortunately, the events of the day had not allowed for an early departure. I wasn't sure if it had been the fire department or the police that had decided to keep most of the building off-limits. Having been up there myself, I had noticed nothing wrong with the structure, but I guessed the strange nature of the incident would have been enough to proceed with caution.

Ellie and the rest of the staff had their hands full with keeping the residents comfortable within the confines of the cafeteria until they could find them suitable accommodations. Fortunately, a lot of the people living in different parts the building had no qualms about offering their rooms to share.

I had stuck around until the night shift arrived. Max hadn't returned, and after looking for him for a while, I'd decided to leave his bag with the night porter and headed home. I wasn't sure which temporary room he'd been assigned, but I knew Ellie or any of the rest of the staff would take good care of him.

The day had gone on way too long, and as I returned home, I felt relieved to find my car still missing. Mom hadn't returned home. This meant I might have to run to work again tomorrow. Once in a while, she'd hit the town with Patty, her best friend. They'd go out for dinner and some fun, but it also meant she'd got home late and might forget to deposit the key in my mailbox.

Despite her shopping excursion, Mom had called me about six times during the day, curious about what had happened, but I guessed she hadn't been interested enough to call off her night of fun. Not that I wanted her to. I was happy for her that she got to do fun stuff once in a while. I just wished she would tell me beforehand that she intended to keep the car for the day.

After a quick shower, I barely had the time to stretch out on the couch with a bowl of instant noodles on my lap before the phone rang. I dropped the remote that I hadn't even used and grabbed my phone. The display read: "Karen Wilder."

"Hey, Kay," I said, calling her by the nickname she'd urged me to use since we'd met.

"Tell me what's going on up there. That retirement home of yours has been on the news all day," Kay said.

"Then you probably know more than me," I said.

"I haven't seen any news all day because I actually had to work a little."

"Don't mock me," Kay replied with a slight growl.

The bowl of noodles started to get too hot for my legs, so I moved it to the coffee table. "They wouldn't let any film crews up close, but from what they did show us, it looked like something blew a hole in the building," Kay continued.

"There was certainly a hole in the building," I said, "but I doubt it was caused by an explosion. The fire department is still investigating, but the surrounding structure didn't seem affected, so..."

"That is so weird."

"Yeah, pretty weird," I replied, and my mind veered to the strange figure standing in Max's room. "Did they mention anything else on the news?"

"Like what?"

"I don't know." I couldn't just ask if there were any mention of a charred, live-sized, creepy statue and as I thought about it, it occurred to me that even if the police had added that to their statement, it would hardly be newsworthy.

"I kept looking up the story on different channels, hoping to see you," Kay said. She sounded apprehensive, as if she were afraid of saying the wrong thing. "I haven't heard from you in a while, and we haven't seen each other in ages." A sense of shame brew in the pit of my stomach, and I felt the heat rise to my cheeks.

"I...I'm sorry. I should've called." The notion was easier said than done when all you wanted to do was to forget about a previous life. Kay was very much a part of that life I so desperately wanted to forget, but she was also one of the best friends I'd ever had. A moment of silence that followed dragged out a bit too long before Kay spoke.

"I guess things aren't as quiet over there as you had hoped them to be." Sighing, I pinched the bridge of my nose at Kay's subtle way of asking how I was doing without prompting my standard reply of "I'm okay."

"Things are quiet enough, although today has been a strange one," I said with a chuckle.

"I bet."

The day had been strange enough that I didn't feel like delving any deeper into my life, and before she could ask anything else, I steered the conversation in a different direction.

"How are things at the office?"

"Okay," she said, sounding timid and nothing like her perky self. "Things are a bit slow, you know, the silence before the storm. Soon everybody will be pulling at all the strings to get that end-of-year bonus." She was right; I knew what that was like. It had been one of the reasons I had to get out of there. "Everybody says hi."

"I doubt that," I replied, a bit too harsh, and regretted it immediately. Kay and I had started at the same time at a company that provided high-tech solar panel solutions, and we'd both worked in the marketing department. Together we'd risen through the ranks until I'd quit about a year ago. From the dozens of colleagues I had worked with over the years, she was the only one I'd stayed in contact with.

"Well, Stella asked after you the other day," she said. "You remember Stella, right?" I did remember Stella, who cleaned the coffee machines every day and had an elaborate bird's nest for hair on top of her head. We used to have a chat about the weather almost every day.

"Yeah, I remember her," I said. "She's nice. Say hi for me, will ya?"

"I will."

"So," I said as I grabbed my fork from the table and started poking my noodles.

After a moment of silence, Kay blew out a breath and then groaned. "How's your mom?"

"She's fine." Another awkward silence followed.

"Okay, you're no fun talking on the phone," she said, sounding a lot more like her usual perky self. I couldn't disagree with her. It seemed I had lost the ability to string together full sentences.

"I'm sorry. I guess my head's not in the right place." My words were followed by a soft chuckle on the other end of the line.

"No offense, Sam, but your head hasn't been in the right place for a while, but don't worry about it. I still love you."

Kay was the only person in the world who could say that to me and bring a smile to my face.

"You know me too well."

"We should get together," Kay said. I was about to object, but Kay continued without taking a breath.

"This weekend isn't good for me, but I have an extra day the next one. What do you say I come up there, and we can go hiking." I opened my mouth, intending to decline. Although I loved hiking, the thought of going out with Kay had me comparing the trip to a psych evaluation, and I've had plenty of those.

Although her intentions came from a good place, she always tried to get me to talk as soon as she got me along. Someone must have told her it'd be good for me to talk about the one thing I just wanted to forget. It was hard for me to judge if this had anything to do with her feeling guilty, even though I'd told her on multiple occasions that there was nothing she could have done. Maybe she just wanted the old version of her friend back.

"Oh, come on, please," she added before I could answer. "I promise it'll be fun."

This time it was me who groaned as I listened to the plea in her voice. She sounded so excited, and a part of me wondered why. I hadn't been that much fun to be around the past year either.

From the day we'd met, we'd started to get together on our lunch breaks and walked around the city or grab a coffee. We'd talked about our days and all the craziness at work that most of the time didn't make any sense to anyone else except to us enduring it. Between the two of us, she had always been the more outgoing one, and she hadn't minded letting me tag along. In fact, she'd often insisted on it.

I'd never been one to hit the town, but at Kay's side, I'd gone to clubs and visited bars I otherwise never would have. I'd also gotten to enjoy her seemingly endless group of friends, who'd embraced me within their circle as if I'd known them all my life. We'd had some good times, but I wasn't that person anymore. Not since that one stupid night, the few memories of which I fought to keep from veering up at the forefront of my mind. Still, I couldn't help but smile at some of the other memories we'd created.

"I don't know, Kay," I heard myself say, instead of the steadfast *no* that came natural to me. "I'm not sure if..." The sentence died in my throat. *How was I going to explain that the mere thought of a trip like that had my heart racing and it wasn't from excitement?*

"It'll be good for you. Please..." Kay said on the other end of the line. "You don't have to answer right now but promise me you'll think about it." I had to appreciate her effort, and she sounded genuine in her offer.

"Okay, I promise I'll think about it," I said with a sigh, even though the idea of considering her proposal made my stomach clench.

After we'd said our goodbyes, I stared at my noodles. Eating them had lost its appeal as my mind was running on overdrive. I closed my eyes and waited for the storm in my head to blow through, but there had been too much to deal with this day. All these questions that were thrown at me by the residents, although I had to admit that most of them had been the same: "Can you help me to the bathroom?" The constant throng of people surrounding me made me miss my tiny office in the adjacent building. And then there was Max and that weird statue and the state of his room; not to mention the even weirder incident with the stones. Which reminded me that I would have to tell Max what had happened to them. This thing with Kay only intensified things. The only good thing was that I hadn't run into Trish again after she'd chastised me by the elevator. I'd probably pay for that tomorrow after she summoned me to her office.

I stared at my phone as the screen faded to black. *Why couldn't it be that easy in life?* Just flip a switch and all the images residing in your head would turn to black. *How could I explain to Kay that although I didn't blame her, every time I spoke to her or saw her, it brought back all these memories?* There wasn't even that much to recall. Kay had been late picking me up and had texted me about it. She had some things to finish up at the office and had stayed late. Afterward, Kay was supposed to pick me up. We'd been going meet some friends at a local bar. It had been my decision to walk the distance instead of waiting for her. I'd even texted her to say that I was going ahead because we had friends waiting for us and it would be easier for her to go straight from the office. Those were the things I did remember.

The rest of the night is a fragmented blur of images and sensations. An arm wrapped around my throat, the taste of metal from the barrel in my mouth, the sound of sirens, and the strong antiseptic smell that greeted me at the hospital.

As I stared at my phone, I fought to keep the memories at bay. This always seemed to happen after an eventful day. It had been one of the reasons I'd had to leave my previous job. That and the constant looks, hushed whispers, and rooms going silent after I entered. Only one thing would work to soothe my mind at this point. I stood and made my way into the bedroom.

CHAPTER FIVE

Running had always been the best way for me to clear my head, and as my feet pounded on the pavement, I found myself heading in the direction of the lake. The sun had set, with only the streetlights illuminating the path. Completely uncharacteristically, I'd left my phone at home, and instead of listening to loud electronic beats, my ears attuned to the sound of my heavy breathing and the drum of my feet on the ground. I kind of liked the lack of noise abusing my ears as I became pleasantly aware of the sounds of nature along with the hum of the town in the background. Closer to the lake, streetlights bounced off the water, giving it an almost magical appeal. It didn't stop the thoughts from running wild inside my head.

As if on autopilot, I ran along the bank at a steady pace. A left turn brought me onto a familiar path, and I stopped as I realized that it would take me to the Grain. The retirement home was the last place that I wanted to go right now, although I felt bad for not returning Max's bag in person and hoped he'd been able to retrieve it.

Not wanting the memories of a strange day and the reminders it triggered to cloud my mind again, I turned to retrace my steps. One of the perks of living in a haven for retirees like Hillside Creek was that after night had fallen, the small town seemed to fall asleep. The path that lay before me looked abandoned, and the rustle of leaves and the sound of the occasional car passing by on the road parallel to the lake accompanied me.

At a slower pace, I waved my arms and rolled my shoulder to loosen my muscles. Overhead, a streetlight blinked several times before it snuffed out. A cold breeze sent a shiver down my back, reminding me that I should pick up my pace and head home.

Ahead, another streetlight flickered, and for some reason, it seemed even quieter than before. As I looked up, I noticed a lack of movement within the trees. A breeze like I'd experienced only a moment ago should at least rustle some of the branches, but everything around me was dead silent. In fact, I couldn't hear anything—not even the sound of traffic in the distance. My eyes veered back to the streetlight, and I froze.

"Now how the hell does that work?" I asked myself as I walked over to the lamppost and stared up at it. The oversized bulb appeared to be on and not on. The light seemed stuck somewhere in between as if suspended in time.

All I could think of was that it was some kind of malfunction, and I was about to move on when a strange sound stopped me. I paused and listened, but as before, I couldn't hear anything, not even leaves rustling in the wind. I narrowed my eyes as I peered into the dark, and I realized that I hadn't stopped that far from the hidden path that led to the small clearing when I heard the sound again.

A soft hum that reminded me of a refrigerator resonated for a moment until it disappeared again. I stepped around the brush cover and onto the hidden path. As I neared the spot that had become my go-to place to eat my lunch, a bright blue light emanating from the small clearing nearly blinded me. It barely lasted a second, but it was enough to send spots flying across my eyes. Still blinking to clear my vision, I started down the path and weaved through the trees.

The stupidity of this situation screamed at me. It was dark, and I was all alone, venturing into a secluded area with no one around to even hear me scream, but I couldn't help myself. Even as I fought the urge to go forward, something seemed to pull me like a magnet. I couldn't stop my feet from moving, even though I tried.

I became eerily aware of my heart beating crazily inside my chest, and it wasn't because of my running. Ahead of me, the blue light grew brighter, and I had to raise a hand to shield my eyes. That magnetic pull also seemed to grow stronger the closer I got to the clearing, and I felt my skin tingle as if hit by a burst of static electricity. My mind screamed to turn around, but my feet just kept moving down the path.

As I rounded a tree, the blue light hit me full in the face, causing tears to spring to my eyes. The short hair on my head rose as the static electricity intensified, and I felt a tiny spark go through my fingers as I wiped at the tears rolling down my face. I jumped at the sound of a familiar but unnerving voice.

"Sam, what are you doing here! Get out!" I couldn't see him, but the urgency in Max's voice was evident. But it wasn't as if I had a choice. I couldn't move except in the direction of the light. Digging in my feet only intensified the currents running through my body, and it had started to hurt.

"Max?" I asked, surprised to hear the old man's voice. "What are you doing here? What's going on?"

"You have to get out of here now!"

I blinked in the hope my vision would return, and it partially helped. Through a blur of tears, I recognized Max's shape, jeans, and hoodie. He appeared to be standing at the center of the light with his outstretched hand at the epicenter of the strange blue illumination that glowed from a stone he held in his palm.

Pain shot down my arms, and my eyes felt as if they were burning in their sockets. I cried out as the burning sensation became too much to bear. I wanted to scream in agony but managed to keep my teeth clamped together.

"Sam, please go," Max called out again as a cloud of black smoke fell down on us. Sparks of fire danced inside the dark veil as if they had escaped a stoked fireplace, as the black smoke tried to engulf the blue light.

My feet skidded over the small patch of grass, and I didn't feel as if I were touching the ground anymore. And then my body collided with Max. The moment our skin connected, I felt as if lightning had struck me. A quick rush of pain ran from the top of my head down my spine, legs, and into my toes until it seemed to retreat into the soil—just before everything turned dark.

As I gasped for air, I felt the last tingles of electricity exit my body. I was pretty sure I must have fallen down and lay sprawled on the grass because something was poking into my back. My eyes had a tough time confirming that. I expected to see branches and leaves against a backdrop of the night sky, with perhaps a star or two, but that wasn't what I was looking at.

I blinked to check if I'd actually opened my eyes, and they seemed to be working fine. A dark, deep blue sky like nothing I'd ever seen before stretched out above me. It didn't resemble anything of the near blackness that night had to offer or the baby blue of a sunny day. A constant shimmer reflected back at me as if the entire surface were made of glass.

"What the..." I muttered as I pushed myself up to my elbows. As I did, I felt my fingers dig into something that felt suspiciously like warm sand. I glanced down and noticed I wasn't lying on grass at all. For a moment, I wondered if someone had dragged me down to the lake, but I wasn't even sure if there were sandy beaches down there. As I looked around, my mouth fell open.

The small clearing was gone, the bird feeder, the bench, even the brush cover and trees were gone. All there was for the eye to see was sand, desert-like sand that seemed to go on forever until it met the deep, dark blue of the sky at the horizon. Frantic, I whipped my head around as I sat up, hoping to find something that would explain what was going on. My mind raced, verging on panic as the thought of having died crossed my mind. Even if I'd believed in life after death while I were alive—which I didn't—this couldn't be it. This placed place seemed too bleak for either heaven or hell. There was absolutely nothing out here, except for...

As if my mind had shut down, it took a while for me to register the figure standing in front of me. When my mind caught up, it dawned on me that I'd been with Max before everything had changed around me, but this person standing before me wasn't an eighty-year-old man—quite the contrary.

"Jesus, who are you?" I managed to say as I stared at the warrior-like figure dressed in heavy armor. I might have focused on the dark blue eyes that stood out against his dark skin, eyes that seemed riddled with confusion. His mouth stood agape as if he were as surprised to see me as I was to see him.

He pressed a hand to his forehead and shook his head in confusion before he raked his fingers through his short black hair. The friendly face stood in contrast to the aggressive-looking outfit he wore from the neck down.

Sturdy leather straps held a well-defined breast-plate in place, and if that was any indication of the physical nature of the stranger's body, I would imagine some serious bodybuilding had been going on. His arms and legs were also protected by armor plating in a color so deep blue that it almost appeared black.

Again, it occurred to me that this guy wasn't Max. *Where the hell was Max?* I wished I could have been the kind of person who would have expressed more concern for the elderly man who seemed to have disappeared into thin air, but I couldn't fight the fears taking control of me.

Within the blink of an eye, time caught up with me, and I scrambled backward. Sand flew everywhere, and I felt it enter my sneakers as I struggled to get to my feet. I turned away from the figure, and I was about to make a run for it when it occurred to me I had nowhere to go. Panic rose inside me as my heart beat frantically inside my chest. Blue sky and sand were all there was. *Where the hell would I go?*

"Sam," a familiar deep voice said, and I froze. It was Max; I heard Max's voice, but as I quickly glanced around, all I could see was the stranger in the armored suit. The hairs on my neck rose, and I felt a cold shiver run down my back. *How did this person know my name?* The thought only lasted for a second before all my instincts started screaming for me to run, and that's what I did.

Without looking back, I ran as fast as I could. It didn't seem to matter that there was nowhere to go. As far as the eye could see, plains of sand stretched out in front of me, and even though it hindered the pace at which I was running, I didn't care. I just wanted to get away from this stranger in his ominous-looking armor.

"Sam, wait!" the stranger yelled as if he knew me. "I can explain."

His voice sounded just as close as it had before I started running, and I realized he was following me.

"Get away from me," I shouted as I struggled to stay on my feet. With each step, my sneakers seemed to sink deeper into the uneven soil. Sweat dripped down my face, and I didn't even dare to contemplate how this place could feel so hot without there being a sun visible in the sky.

All I could do was keep my eyes fixed on the uneven surface that lay before me and remain focused on staying upright. I couldn't afford to fall down, not with this stranger so close on my tail. *Was he still there?* I didn't dare look over my shoulder. The sounds around me seemed to dissipate until only my heavy breathing and the constant pounding of my heart resonated within my ears. I could almost imagine having managed to get away from the stranger when an arm suddenly wrapped around my waist.

I yelped in surprise but then screamed in despair as the stranger pulled me to a stop.

"Get off me!" I shouted as I struggled against the arm holding me captive.

"Sam, please," the stranger said, "you have to calm down."

Ignoring him, I screamed again and beat my fist against the arm holding me. Having seen the stranger's build, I could have guessed it wouldn't do me much good, and the armor that enveloped the muscular arm probably hurt my hand more than it did him. As suddenly as the stranger's arm had gripped me, he released me, and I fell to my knees.

Sand stuck to my sweaty palms as I caught myself on my hands. I struggled to get air into my lungs. Every muscle in my body seemed to have taken on a life of its own as I felt uncontrollable tremors run through me. I closed my eyes and focused on taking steady breaths. It wouldn't help my situation if I started to hyperventilate and pass out—although that might make it easier. At least, I wouldn't feel it if he killed me after I passed out.

A tentative hand on my shoulder brought me out of my morbid thoughts, and I flinched. I pulled away from the hand, swirled around, and, in doing so, launched a considerate amount of sand into the air. Shifting to my butt, I leaned on my arms and dug my feet into the ground for traction in case I needed to get up quickly.

I had to squint until the dust cloud I'd created settled. Realizing that running wouldn't get me out of this situation, I froze and focused on the stranger a mere three feet away.

He knelt in the sand and held his hands up, palms out, as if he wanted to convince me of his nonthreatening nature.

I swallowed hard as I waited for what was to come next, and dug my fingers deeper into the sand to keep my hands from shaking.

"Please," the stranger said again. "I can explain...just try to calm down."

If it weren't for the fact that I was staring at a stranger, I would have sworn that I was listening to Max's voice—him or James Earl Jones. But the image of the man dressed in armor did not jibe with the memory of the sweet old man that I shared a bench with.

I glanced around to check if my situation had changed. It clearly hadn't. My hands balled into fists, squeezing the sand as I closed my eyes and took a deep breath. The stranger hadn't killed me yet, so that was a good thing, and the way he seemed to be sitting there patiently waiting for me to compose myself might be another good sign. As my breathing evened out, I felt confident enough to trust my voice, and I opened my eyes.

"Who...are you?"

"You know who I am," he said.

I shook my head because I didn't think I'd be able to force the words out. I closed my eyes again. Taking a deep breath, I forced myself to think. Being miraculously transported to a desert was something I didn't think I'd be able to figure out, so I tried to focus on the man who knelt before me and apparently seemed convinced that I knew him.

With the fear momentarily overruled by curiosity, I narrowed my eyes and scrutinized the face staring back at me. The man looking at me was young and strong, and even though he resembled a younger version of Max, it couldn't be him. Besides, Max's eyes were brown instead of blue. My eyes teared up as I glanced around at my surrounding again. *What the hell had I gotten myself into?* I flinched as the stranger leaned in and reached out a hand.

"Please...please don't...I just..." I could hear myself fumble the words—not sure if I wanted to beg for my life or cry for help.

"It's okay, Sam," he said in that soothing voice of his. "It's me, Max. It's really me. Just give me a chance to explain everything." His brows furrowed as he contemplated his words. "Well, maybe not explain all of it, because, who knows everything, but most...I mean *some* of it." He smiled, and it made the similarities to Max even more evident.

"You can't be Max," I said, throwing up a hand to wave at him but inadvertently creating another cloud of dust. "You're all...young and stuff." He shifted closer on his knees with his hand still stretched out, and on pure instinct, I pushed my legs to edge back. I raised a hand in defense. "Please don't come any closer."

I felt like a rabbit caught in a noose as my eyes scanned the horizon. I'd already tried running, and that hadn't worked out very well. Despite the lack of a sun hovering in the sky, my feeble attempt at escape had left me hot and sweaty. My breath still came in short bursts, and my chest ached as I tried to get air into my lungs. Sand caked the hand I was holding up, but it didn't stop it from shaking, and so I dug my fingers back into the loose soil. I had no choice but to face whatever this stranger had planned for me.

"Your name is Samantha Judd, and for the past year or so we've been sharing lunchtime together," he said. "During that time, we've had some interesting conversations and shared a lot...well, mostly I shared, and you listened."

I shook my head in defiance. What he was telling me wasn't possible.

"Is he your dad or something?" I said. That had to be it. Max had a son, although he had never told me about having children.

"Sam, please just look around you. You're not home anymore." He paused to let that sink in. At his request, I looked around again as if that would reveal something more than the sand and the deep blue sky.

"This isn't possible," I muttered under my breath.

"Trust me: it's me," he said as our eyes reconnected, "and I can help you get home again."

"What are you?" I asked with a tremor in my voice.

"Well, I'm not from Earth if that's what you're asking." My eyes grew wide as my mouth fell open.

"You're...you're..." I stammered, "an alien."

A broad smile lightened up Max's face as he said, "Take me to your leader."

CHAPTER SIX

I just glared at him.

"Sorry," Max said, "I always wanted to say that."

I couldn't reply, and I couldn't take my eyes off him. Unable to move, I just sat there.

"Okay," he said, "let me make you a deal. Why don't we just walk a little. I hear it's good for your health, and I'll explain what I can?"

"What you can," I repeated under my breath, too stunned to make a normal sentence.

"Yeah, what I can," Max said as he offered his hand for me to take. Stuck in the middle of a desert on what might be a different planet, I figured there wasn't much else I could do.

I pulled my hand from out of the sand and raised it to meet his. I hesitated before I placed my hand in the palm of his, and he gently pulled me to my feet.

As soon as I stood, I jerked my hand from his as if he'd set it on fire.

My vision swayed a little, and I bent over to grip my knees. Grains of sand ground the palms of my hands, and I patted my pants in the hopes of clearing some away. The more I did, though, the more it became clear that the pesky, gritty particles had infested my clothes.

"You okay?" he asked. I straightened and had to look up to meet his gaze. This version of Max stood at least six feet tall, while the old Max was closer to my height. It seemed impossible that these two distinctively different people could be one and the same person.

The glare I shot him must have conveyed my thoughts because he stepped back and gestured for me to follow.

"That's it," he said as if he were coaxing me out of my shell. My feet started to move, and before I knew it, we walked side by side. Max kept his distance, and I appreciated that. I also appreciated that he didn't start his explaining right away, and I used the time to get my head on a little straighter because I felt as if I were on the brink of a nervous breakdown. By the time he did speak, I'd lost all track of time.

"How are you doing over there?" he asked.

I scowled at him, annoyed that he even had to ask the question.

"How do you think I'm doing?" I replied harshly. "I'm on the verge of freaking out." It seemed the fear

I'd suffered from before had morphed into anger, but that didn't stop me from feeling unsettled.

"Hmm," he said as he stared ahead with a thoughtful look on his face that stirred my irritation.

"Not *hmm*," I said and stopped walking. "What the hell am I doing here and how do I get home? No, better yet, where the hell is here?"

Max moved toward me but stopped at an arm's length. He glanced at the empty desert as if it were something special before he raised his arm.

Embedded in his armor sat a device that took up most of his forearm with a built-in screen. As he touched it, there was a soft beep, and he narrowed his eyes at it before he turned to stare at some point in the distant.

A combination of concern and contemplation marred his face that rekindled some of that uneasiness brewing in my gut. His gaze settled back on me, and despite the strange blue color of his eyes, I could see the old Max staring back at me, just like he had the last time we'd sat on that bench in the clearing. After the morning I'd had then, I must have looked like shit to him, and I could only imagine how I appeared to him now. It seemed impossible that this was still the same day.

Max opened his mouth to speak, but then closed it again. He seemed to hesitate, as if he were worried about how I'd take it. Considering how I'd reacted not that long ago, that seemed reasonable, but I needed him to tell me what was going on.

"I don't know why or how you're here," he finally said.

That wasn't the answer I was looking for. I swallowed. "But you can get me back, right?" I couldn't hide the despair dripping from my voice. I wasn't exactly cut out for this kind of stuff—whatever this was.

With an easy smile gracing his face, he said, "That won't be a problem," with enough confidence that it soothed my mind a little.

I blew out a breath and felt some of the tension flow from my body. My heart still pounded faster than it should, but the franticness that had taken control of me before had dissipated. Despite the apparent differences, I felt a sense of familiarity around Max that seemed to help calm my nerves.

"Then please, take me home," I said in a pleading tone. "I would like to go home now."

Max's eyes never wandered from mine as he shot me a sympathetic look.

"I am not sure if that is a good idea right now," he said. "I don't even know how it was possible for you to end up here." The words struck me like a fist, and before he could explain, I lashed out at him.

"What?" I shouted. My nerves hadn't even begun to settle, and my heart had never stopped firing on all four cylinders. "You just said that it wouldn't be a problem and now you're telling me you won't." I couldn't tell if it had been anger or fear that had taken over, but it didn't stop me from taking a step to close the distance between me and this supposedly younger version of Max.

"Please," Max said, raising his hands again in that nonthreatening manner that he had used before. "I will explain, but I need you to calm down and breathe." He waved his hands as if he were some kind of yoga-teacher who had no idea of what he was doing.

Max was right, though, and I needed to calm down because if this got any worse, I was going to pass out. Feeling my knees go weak, I gave in and sat down in the sand before my legs could collapse on their own.

As I closed my eyes and lowered my head between my legs, I sensed Max kneeling by my side.

"Alright, I will get you home," he said with enough conviction in his voice that it would be hard to doubt him. Taking a deep breath, I raised my head and stared into those dark blue eyes of his. He looked at me with that same grandfatherly concern that I had witnessed not that long ago at the small clearing. Intellectually, I still couldn't fathom that this strong warrior-like man was the same person as the warm and gentle elderly man that I spent my lunch hour with, but with that look, something deep inside told me that they were one and the same.

Max checked the device on his wrist again before he tugged at a delicate chain around his neck and pulled what looked like a pendant from behind his armor. On closer inspection, I realized that it was a sparkling stone, which I recognized from that afternoon. It was one of the gemstones that had fallen from the box. Unlike before, it sparkled like a diamond. Drawn in by the color, I looked up at the sky and saw it had the exact same dark blue color.

A hand on my knee caused me to return my attention back to Max, and I noticed that he had his eyes closed. I froze at the sight of his furrowed brows that revealed a look of concentration. *Was this it? Was Max going to take me home?* I held my breath and waited for whatever was about to happen. A long moment later, I was still waiting.

Unable to hold my breath any longer, I exhaled in a deep, long sigh and triggered Max to open his eyes.

"What?" I asked at the look of confusion on his face. A bead of sweat ran from his hairline down his temple as Max shook his head.

"I'm..." he started to say, but instead of finishing his sentence he glanced at the device strapped to his forearm.

"Max," I said in an attempt to recapture his attention, "whatever you were doing right now, was that supposed to bring me home?" My voice held a tremble that I couldn't control, and I felt my heart rate pick up again. If he had just tried to take me home, then, given the fact that we were still here, something was wrong. When Max didn't answer, I tapped the device strapped to his wrist as I said,

"Please don't tell me that thing is broken."

He finally lifted his head, and the concern that I had seen on his face before had been replaced by a kind smile.

"No," he said, "the device is not broken, but taking you back so soon after we've arrived, is inadvisable."

"What, like the batteries need recharging or something?"

He smiled again as he took my hands and pulled me to my feet.

"I'm afraid it's a bit more complicated than that," Max said, "but you don't have to worry."

"But I am worried," I said. "In fact, I'm scared out of my mind, and I don't even know where I am or how I got here."

"Yes, well, that might be a bit hard to explain," he said. It felt as if he were giving me the turnaround with his vague answers and I had enough of it.

"Try me," I said in a harsh tone.

Max took another quick look at the device strapped to his arm and faced the horizon in the direction we were heading.

"Have you ever watched that TV series called *Doctor Who*?" he asked as he started walking again. I glared at his back, but he wouldn't be able to see, so I hurried after him.

"If you're about to tell me you're a Time Lord, I'm going to scream," I said in a loud voice, "and I won't care how old you are...or were." He grinned, and for an instance, I could see the old Max sitting on that bench in the small clearing.

"No, I'm no Time Lord," he said, "but you know the show. That's good." He scanned the horizon again and took another glance at the thingy on his arm.

"Then you know how he uses that phone box to travel through time and space."

Hoping that this conversation would be going somewhere, I nodded.

"Instead of a phone box, I use this."

Max grasped the necklace around his neck again and showed me the sparkling stone hanging from it. I had guessed that the device strapped to his forearm was supposed to get me home. It turned out I was wrong.

"You use a diamond to travel through space and time," I said indignantly as I faced him again.

"Not exactly. We haven't traveled through space or time" he replied, "and it's not a diamond—it's a sapphire."

Unable to care about what he was holding, I rolled my eyes.

"Then what?" I said as I stopped again and felt the frustration sear inside me.

"We should keep moving," he said as he glanced at the device again.

I threw up my arms and growled.

"I've got sand in my shoes, and I'm hot without there even being a sun in the sky, and you keep talking in circles," I said. "I'm not going anywhere until you tell me what's going on and tell me where the hell we're even going anyway in this godforsaken place because there is nothing out here."

"That last question is easy," he said as he pointed a finger. My eyes settled on the direction that he pointed in and I blinked.

"What the...how did...where..." I said, but I couldn't form a coherent sentence. Even though there wasn't a sun in the sky that could hinder my vision, I lifted my hand above my eyes as if to shield them. In the distance, I could make out a structure of some kind. From this far away, it looked like a wall that stretched out along the horizon. That thing must be bigger than the Great Wall of China. I couldn't tell where the structure ended, and the sky started while reaching along the entire horizon, and strangely enough, it seemed to have appeared from out of nowhere.

"C'mon, let's keep moving," Max said as he tugged the stone back behind the protection of his armor. "Once we're there, it'll be better to talk."

Lights evenly spaced along the length of the wall blinked on and off in intervals. The lights had the same color as the sky, and as they simultaneously flashed on, it looked as if the wall was one with the sky.

"What am I looking at?" I asked as we headed toward it.

"That is the border fence," Max said.

"That is a fence?" I asked and stopped walking. "That thing is massive."

Max reached out to touch my shoulder and nudge me forward. I flinched at the harmless gesture and didn't even know why.

He raised an apologetic hand and said, "I'm sorry, but it's best if we keep moving." He glanced at the device embedded in his armor and then did the same thing with our surroundings. For the first time, I noticed beads of sweat had gathered at the edge of his hairline again.

I glanced down at the running gear I was still wearing. My training tights and long-sleeved running top were made from a material that kept my body from overheating, but I guessed it wasn't designed for a desert workout. I wiggled my toes and felt the sand scratch my skin. My feet were already hurting, and I feared that blisters were bound to show up.

"Sam," Max said and gestured toward the fence. I wasn't sure if it were just me or if he was getting antsy.

We started walking again, and soon I was breathing heavily. Max had picked up the pace considerably as he kept scanning the area. He might have invoked a nervous tick within me, because every time he looked around, I started to do the same. I never noticed anything out of the ordinary, though—except for the fact that I was stranded in an alien desert and apparently without traveling through space or time.

It might have looked like a solid structure from a distance, but as we neared, I could tell it was a fence— a massive fence. Poles rose up from the ground every fifty feet or so and large beams intersected it to create a platform on which another section was built. With all these layers upon layers, the structure must have been as high as the Space Needle back home, but instead of wire mesh or bars, the actual fence part looked to be see-through.

The fluctuation in the fence seemed to increase with every step we neared. By this point, I could see figures in armor similar to what Max was wearing, standing on every layer of the fence.

"Is this home for you?" I asked.

"Huh, what..." he said taken off-guard, and I couldn't contain a grin.

"No, it's not. What gave you that idea?"

I looked up at the guards and pointed at them.

"You dress alike," I said.

"Ah, no," he replied. "What you're seeing when you look at me is a 'projective' cover."

I blinked. "A what?"

"It's like camouflage used in the military except for this camouflage allows the natives to see what they are most comfortable with," he said and paused as if to see if I'd gotten all of that. "It makes it easier for them to accept me."

"Ah," I said as I thought about it for a moment. "So why am I not seeing an eighty-year-old man, because that might have made it a little easier for me to get my head around all this—although not that I have my head around this at all..." My voice trailed off as my thoughts veered in a different direction.

"Is that why you look like a cross between Denzel Washington and Brad Pitt?" I asked.

Max shrugged as he shot me a lopsided grin.

"My brain projects what it needs to overcome its

obstacles. Sometimes these are the result of the things that I enjoy."

I stared up at him as I tried to make sense of what he'd just said. Had he said, "*What it needs*"? My foot caught in the sand, and I stumbled. Max reached out a hand to steady me, and he shot me a nervous smile before he returned his gaze to our surroundings. *What the hell had him acting so nervously?*

It turned out the fence wasn't exactly see-through. Well, it was, but I didn't imagine I would be able to walk through. The middle sections seemed to be made out of glass similar to the gemstone Max had shown me with the exact same blue color. As something that looked like a bolt of lightning flashed through the see-through barrier, the blue color magnified. No wonder the structure seemed to melt into the sky from a distance; the two looked exactly the same.

"Whose border is it anyway?" I asked as we approached the fence.

"I would prefer to go into that once we're safely behind the fence," he said as he glanced around again.

I followed his gaze and then threw up my arms. "Safe from what?" I asked as I spun around. "There is nothing out here." In the next moment, I felt as if I were in one of those movies where everything turned sour after someone had spoken a typical cliché like "I'll be right back."

The earth beneath my feet started to tremble, and the desert sand visibly shifted. In the distance, a cloud of smoke billowed up into the sky, but it dissipated as quickly as it had appeared. As it happened again, much closer this time, I noticed that it wasn't smoke at all. Desert sand shot up from the ground as if it had been sucked up by some localized vacuum cleaner and then spat out again. Dumbstruck, I stared at it until I felt a hand on my shoulder.

"We have to go now," Max said. The urgency was apparent in his voice. Before I'd turned, he'd already started running toward the fence. For a second, I was amazed by the speed at which he managed to run while he appeared to be talking into his forearm. This actually shouldn't have come as a surprise because he'd caught up with me pretty quickly before, but then I hadn't seen him move.

Behind me, I heard another burst of sand shooting up into the sky. It seemed even closer now, and the sound made me jump. In the next instance, I was running flat out to catch up with Max.

On the first platform, I noticed one of the guards waving his arms at us while he shouted something. I couldn't decipher his words, but I figured he meant hurry. I refused to let myself think about whatever it was that the guard was trying to convey. Thinking always got me into trouble, and I had a feeling this was a time to act.

I'd nearly caught up with Max, who had stopped before the fence as the sound of another burst of sand behind me led me to sneak a peek over my shoulder. I wasn't even sure what I was running from, but as soon as I looked, I wished I hadn't. The desert seemed to disappear into nothingness only a few feet behind me as if a giant sinkhole had opened up.

"Oh shit," I yelled as I tried to move faster, but the sand started to shift under my feet. I stumbled, but on hands and feet, I managed to stay moving as I felt a cold rush of air touch my sweat dampened skin. A shiver ran down my spine, but I wasn't sure if it was from the cold air itself or the fear of how deep this hole might be if it meant it was that cold. Ahead of me, I saw the fence open up and figures in the same armor as Max came rushing toward us.

I'd almost reached Max, but as our eyes met, his grew wide. His mouth moved, but I couldn't hear his words. He started in my direction, and I wanted to tell him that he was going the wrong way, but the ability to speak left me as I felt the ground disappear from underneath my feet, and all I could do was scream.

"Hang on!" Max shouted, but I wasn't hanging on to anything. He'd grabbed my arm and he was hanging on to me. I was just dangling over the edge of an abyss. My feet dug into the sand, trying to get perches, but the desert sand kept displacing itself, and my sneakers didn't allow me to get a foothold.

"Please don't let me fall," I begged as I looked up at Max. He was hanging halfway over the edge, and I couldn't imagine how he'd managed to not slide into the hole with me, but at this point, I didn't care. He was the only thing keeping me from falling down this black hole.

"Grab my other hand," Max yelled as our eyes met.

"No," I called back. "You'll fall in." His free hand was already reaching for me, so my reasoning didn't make any sense. Neither did Max defying gravity, but that was something we could get into later—if I made it out of this. I reached up to grab his hand but flinched at the sound of a loud crash, and I lost it again. The noise continued, and it reminded me of gunfire, but different. Another different sound that seemed like a cross between the hiss of a snake and a squealing pig times ten made my blood run cold, and I scrambled to grab hold of Max's hand.

The loud bangs seemed unending as Max looked over his shoulder and shouted, "Pull." Seemingly without effort, I was lifted from the hole and over the edge into Max's arms. Breathing heavily, I held onto him, afraid something would grab me and drag me back down.

"Thank you...thank you," I said between gasps. I looked over his shoulder and noticed the two men in armor behind Max. They must have been holding his legs, so he wouldn't tumble down into the hole after me. Before I could thank them, they were already on their feet pointing weapons at something and firing. They didn't look like the guns I was used to, more like staffs shooting bolts of lightning, but I guessed I hadn't been that far off in my assumption of hearing gunfire. None of that seemed to matter because my instincts screamed for me to get out of there.

Before I could act on my own, Max pulled me to my feet. My gaze shifted to my left, where half a dozen armored men stood and pointed their weapons up at the sky as they fired a constant barrage of lightning bolts. Max tugged at my arm, forcing me to move along with him, but I couldn't help my curiosity. I glanced over my shoulder in search of whatever it was that needed firing at, and my breath caught as I simultaneously stumbled over my own feet.

"Wha-what the hell is that?" I yelled as Max wrapped an arm around my waist. He was pulling me backward, while I couldn't seem to get my legs to work along with him. My brain couldn't fathom what I was looking at. Well, perhaps it could, but it just seemed impossible.

A snakelike creature rose up from a hole in the ground and stood as high as a three-story building. It had the misshaped head of a dragon with a mouthful of teeth that would make a great white jealous. Its eyes were as black as coals, while scales that looked like shiny plates ran up and down the length of its enormous body.

"Let's go, Sam," Max said close to my ear. It must have been the urgency in which he said it because my legs started to move. We had almost reached the fence as the creature hissed and snarled at the men firing their weapons at it. On the surface, the lightning bolts fired from the staff-like weapons did not seem to damage the creature, but I couldn't help but think that the strange-looking animal must be suffering in pain.

The men in armor started to move along with us. They kept firing their weapons in an even rhythm that seemed to be more about keeping the creature at bay than damaging it. Max and I reached the fence, and it felt as if I was doused with static electricity as we passed through the opening. The hairs on the back of my neck and all over my body stood up. If the hair on my head hadn't already faced every direction before, I was sure it would now.

"Move," Max shouted. He was still holding on to me, directing my every move, so I didn't think he would be yelling at me. Three men in armor joined us and found safety behind the fence as they took up positions at our side. Four of them were still out there as the creature lashed out. Even with the men up on the fence firing at it, the creature thrust its enormous head forward. Two of the men managed to duck in time to escape the blow, while the other two weren't as lucky. One of them was hit full on, and his body flew through the air until it hit the ground.

Without thinking, I pulled myself free from Max's grip and crossed the few yards to kneel at the man's side. The suit was bulky, and his face was hidden behind the visor of his helmet. I couldn't detect anything immediately wrong with him, except that he'd been knocked unconscious.

From my peripheral vision, I could see the fourth man being lifted off the ground as I heard his screams. I shivered at the sound that could only have been bones breaking, but I refused to look. Instead, I grabbed the man laying at my feet under his arms, intending to pull him behind the fence.

I'd managed about five feet and felt out of breath. I didn't know if it was exhaustion or if, more likely, his suit was just that plain heavy, but I needed help. The guards standing close to the fence were still firing their weapons at the creature as they waited for the remaining two men to make it behind the fence line. Fortunately, Max had noticed my struggle. He took the man's other arm, and together we dragged him behind the line.

CHAPTER SEVEN

Another burst of static sent a shiver up my spine, and I felt the hairs on the back of my neck stand up again. I turned to the fence in time to see a blue shimmer stretch across the entrance. It turned solid right before my eyes as if I were looking through glass. The snakelike creature was still out there, and it appeared angrier than before. I jumped as it struck the glass with its head. A lightning bolt flashed across the area it touched and into the creature. The thing screamed like an animal knowing it was about to be slaughtered, and I breathed easier as it shook its massive head before disappearing down the hole from which it had come in the first place.

"All clear," one of the men who towered over the rest shouted and gave way for the other men in armor to cheer in victory. I watched them as they held their staff weapons in the air and shouted something that sounded like *anguish*.

The tall man pressed a hand to his chest and bowed his head. The others followed his example as if he were the one in charge.

"To the fallen," he said in the same language as I had learned to speak as a child, "may they live in our memories—always." I wasn't sure why it surprised me that the man spoke English. Aliens always seemed to grasp the language perfectly in the movies or on TV—although this wasn't a movie or a TV show.

The guards that had gathered around the tall man repeated his words, and the silence that fell was only broken by the soft words of two men who asked me to step aside. As I did, they kneeled by the lifeless form Max and I had dragged behind the fence. They looked like first responders as they seemingly checked vitals before lifting the injured guard onto a stretcher and hurried off.

I felt an urge to follow them. This mere stranger had ventured beyond the safety of the fence to risk his life for Max and me, and I couldn't help but feel responsible.

Before I could follow, the tall man who had shouted the all clear briefly stopped the men holding the stretcher. I couldn't hear their conversation, but I could see the movement coming from the man lying on the stretcher. The tall man patted the injured guard's arm before he let him get carried off. I couldn't know for sure if the guard would be all right, but I felt a sense of relief that at least he would have a chance.

As I stood there and watched the guards drag off the injured man, it felt as if all the energy started to drain from my body. Beyond the entrance, it seemed the creature had lost its interest and had backed off from the fence. I stared at it, not quite sure what I was looking at. *Was this for real?*

"Hey," Max said as he stepped into my field of vision. I blinked to regain focus and looked up to meet his gaze. "You look a little pale there. You okay?"

I didn't know what to say because I didn't know how I was feeling. It seemed as if my brain had overloaded and couldn't deal with all the information it had absorbed. As if out of self-preservation, it had returned itself to idle mode.

"Just take a deep breath," Max said as he placed a gentle hand on my shoulder. It took a moment for his words to register, but I did as he asked. "That's it."

It wasn't hard to read the concern in those strange blue eyes, but I didn't want him to worry about me.

"I'm fine," I said, but from the look on Max's face, I didn't think he'd bought it. He was about to say something when someone calling out interrupted him.

"Maximus," that same tall man from before said as he approached us. He removed his helmet and held out a hand before both men grabbed each other's lower arms. "It is good to see you, old friend." Max didn't just reciprocate the arm shake but pulled the man into a hug.

"It has been too long, my friend," Max replied. They slapped each other on the back before Max released his apparent friend and gestured for me to join them. I took another deep breath and felt rather relieved by the distraction.

"Is he going to be all right?" I asked as I pointed in the direction they had taken the man on the stretcher. The words flew from my mouth before I had a chance to think about them and before Max had an opportunity to introduce me to his friend. I couldn't help it. Those guards had willingly left the safety of behind the fence to make sure the snake with the dragon head wouldn't eat Max and me. I tried not to linger on the absurdity of that. Still, I felt a need to know if the injured guard would be all right.

Max's friend grinned, and his eyes held a playful glint as he replied, "She shall be just fine."

Even though I had no way of knowing the guard's gender because of all the armor and the helmet she'd been wearing, I still felt heat creep up my neck at the apparent mistake.

"Cyril," Max said, "this is my friend, Sam."

I had to look up at the man, who must have been at least six foot three, and I imagined his body to be just as solid as his armor looked. He would have been intimidating with his dark eyes and sword handle poking out from behind his bald head if it hadn't been for the friendliest smile I'd ever seen spreading across his face.

"Sam, this is Cyril," Max added. "He is the leader of the Ora guards."

"Welcome to Ora," Cyril said as he grabbed my arm as he'd done with Max. The firm grip on my lower arm hurt, but I didn't want to insult the man, so I clenched my teeth and tried not to show the agony on my face. Cyril shot me a curious glance and then turned his eyes to inspect my arm. "Strange armor your friend wears."

He kept turning my arm and tugging at my shirt as if it were some commodity, and as he started to twist it, it was time to let him know I'd had enough.

"Hey," I said, "that hurts."

"Cyril, my friend," Max said as he intercepted Cyril's arm, "Sam's clothing is not armor."

That disclosure earned Max a disapproving glance from Cyril. The tall man let his eyes roam over my running attire and frowned.

"You dare to let your friend breach the dunes without armor," he said and sounded appalled before he turned to me. "You must forgive me for my friend's ignorance in leading you out into the dunes without proper protection." He reached down and took my hand again but used a gentle touch this time. He kissed the back of my hand. "A strange and beautiful woman like yourself should never have been subjected to the likes of the Anguis without the ability to defend herself."

There was that word again, although this time it didn't sound like "anguish," but more like "an-gwis." For a second, I wondered if it were the snake-crea-ture's name, but the rest of Cyril's words combined with him looking straight into my eyes, caused my cheeks to flush red. The blue light from the fence bounced off his bald head and distorted his bronze complexion as he slightly bowed.

"Yeah, yeah," Max interjected, "that's quite enough."

With a wink, Cyril released my hand and spread his arms.

"Welcome to Ora," he said again and took a deep breath. Feeling a bit overwhelmed by all the sensations hitting me, I also took a deep breath in the hopes of calming my nerves. Instead of the warm desert air that I'd expected to inhale, I noticed the temperature had dropped significantly. My mouth dropped open as Cyril moved his large frame and allowed me to take in my new surroundings.

"Impossible," I said under my breath as I peered across the green pastures filled with grazing animals that looked suspiciously like sheep. Wooden fences lined the grassy fields so the animals wouldn't stray into the forest surrounding the land. In the distance, I could make out small structures that gradually increased in numbers to form a village. The sky above still looked like a deep blue glass ceiling, but nothing else resembled anything of the desert we had encountered on the other side of the fence. It seemed as if we'd stepped into yet another different world.

"Not impossible," Cyril commented after he noticed what must have been a look of utter amazement on my face. "Perhaps unlikely, but very much possible. You should know these things if you're traveling with Max."

I wasn't sure how to reply to that and searched

Max's face for support. As if he were able to read my mind, Max turned to Cyril.

"What has Anguis so aroused so early in the season?" Max asked. From the context of his question, I determined that indeed Anguis was the creature's name, but I still didn't have a clue to what that thing was.

Feeling out of place, I quelled the urge to ask Max yet again what happened to my surroundings. Everything kept changing so fast, and it was hard for me to keep up, but Max's abrupt change on the subject made me wary of asking the question with Cyril around.

A crease formed on Cyril's face, changing his demeanor to serious as he replied, "She's been at it for a couple of days now; I think something has her spooked. There have been a lot more sightings of her on this side of the dunes, but we don't know why."

"Anguis?" I asked.

Cyril raised an eyebrow at me before narrowing his eyes and shooting Max and angry look. "You haven't even—" Cyril started to say, but Max cut him off with a wave of his hand.

"She's the snake thing you've seen, and she's usually pretty domestic," Max said as if it were something I'd come across daily. My mouth fell open. That thing had killed a man, and apparently, it lived in the dunes where Max and I had been strolling around for most of the day, and they were talking about it as if it were some kind of pet.

"You call that domestic!" I said. "That thing—"

"Sam!" The harshness of Max's voice made me flinch, and I swallowed the rest of what I wanted to say. He shot me a stern look as if he were berating some small child. I felt as if I were standing before Trish telling me how to do my job even though I could probably do it with my eyes closed—except this wasn't about my job.

The strangeness of my surroundings, the men in weird armor, a fence bigger than anything that I'd seen before registered as my eyes strayed away from Max's. I'd felt out of my element for over a year now, but that was nothing compared to this. My hands were shaking, and I balled them into fists. All I could do was follow Max's lead and apparently that meant keeping my mouth shut—for now.

"Have you heard from Danara?" Max asked. "Has he had the same trouble with Anguis?" Cyril shook his head.

"Nothing, except that most of the people who had joined him have returned to Ora."

The frown on Max's face told me this wasn't a good thing. "Why have they returned?"

"It seems that Danara has been secluding himself and has denied them access to the library and other parts of the main building, so they haven't been able to get much work done. They figured they might just as well make themselves useful during the harvesting season in the village. I have asked Deyo to return to keep an eye on things."

"I see," Max said as his gaze drifted toward the

fence. "I wished I had more time, then I might have gone out there and—"

"Do not dwell on it," Cyril interjected. "You should focus on the alignment."

Their eyes met, and Max nodded. As the smile returned to Cyril's face, he added, "Beg your pardon for a moment." He didn't wait for a reply and set off to talk to one of the men in armor.

I turned to look up at the massive fence, that from this angle looked to be one with the sky. To my left and right the fence seemed to go on forever and as far as I could tell, armored guards stood posted every couple of hundred feet or so.

"Sam," Max said in a gentle voice. My breath caught as I turned to look at him and I had to clear my throat before I could give him a reply.

"It's just a lot to take in," I said and hesitated.

"I'm sorry," he said, and it wasn't hard to read the sincerity from his face. "But I need them to think you're with me. I don't want them to wonder or worry about you or who you are."

"Why?" I noticed the harsh tone in my voice, but I figured I had the right to sound a little upset if I didn't just have to worry about being stranded in this strange place but also had to worry about the inhabitants.

"Basically," he said and paused. He shot me one of those looks that told me he intended to hit me with something and he was trying to figure out if I could handle it. "I'll be honest with you, so please don't..." I recognized the hesitation in his voice. It wasn't just with him. I'd heard it before with Kay or even Ellie and it was one of the reasons I'd run from my previous life. People who had witnessed one of my episodes tended to react like that afterward as if I were made of glass and needed special treatment. I knew there was validation in that kind of a response, but that didn't mean I liked it. Max scratched the back of his head as he considered how to continue.

"The truth is, I have no idea what has happened, or how you've come to be here."

At the utter look of disbelief on my face, he quickly added, "But that doesn't mean I don't know how to get you home."

I tried to swallow, but my throat felt as dry as the desert that lay beyond the fence. Despite the lack of saliva in my mouth, I opened it anyway, but before I could say anything, Max raised a hand.

"It's just easier for them and for me when they just assume that things are the way they are supposed to be. These people have enough to worry about, and I don't want them to worry about you."

"Do..." I started to say and hesitated. I met his unfamiliar blue gaze, that even though it was so far removed from the dark brown ones that belonged to the old Max, I felt oddly comforted by. "Do I have to worry?" A brief smile curved his lips but vanished as quickly as it had appeared.

"I have a feeling you're always worried."

He wasn't wrong about that. I did have a tendency to worry about things, and it usually meant avoiding the aggravating stuff that inclined me to make a fool out of myself. Despite the reasons for me being here, this situation had already proven to be a challenge, and I had a feeling there would be more to come. Running away like I'd done with my job wasn't an option here, and there was nothing I could do about that now, except deal with it.

In the hopes of finding some reassurance to do that, I asked, "Do you promise you can get me home?"

Without hesitation, Max gave me the confirmation I needed.

"I promise."

He looked me straight in the eyes, and I knew he was telling me the truth—at least a truth he believed himself.

"Okay," I said, hoping to sound convincing, "I believe you."

Max kept his eyes on me, and he hadn't actually asked a question, but the concern was evident on his face.

Blowing out a breath, I added, "I'll be fine—I think." I hadn't intended to voice my afterthought, but Max merely nodded.

"Maximus," Cyril shouted from a distance, "I shall see to Moira. You two go ahead. The alignment isn't until the day after tomorrow, so we'll have plenty of time to catch up." Max threw a hand up and waved at Cyril.

"Will do," he shouted before turning to me. "C'mon, and this time around you can ask as many questions as you'd like."

I managed a smile but despite my internal pep

talk, I still felt unsettled. My brain was screaming at me to read the warning signals and kept the fear inside me alive, but at the same time, I felt exhilarated—a sensation that had eluded me all my life. Strangely enough, I welcomed it.

I couldn't keep my eyes from roaming the landscape. Walking along the narrow dirt road toward the village made me feel as if I were strolling that yellow brick road wearing sneakers instead of those godawful ruby slippers. Beyond the plains of grass with their grazing animals and fields holding crops that I couldn't iden-tify, the land reached out for miles to where it was bordered by trees. A thick forest rose up out of the valley until it was stopped by the rock-faced mountain range that stretched along the horizon with a single peak that stood out against the deep blue sky.

As Max and I made our way to the village, a few of the smaller animals had gained an interest in us and had started to follow on the other side of the wooden enclosure. On closer inspection, the animals turned out to look like sheep and probably were sheep. In one way, this seemed odd to me, but then, every-thing about this was weird.

We hadn't spoken since we had left the fence even though he'd offered to let me ask any question I'd like. I didn't think I'd be able to keep the tremor from my voice, and I wanted to calm my racing heart a bit before I aroused myself again by grasping at things I'd probably never understand. My hands still shook; I knew the signs far too well and forced myself to focus on the surroundings and the things that might trick my mind into thinking I was home—like grass. Grass was good.

As the small buildings of the village ahead of us grew a little bigger, it occurred to me that I might not have another chance to talk to Max about what was going on. It had become clear that he didn't want me asking questions to any of the inhabitants of this world.

I returned my gaze back to the grassy pastures as I sensed my vision starting to blur around the edges. If I wanted to get some answers, then I needed to get my head on straight. I balled my hands into fists, determined to stop them from shaking, and took a couple of deep breaths. Experience told me this wasn't the time for an in-depth conversation, but it didn't seem circumstances left me any choice.

Max had kept his distance as we walked, but each time I shot him a sideways glance, I noticed him keeping an eye on me. He looked kind of impressive in his armor—strong and handsome. Instead of an old man with white hair, a wrinkled face, and the hint of a beer belly, I was faced with this warrior-like younger version of Max with jet-black hair and well-toned arms. Having him tower over me felt a bit daunting. I couldn't remember the old Max being this tall. Despite the differences in height and those out-of-place piercing blue eyes, there wasn't a doubt in my mind that it was Max walking by my side. Perhaps it had something to do with his oh, so recognizable voice. With this idyllic backdrop, he looked as if he'd stepped out of a history book or perhaps even out of the legends of King Arthur's court.

I raked my hands through my short hair and over my face as I felt unsure of where to start. The how of all this seemed magical to me, and even if it were scientific, which I guessed with Max claiming to be an alien and all seemed more likely, I doubted I'd understand any of it. The why of things would be the more prudent approach although Max had already stated that he didn't know what had happened. Max had shouted more than once for me to leave the clearing before any of this happened—still...

"Why are we here?"

Max grinned as if he were expecting the question. "I don't presume you'd settle with me saying to appreciate the view?" he said. I shot him a hard glare, and he added, "I guess not." Max drew in a deep breath as he purposefully glanced around the area. "It is quite beautiful, isn't it?"

"Don't bullshit me, Max," I said. "This shit isn't funny." My voice reached a higher pitch than usual, as it peaked along with my agitation. "Look at this." I threw a hand up to indicate the fields and animals surrounding us. "I mean, I should be home in bed and not in freaking New Zealand with sheep and a glass roof."

To emphasize my point, I turned and pointed at the massive fence with its blue lights. "Look at that and don't even mention that snake thing beyond the

fence that for all intent and purposes tried to kill us
—*kill us*."

I was still pointing in the direction of the fence as a memory of hanging over the edge of that sinkhole flashed through my mind. Along with the image, I felt a sudden rush of cold as if I were back there all over again, suspended above a black hole that would have swallowed me up if Max hadn't caught me.

A sudden rush of fear fell over me like it hadn't done in almost a year. I silently cursed myself. The signals had been there, and I should've listened to my body. *Wasn't that why I'd gone running in the first place before this happened—to clear my head?* Instead of clearing it, stuff had been piling up in my brain, including the most unimaginable circumstances, and I've been walking around in an alien place, mulling it over. Overthinking always got me into trouble.

My eyes stung as I fought the tears threatening to spill over. Bending forward, I pinched the bridge of my nose and took a couple of deep breaths. It felt as if everything that had happened this past day just hit me in the face. I wasn't sure if it had been Max's dismissive comments or just the pile-up of things accumulating in my brain.

My knees buckled, and as my butt touched the ground, I pulled my legs up and lowered my head, hoping to catch my breath. After what my shrink liked to call my trigger event, a day like I'd had at the retirement home today might have triggered an episode like this. Fortunately, those days rarely occurred, and running helped clear my head. Today, though, things had kept going from bad to worse, and it had caught up with me.

Max kneeled at my side as I closed my eyes tightly shut and tried to keep myself from hyperventilating. He placed a hand on my back as he said, "Breathe, Sam."

I wanted to lash out at him at the apparent stupidity of his comment, but fortunately for him, I couldn't utter a word. "In through the nose...two, three, four," he added. "Hold it...and out through the mouth, two, three, four." He kept repeating his words, and I focused on his rhythm. Slowly, I managed to regain control over my breathing and lifted my head. Tears rolled down my cheeks as I opened my eyes and quickly used the sleeve of my shirt to wipe them away.

My heart pounded like crazy against my rib cage, and my hands trembled. Even as my vision cleared, I kept my eyes riveted to the ground. There wasn't any reason for me to feel ashamed, I knew that, but knowing something and acting upon it were two very different things.

Max took a seat by my side and kept his hand resting on my back as I took another deep breath. He didn't say anything, and I appreciated that. It gave me time to collect myself. I swallowed to get rid of the lump in my throat and managed to raise my head. If it weren't for the deep blue sky and the lack of a sun, I might have enjoyed the view of the two sheep staring at me as they chewed.

"So..." Max said after a while, "I'm not entirely

sure how to proceed right now or how you want to deal with this."

Somewhat surprised, I looked up at him. One of my episodes had never triggered a response like that. Usually, people reacted with a bunch of sympathy and pity—which I hated. Max looked at me as if he knew what I was thinking.

"I'm guessing you've seen this kind of reaction before," I replied. It seemed obvious, knowing how he'd helped me focus on my breathing to keep me from hyperventilating.

"I might look young," Max said with a grin, "but I've been around." In comparison, looking young might have been an understatement. The old Max back home was in his eighties, with a wrinkled face and gray hair. This version didn't even have a single crow's foot around the eyes.

"I guess," I said as I realized that with Max being an alien, he might even be older than eighty.

"In my experience," he said, "there are some people who want to talk about what's going on inside their heads, while others don't, but I'm thinking you're more of the latter."

I managed a smile but knew he was right.

"I tend to think too much about the things I can't control and then get worked up about them."

"I see," he said and nodded his head. He didn't add anything else, as if he were waiting for me to fill in the gaps.

"Maybe if you could tell me a little more about

this place and what's going on, it'll stop me from conceiving a bunch of crazy shit on my own."

"Okay," Max said in a subdued tone, "but first, I want you to know that I never intended for this to happen. I don't understand how you got dragged into this. You have to believe me." I recognized the remorse in his voice, but at this point, it didn't make sense to lay blame. Sometimes things just happen; I just wished it wasn't always happening to me.

"I believe you," I said and meant it.

Taking a deep breath, Max said, "I am here to align the Sapphire Twins." He removed his hand from my back and used it to fiddle with the necklace around his neck. He retrieved the stone from behind his breastplate and held it out.

The small gem lay in the palm of his hand. It wasn't shining as brightly as it had before, but it was the same stone that I'd held after I'd dropped a bunch of them in the grass at the clearing and the same one that the older version of Max had held before transporting us to this place. I stared at his hand, holding nothing more than a piece of shiny rock—at least that's what it looked like to me. "This stone is part of a network," he continued. "It has a twin here within this place." He gestured toward the town. "The day after tomorrow, I'll be able to align both of them so they will be calibrated to the same frequency again, and then I'll be able to take you home."

I pulled my gaze from the stone to glance up at Max. There wasn't any pity in his eyes, only concern, but it seemed safer to keep the conversation away from me. Max clearly knew what had just happened, but I didn't think I'd be able to explain the reason behind it.

"Why..." I started to say. My voice sounded scratchy, and I coughed to clear it. "Why does it need aligning?"

Max shot the stone a sideways glance before turning to me.

"Well," he said with a look of contemplation, "I guess the best way to describe it is to compare it to the sun."

"There is no sun," I said as I briefly looked up. He shook his head in a way I remembered the old Max would when he thought me to be impatient.

"You know how the earth rotates around the sun along with Mars, Jupiter, and all the other planets," he said.

"I think I heard someone mention that, yeah."

Max shot me a wry smile before he continued.

"The stones are part of a network that works on a similar level. Except to keep them in orbit and their proper position from the sun, they need to be aligned once in a while."

"But these are stones, not planets," I said.

"True," Max replied as he slipped the stone back into its hiding spot, "but the blue sapphire stone has a connection to this world and its twin." With a little effort, Max got to his feet in his heavy armor and held out a hand for me. I took it, let him pull me up, and followed as he started to walk in the direction of the village.

"So...if you don't align the stone, this planet will

get knocked out of orbit," I said and tried to keep the incredulity from my voice. "That doesn't sound like a sturdy system."

Max shook his head again before saying, "I said it could be described as planets rotating around the sun."

"But you also said that the stone was a connection to this world."

"Exactly, but worlds come in many forms," he said. I couldn't hide the look of confusion on my face, and Max grinned.

"You lost me," I said as I walked up a bridge that crossed a narrow stream. Max laughed, and his eyes sparkled with amusement.

"Everything that happens around you exists in your world: your friends, your family, your life. Other people live in their own worlds. Sometimes worlds only exist in books or the movies or even in someone's head, but that doesn't make it less real—at least not until you flip the last page."

He eyed me with curiosity as I absorbed the information, and it made me wonder if his analogy was just a vague explanation or if it held any kind of truth. Not sure if I wanted to understand, my gaze followed the stream of water from where it came down the mountain when something occurred to me.

"So the same goes for the other stones?" I asked. "Are they like this one. Do they lead to other worlds?"

Max's eyes grew wide as he stared at me.

"How do you know about—"

"I dropped them," I quickly said before he could finish his sentence, "when I went back for your bag."

"Ah," he said as I witnessed the dawn of realization on his face, "that's why they were all in disarray. I'd almost accused the night porter of going through my stuff."

I shot him a meek grin as I pulled a hand through my hair.

"Sorry."

"That's okay," he replied. "So you touched them?" I grimaced at the memory of gathering the stones.

"I all but burned my hand holding them."

"Really?" Max frowned before he shot me a look that I couldn't decipher.

"Do you think that's significant?" I asked.

"It might be," Max said. "I just don't know how." He looked contemplative as I prayed that I hadn't broken the stone that was supposed to get me home. "It could explain why the stone reacted the way it did when I activated it and it pulled you in. It recognized you," he added.

"The stone recognized me," I replied with raised eyebrows and a hint of incredulity in my voice. Ignoring my signs of disbelief, Max nodded as he said,

"I'm afraid that's the reason why you won't be able to leave until after the alignment."

"Then why did you say it was inadvisable to travel back so soon," I said, "you made it sound as if it weren't a big deal."

Max sighed before he said, "I'm sorry, I shouldn't have given you the runaround like that, but I wasn't exactly sure what was going on when I couldn't make it work, and I didn't want to worry you."

My blood ran cold as I considered the implications. I tried to voice my concerns, but had trouble forming the words.

"But, but...Cyril said, and you said that...that wouldn't be until...until—"

"Until the day after tomorrow," Max added to finish my sentence.

He cocked his head and watched me patiently as I absorbed the information. Under Max's scrutiny, I inhaled deeply and let it out in a long breath.

"Will you be okay with that?" Max asked. It wasn't as if I had a choice, I was stuck here. I shook my head, feeling helpless, but as I opened my mouth to reply, the word that came out was a surprising "Yes."

"Good," Max said with a hint of a smile on his face as his gaze drifted in the direction of the village, and I realized we had nearly reached our destination.

Small, cozy-looking buildings stood in a tangle on the outskirts of the village. There didn't seem to be any logic applied to the haphazardly placed homes, and as sophisticated as the fence we had encountered might have looked as simple as these small buildings appeared. With each step that I took, taking me closer to the village, it dawned on me that I was probably going to spend some time there. As much as that thought frightened me, it also triggered a sense of excitement. *Who would be able to say that they had visited an alien village? Or well, sort of alien, but still? Who would believe me if I told them?* Besides, I'd have to get home first. Max might have said that he believed that he could take me home after the alignment, but I had a feeling that he didn't have a complete grasp of what was going on. *So how would he know if it would work?* Unwilling to let myself get worked up again, I tried a different approach.

"Tell me about this place," I said. Max smiled, looking pleased with himself. I returned the gesture and felt a bit more relaxed. Maybe this talking about stuff wasn't such a bad idea after all. I should remind myself about that the next time I spoke to Kay.

"Well," Max started, "as mentioned by Cyril, this place is called Ora, and most of the people living here keep themselves busy farming the land, keeping livestock, and acting out their creative tendencies. Basically, they enjoy...life, so there is no need to worry about them." There was a slight hesitation as he said *enjoy life* as if he couldn't find the right words to describe what these people were doing here. This seemed a little odd, but he continued before I could mention it. "There is also a small settlement on the other side of the desert called Laeva, which is a place some of the residents go to if they want to get away from all this." Max waved a hand in the air, indicating our surroundings.

"All this," I echoed.

"You'll see," Max said with a grin.

A bell sounded as I admired the contrast between the high-tech, structured fence and these simple farmhouses. The noise seemed to emanate from a taller building that reminded me of a church—a tiny church.

"What's that?" I asked.

"That would be the welcoming party," Max replied. "Just relax and remember: Act like you've known me for years. I'll answer any questions they might have."

CHAPTER EIGHT

It appeared that the entire village had come out to greet us. People approached us from every home and narrow alley as we walked down a street between a row of small buildings and ventured into what looked like a market square. Small stalls stood in a line, with various goods displayed on them. One of them held a variety of breads, while another stood piled with baskets of weird-looking fruits—at least, they looked like fruits.

From this angle, there seemed to be more order to the buildings surrounding the square. Narrow streets and alleys running between the small wooden structures all converged on this square, and it wasn't random at all.

A small group of four stood clustered together, playing a catchy tune on weird-looking instruments, while several other people homed in on Max as they greeted him. He returned their greetings with a big smile and threw his arms around every other person. As we moved among the villagers, I noticed a small structure in the center of the square, and it seemed the crowd of people was maneuvering us toward it.

An elderly man stood at the top of the steps that led to a simple, raised platform. The white of his hair matched his old, wrinkled face, but it didn't detract from the sparkle of joy that emanated from his face. As we walked in the direction of the raised platform, I took a moment to take it all in.

Nothing resembled the level of technology that we had witnessed at the fence. None of the people who had come to greet us were wearing anything like the armor I'd seen on the men guarding the fence. Neither could I detect any of the staff weapons or swords carried by the guards. These people wore simple clothes that reminded me of ancient Rome or Greece. Lightly colored garments hung loosely around their bodies, tied off around the middle with a simple rope. I felt as if I'd taken a trip back in time instead of being transported to some distant alien planet—if this even were a distant alien planet.

Max hadn't elaborated that much about his comments about worlds coming in many forms or about his persisting that we hadn't traveled through space or time. I didn't have a clue of what he'd meant by that, but the suggestion applied that this might not be an alien planet. *But what else could it be?* It wasn't Earth. The more I thought about it, the more confusing all of this became.

I felt the sudden urge to crawl into bed and

pretend this was all a bad dream. Perhaps it even was a dream, and I just needed to wake up. *But what if it wasn't?* Max seemed convinced that we'd be able to go home in two days, but that wouldn't stop my mom from freaking out if she didn't hear from me tomorrow. *And what if Max was wrong? What if it would take months to get home*—I could lose my job, and I didn't even want to think about what it would do to my mom.

A pang of guilt settled in my stomach as I realized I hadn't even considered what this might do to her. Cyril and Max had mentioned that the alignment wouldn't happen until the day after tomorrow and I wouldn't be going home until Max had aligned the stones. Mom and I might not have the most conventional relationship, but that didn't mean she wouldn't freak out if she didn't catch me going to work tomorrow morning. *What was she going to think? Would she go to the police or worse would she call Trish?* About a dozen variations of how my mom was going to work herself into a frenzy popped into my head.

As soon as I realized that the wheels inside my head had started churning again, I had to stop myself. I wasn't eager to experience another episode as I had before, not with all of these people around or at any time, so I took a deep breath and banished the thoughts from my mind—for now.

As we neared the raised structure, the elderly man lifted his arms in greeting. Except for a black robe that made his white hair stand out, the old man wore the same simple clothes as the rest of the villagers. There was something familiar about him that triggered my memories. I felt as if I had seen him before, but I couldn't quite place him. It could be that I had spent too much time among the elderly today while helping in the cafeteria, but I couldn't get past the feeling that I had seen him before.

"Maximus," the elderly man said with a big smile on his face, "how good to see you, my old friend."

"Oman," Max said as he took the few steps up toward the platform and greeted the elderly man with a hug.

"You haven't left yourself much time," Oman said.

"You know me, always trying to make an entrance," Max replied, "and it is good to see you, too."

"Maximus!" a voice shouted over the friendly crowd. I half turned to see a woman with a small child by her side hurry toward us. The woman's dark hair framed a beautiful face with dark eyes that held an Asian quality—perhaps Chinese.

She too looked familiar somehow, but as with Oman, I couldn't place her. Strangely enough, a bunch of the faces among the crowd evoked that feeling inside me—like I knew them, but not really. As if they were part of a dream in which all the faces got jumbled up, although I figured I'd remember meeting a woman with a face as flawless as the one heading our way.

The woman's lean but muscled arm held on to the tiny hand of an equally beautiful girl with no apparent resemblance to the woman. I didn't think the child to be hers, but the small frame clung to the strong-looking woman as if she were her mother.

Both of them whisked by me as if they hadn't even noticed me, even though I must've stood out in my black running clothes. The woman hurried up the steps and threw her arms around Max. He hugged her back before he knelt and greeted the young girl. The child's golden locks had been pulled back into a pony-tail, while the strands of hair that had escaped created a messy effect. The child apparently recognized Max and did not protest as he lifted her off the ground.

I raised an eyebrow as Max turned with the child in his arms and waved at the crowd that had gathered around the small structure. As soon as he did, the group playing instruments hushed their music, and everyone around fell silent.

"Greetings, my friends," he said. "It is good to see you all, and it is good to be back here in Ora. I know this is on short notice, so perhaps I will not get to greet everyone in person, but I'll promise I'll be back sooner next time."

Some shouts of welcome sounded from the people who surrounded me before they slowly started to disperse. As the noise level died down and Max had exchanged a few words with Oman and the woman, who were standing with him on the platform, Max seemed to realize that I was still there. He held on to the child as he came down the steps and gestured toward me.

"Oman, Lana, please allow me to introduce you to my friend Sam," he said. Oman and Lana followed him down the steps before they greeted me with the same welcoming hugs with which they had greeted Max.

"I've known my dear friends Oman and Lana all my life. They keep me grounded as it were." Max gave Lana a sheepish grin as he shifted the young girl in his arms.

"I doubt you need us to ground you," Lana replied with a gentle smile spread across her beautiful face.

"You have no idea," Max said. He playfully bumped her shoulder, but as he smiled, I noticed a wistful glint in his eyes that seemed to convey to me that he truly needed her to keep him grounded.

There clearly hung a hint of old familiarity among these people that seemed stronger than mere friendship. I didn't think there were any blood relations, though, because Lana looked like an Asian princess, while the little girl reminded me of a young Shirley Temple, and Oman seemed to have Arab blood coursing through his veins.

"And this young beauty is Juni," Max said as he tickled the small child on her chest. The girl giggled as she swatted at his hand. "This is my friend Sam," Max repeated in a bit of a singsong voice. The girl looked at me with big blue eyes, and I had to keep myself from glancing up at the sky. The color of her eyes nearly matched that deep blue color that surrounded us and looked the same as Max's.

With a brilliant smile, she said, "Hi, Sam."

"Hi, Juni," I replied and couldn't stop a smile from lifting on my face.

"Come, come," Oman exclaimed, "join us for supper."

Oman lead us away from the square, and Max remained close by his side as we walked along the narrow streets and alleys. Small buildings with sloping rooftops that looked like cozy little homes stood in the strangest arrangements. Standing in the middle of the square, the placing of the structures had come to make sense, but as we ventured deeper into the village, the randomness reappeared. I felt as if I were making my way through a maze.

With a quick look over my shoulder, it was easy to determine that I would never make it back to the edge of the village without assistance. As we rounded another corner, a woman carrying a basket loaded with laundry greeted Oman with a broad smile. She greeted Max with the same courtesy, but all I received was a curious glance. I'd been getting a lot of those as we moved along.

With Max and Oman in deep conversation, I let myself fall back and walked as the last of our small group. With every step, it became harder to keep my eyes fixed on where we were going. There was so much happening around me. Everywhere I looked, people kept themselves busy by either making something or just playing a tune on a weird-looking instrument, and the street seemed to be the place to do it.

On my left, a man looked utterly out of touch with

the world around him while he carved away at a statue that seemed to be made out of a piece of glass that held the most beautiful array of colors. To my right, someone was painting the facade of one of the small buildings, but she wasn't just giving it a fresh coat of paint. It looked more like something someone like Claude Monet would have painted on a canvas. Each corner we took, I'd find a different surprise, and I'd be drawn into some other kind of beautiful creation.

A few steps ahead of me, Lana held Juni by the hand. The little girl had Lana's full attention, and she greedily took advantage. The child was as curious as I'd ever seen. She kept pointing her tiny fingers at anything and everything she noticed, and around here that was a lot. Every time she did, she asked Lana a question. Lana, in turn, answered Juni with what seemed like all the patience in the world.

"Why is it always so hot as we pass Mr. Oban's workshop?" Juni asked in a high-pitched voice.

At the question, I looked in the direction of what had to be Mr. Oban's workshop. Juni was right. Heat poured out in waves from the open portal, and the air wasn't pleasant to inhale. Inside, a broad-shouldered figure with muscular arms held a red-hot piece of metal with giant forceps and banged it with a hammer. From out here it almost looked like the workshop of an old-fashioned blacksmith—almost. It would have looked exactly like that if it weren't for the digital numbers on a control panel that I figured to be reading the temperature.

"Because Mr. Oban works with all kinds of metals,

and they need to be heated before he can mold them," Lana answered.

A moment later, Juni tugged at Lana's sleeve. She glanced up at the tall, slender woman and urged her closer. It seemed as though the girl had another question but did not intend for anyone else to hear. Lana shot her a smile before she lowered herself to Juni's level. Juni whispered something near her ear, and Lana shook her head.

"I do not know," she replied in answer to the little girl. "Why don't you ask her yourself?" Juni blushed and shook her head vigorously. "Oh, come on, you are never this shy," Lana added.

"You come with me?" Juni asked. Lana grinned as she grabbed the child underneath her arm and lifted her off the ground. Lana settled Juni on her hip and glanced back at me before she slowed her pace. We rounded another corner and passed a small structure with what looked like a storefront. Several people stood in the line waiting patiently as a man behind a counter wrapped something in a piece of paper and presented it to the woman at the front of the line.

Several burly looking men occupied a small porch in front of the adjacent building and seemed to be playing a game. They laughed and drank as they lounged on wooden chairs.

Before I could determine if I knew the game, Lana obscured my view. She smiled at me kindly as she matched my stride.

"I am sorry," she said with a sparkle in her eyes, "but would you mind if Juni asked you a question?" I shifted my gaze to the girl, who was watching me expectantly as she held a tight grip on Lana's neck. I smiled at her.

"Not at all."

The girl beamed at me as she asked, "Are you from the Old World like Max?" I looked at her a bit stunned and not sure how to answer. I wondered if she'd meant Earth or someplace else. It wasn't as if I had any knowledge where Max had come from. He might not be from Earth, but that couldn't mean that it wasn't his home. It was where he lived after all.

"Well," I said as I struggled for an answer. In not so many words, Max had warned me not to raise any suspicion toward me. I didn't want to complicate things for myself and what the girl had suggested came close to the truth. Not that I would call Earth the Old World, but I did live where Max lived, and it felt best to stick to the truth as close as possible.

"I am," I said. "To be more specific, I'm from a town called Seattle."

Juni scrunched up her little nose and seemed deep in thought before she said, "I don't know of a Seattle."

"I'm not surprised," I said, "because I think it's pretty far away." It had to be, hadn't it—*right?* For things to be so different from home, it had to be a place very far away. I sighed at the memory of home, and it occurred to me that I'd mentioned Seattle as being my home. While I didn't live far from the city, it hadn't been my home for over a year. Perhaps I missed my old life more than I wanted to admit.

Before the melancholy I'd started to feel could overtake me, Juni asked, "Will you tell me about it?"

"Juni, I think Ms. Sam could use something to eat before you pester her with all your questions," Lana said as she gave the child a stern look.

"That's all right," I said as I noticed that the narrow street that we traveled started to climb.

This section of the village appeared more like what I was used to, with normal-length streets. We hadn't rounded a corner for at least fifty yards. My calves started to ache as the incline became steeper, and I glanced ahead to where we were heading.

A structure that looked bigger than the other houses we had come across stood at a distance beyond the narrow street. As with the other structures, it too had a sloping roof along with a considerably large porch at the front of the house. Max had already climbed the few steps that led up to the porch as he turned to face us.

"We'll start dinner," Lana said as she too ascended the steps. "You two relax for a minute. We'll be ready soon."

"Thank you," I said before Lana disappeared inside the house. Oman had also ventured inside, and I was left with Max standing on the porch. Facing him, I couldn't decipher the look in his eyes. I would've asked, but before I could, he turned to peer in the direction of the village.

"Welcome to Ora," he said under his breath. I'd heard the welcoming phrase several times by now, but as I followed Max's gaze, I understood his remark.

The incline hadn't appeared that steep, but as I looked out over the rooftops of the village, it became obvious that it had been. It also gave me a better view of the village's layout, which, as I'd suspected, had quite a liking to a maze. Movement along the narrow streets and the smoke plumes rising from some of the chimneys gave the place a homely feel. Beyond the village, I could see the fields, and I even spotted the tiny dots of distant sheep. The fence seemed miles away as it lit up the horizon like a blue beacon. The contrast with the village seemed too odd.

"It all looks like some primitive town from a fantasy novel, but it really isn't," I said as I glanced up to face Max. "Is it?"

"Well, it is anything but primitive, if that's what you mean." Max leaned forward and leaned his elbows on the railing. He narrowed his eyes as he regarded me.

A question sat behind those eyes, and despite the fearful feeling of facing that question, I asked, "What?"

Max's gaze didn't waver as he shifted to lean on one elbow and fully face me. "Before...back in the field," he said and hesitated.

I clamped my teeth together and locked my jaw in place in anticipation of a question that I wasn't going to like.

"Can you tell me what happened?"

"I...eh...," I started to say but had to clear my throat before I could continue. "I just got a bit over-whelmed."

Max nodded his head in understanding, but I had a feeling he wasn't done with his line of questioning.

"Considering the circumstances, I guess that's understandable," he said, and I felt a *but* coming, "but that's not exactly what I meant." He paused as if to gage my reaction. "This isn't just about what's happening right now, is it? Something else is causing this."

I turned my head away from Max, unable to look him in the eyes anymore, and wrapped my hands around the railing. *Why couldn't he just leave it alone?* It wasn't as if it were any of his business. Although I could understand him wanting to know considering our situation, that was his own damn fault. Max waited patiently for my reply as if he anticipated that my mind needed to play catch-up.

"It's not something that I tend to share," I finally replied. In fact, it wasn't. Mom knew, but she was the kind of person that shoved these things under the rug and only because she was raised in an *if-you-ain't-bleeding-then-you-ain't-hurt* kind of way. Back at the retirement home, Trish knew because I had to disclose any medical problems on my job application and she was my boss. Besides Trish, only Ellie knew, and that's only because she'd found me hyperventilating in the restroom once. Both of them knew of the disorder and not the reason behind it—only Kay knew that.

"I can be a good listener," Max said.

"Well, I don't wanna talk about it," I said, "especially not with a stranger." Max flinched a little at my harsh words, and I instantly regretted what I had said.

Max wasn't a stranger, not exactly, but I wanted him to drop the subject, and I needed to find a way to steer the conversation in a different direction.

"Sam, how long have we been sharing our lunch together. Hell, you practically know everything about —" He broke himself off as I raised an eyebrow. The words had fallen from Max's mouth as if he believed them himself. At the look on my face, he shot me a shy grin. "Well, almost everything."

"Everything except the fact that you're a shapeshifting alien," I said and managed not to cringe at the absurdity of the statement.

"It's not what you think," he said and sounded defensive. "Back home, I am the old man that you know—an old man with aches and pains, an old man with regrets, the same as every other man, and some-times...I get to go...on a trip. And after all this time, I wished you wouldn't consider me a stranger."

I shook my head in wonder as my eyes swept across the strange village at the foot of the hill. *How could a man caught in something as amazing as this, looking like some tall, dark, and handsome action hero, think of himself as an old man?*

"Is it?" I asked. He raised an eyebrow, and at his questioning gaze, I added, "Earth, is it your home?" He watched me for a long moment before he sighed, and I knew he could see right through me as I tried to steer the conversation away from wherever he'd intended it to go before. For whatever reason, he seemed to relent.

"As much as a place can be a home." Max's voice

had lowered an octave and reminded of the lion from a Disney movie.

"But, no, I wasn't born on Earth if that's what you mean. I needed a place to stay, and I figured Earth would be a good a place as any."

"Why did you leave your home?" My question came out of a natural progression of the conversation, but from the long stretch of silence I faced, it seemed Max either hadn't anticipated the question or felt reluctant to answer. I leaned toward the latter as he shot me a contemplative look.

"Let's just say that it was a mutual agreement."

I eyed him for a second, not sure of what to make of that reply. *A mutual agreement between whom?* Before I could ask, Max seemed to have found his voice again.

"Besides, Earth is such a colorful place with a multitude of diversity living under the same roof."

I snorted a laugh at his choice of words. I couldn't help it. He made it sound as if we were all living a happily ever after while all that diversity he spoke off was usually the reason for a lot of upheavals.

"I know what you're thinking," he said, "but it's true. On a larger scale, it might look like your world is all in shambles with your wars, hunger, and politicians with overblown egos, but there is also beauty in it."

"Like what?" It wasn't that I didn't know what he was talking about, but it would be interesting to hear an alien's perception of things.

"Like the act of creation," he said without hesitation. "You make up stuff with your minds and then create them with your hands. I can still remember the first time that I saw the Great Pyramid of Giza or read the works of Shakespeare."

An infectious smile spread across his face as I watched him indulge in the memories.

"I hate to break it to ya, but the pyramids were built by slaves."

"I could introduce you to some researchers who would beg to differ, but you are right," he said. "Things aren't all roses, but coming from a place so bland that it looks like cream cheese spread on toast, you'll come to appreciate these things. Besides, I'm a true believer in suspension of disbelief."

For a moment I thought about making a comment about the cheese thing but decided otherwise.

"Is that why you chose to mimic iconic figures from Earth?" I asked.

The feigned innocence he projected was endearing. With a crooked smile, he said, "You didn't miss that, did you?"

"It's kind of obvious once you know you're dealing with a shapeshifting alien." Max cringed a little at the mention of the word *alien*. I guessed he didn't see himself like that, and maybe I was the alien here. He recovered quickly, though.

"It's just because you've got this great range of characters to choose from. There is none of the pretend entertainment on any of the other places I get to visit." Max's eyes sparkled as he spoke, and he reminded me of a little kid taking his pick out of the most awesome Halloween costumes. "My photonic manipulator needs a template for input and who better than the guys that played Achilles and Rubin Carter."

"With Darth Vader's voice," I added. Max grinned and nodded. So, he did know who Vader was.

"So, what do you really look like?"

"I don't think it's a form your eyes would appreciate," he said unapologetically.

"This is so weird," I said under my breath as I pinched the bridge of my nose.

Juni's laughter reached us from inside the house, and the sound made me smile. This village was so peaceful, and its residents had welcomed me with open arms.

"What happens if you don't align the stones?" I asked.

My gaze had returned toward the town as Max replied, "The realms of existence will start to fall." He'd said it in such a nonchalant way that I thought he was joking.

"If you put it like that," I said with a chuckle and turned to face him. As soon as our eyes met, I knew he wasn't joking, and his grim expression triggered an involuntary shiver. His lips turned into a thin line as he added, "Well, at least mine will."

"What does that mean?" Max stared at me for a while, and as I held his intense blue eyes, I felt a feeling of unease creep up on me.

"It's hard to explain, just as I might imagine it is for you to explain what brings on or happens to you when you experience one of those...episodes." I should've known he wasn't going to let that subject rest so easily.

"I think it's hardly anything like that," I snapped.

"Are you sure?"

Unable to decipher the meaning behind his words, I stepped away from the railing. I felt a sudden urge to get away from Max. Not sure what to do, I let my eyes roam over the porch. There was a seating area on the other side of the door. I didn't feel like sitting out here. Heading into the village didn't seem like a smart thing to do, so going inside remained my only option. Something occurred to me as I took a step toward the door and stopped.

"Is Earth involved in this?"

I didn't want to face him as he gave me his answer, so I kept my back turned to him. Perhaps it was because I already knew the answer.

"It is." Although I anticipated the reply, his words felt like a slap in the face, and I turned around. Our eyes met, and as I held his gaze, a million questions popped into my head. "But not in any way you think," he quickly added as if that would soften the blow.

"Well, I'm thinking the world on fire, the apocalypse and all that, does that come close?" With each word, my voice became louder.

Max pushed away from the railing. He held his hands out as he stepped closer.

"What the hell am I supposed to think. First, there's all of this." I waved a hand as if the gesture could even come close to indicate everything going on. "Then you tell me—"

Behind me, something clattered to the ground inside the house that made me flinch. Somehow the sound worked as a warning chime telling me to slow down. My chest heaved as it would after one of my runs, and I tried to take a deep breath.

"I'm sorry," Max said. He reached out a hand, but I stepped away from him. "I hadn't meant to get you caught up in all this; but it's not as dire as you think, I just don't know how to explain, not without..."

He looked at me with pleading eyes as the words died in his throat. I shook my head and raised a hand to ward him off.

"I need...just give me some..." I couldn't get the words to pass my lips. I needed time to let things sink in, although the circumstance made that incredibly difficult. Without another word, I turned to open the door and walk into the house.

The inside of what I'd come to learn was Oman's home looked as warm and cozy as I'd expected it to be. I wasn't sure why, but it matched the outside of the endearing structure. As with the rest of the village, it had a historical look and feel to it.

A fire burned inside a hearth close to a long rectangle table that took up most of the room and that could seat at least ten people. I walked over to the shelves stacked with books where they lined the walls and glanced over at a seating area that sat tucked into a corner. Windows at the front of the house gave a view of the village at the foot of the hill, and I figured it would be nice to lounge in one of the comfortable-looking chairs while reading a book, although, despite giving it some effort, I couldn't decipher any of the titles written on the spines of the books. This was probably for the best because it didn't seem right for me to cozy up with a book while, for all I knew, my mom sat inside a police station filling out a missing-person report. Forcing the thought from my mind, I glanced around the room.

The only thing that seemed out of place in the room was the large flat screen that hung in the center of one of the walls. I remembered Max mention something about the lack of entertainment like we had on Earth, and I expected the large screen to have a different purpose than for watching TV shows.

An elderly woman who had introduced herself as Cora moved with efficiency around the kitchen on the other side of the room. She had no trouble lifting the heavy pots and pans on and off the cast-iron stove. Even with a cane, the ancient-looking woman was getting on better in a kitchen than I ever would.

As with some of the other villagers who I had seen or met, Cora held a familiarity that this time, I managed to place. I had seen her before, and it wasn't even that long ago. She had been one of the women who had gotten hold of Beth's lipstick. While telling the story, Ellie had pointed out the table where she sat with her lipstick-abusing friends. According to Ellie the lot of them always occupied the same table for their daily game of cards.

Both women looked exactly the same, down to the thick curly hair on top of their heads. The only thing that differed from retirement-home-Cora was that she had to be wheeled around in a wheelchair and this version hauled around cast-iron pans as if it were nothing.

I wondered if the two women were different versions of each other because I couldn't imagine them being one and the same person. That was strange enough on its own because apparently, I was able to believe the old Max and this younger version being one and the same person. Max had mentioned something about a photonic manipulator that he used to create his own appearance. Perhaps that thing had something to do with the fact that I was seeing familiar faces all around me. If that device used existing templates, then it could be that Max had pulled his inspiration from the people around him and those happened to be the people around me.

I shook my head to keep my mind from going around in circles. I had no idea why these people triggered this feeling of familiarity or why Cora had a look-alike back at the retirement home. Maybe it was all just a coincidence, but I would have to ask Max about it.

Fortunately, Max had kept his distance, and this gave me the time to collect myself. None of the people inside the house had given any indication that they had noticed something wrong or had overheard my conversation with Max.

To keep my mind off things, I offered to help Cora

and Lana, but the old woman just shooed me away. It took some persistence and a mention that I wouldn't be able to eat unless I'd done something to help before Lana offered me an empty bowl and a basket filled with some type of vegetable. I still felt as if they had succeeded in removing me from the kitchen area as Lana guided me to the large table and seated me across from Juni.

The little girl busied herself by drawing pictures as I managed to get the hang of cleaning the roots Lana had entrusted to me. The roots looked a bit like a potato without the skin, and Lana had shown me how I only needed to remove a small piece off the top and the bottom of the strange-looking potato before cutting it into pieces. The task was easy enough, and I dropped chopped pieces of the root into the bowl as I watched Juni work on her drawings.

I'd gone halfway through my basket when Max entered the room along with Oman. Our host gave me a curt nod before he gestured for Max to sit. Despite the offer, Max stayed where he was. He had removed the upper half of his armor and replaced it with a simple cotton shirt. His broad chest pulled the fabric taut, and the sleeves were tight around his muscled arms.

Oman hurried over to the kitchen area and greeted Cora with a kiss on the back of her hand. They exchanged a few words I couldn't decipher before he returned to the table with a carafe and several mugs. I thanked him as he filled one and handed it to me.

Max stood awkwardly at the head of the table. His eyes seemed downcast, but I knew he was watching me. A simple task like cutting vegetables had eased my nerves, and I felt more like myself again. I still hadn't come to grips with the situation, but I couldn't lay that on Max—this wasn't his fault, and even though I still felt a sense of dread looming over my head, I managed to smile in his direction.

After that, Max seemed to relax a bit and found a seat next to mine. He smirked as he glanced over the rim of the basket.

"I never knew you had it in you," he said. I shoved an elbow into his side before I grabbed another root. Only then, I wondered about the familiarity of the gesture. The older version of Max always managed to tease me as I joined him for lunch at the small clearing. He was never very appreciative of my reluctance to cook a decent meal every day. According to Max, takeout and microwave dinners didn't count as real food, and he always found one way or another to point that out in a playful tease.

"Tell me, my friend," Oman said as he eased down into a chair, "how come you are so late in the season?"

Max hesitated and glanced my way before formulating his response.

"Things have gotten a bit complicated," he said in a low voice. I tried to keep my face void of any reaction as I wondered if I were Max's complication. It wasn't like I had any choice in the matter, and I wanted to interject, as I remembered something. I hadn't been the only thing that had recently intervened in Max's life. His room at the Grain had been destroyed, and somehow an ominous-looking statue had stayed behind. I'd almost forgotten about that. *Could it be that this statue thing had been Max's complication?*

My eureka moment didn't last long as the conversation veered into a different one, and what he said next did not make any sense to me. "We have been friends for too long, Oman, so I cannot lie to you, but I do not wish to worry you."

Oman shifted forward and lay both his hands flat on the table, his full attention riveted on Max as he said, "Is it Jasper?"

Max nodded in confirmation.

"He is getting closer, isn't he?" Oman added.

Max nodded again. "He is getting closer," Max replied. "I barely got away from him last time. That is why I was late in coming here."

My hands had stopped moving as I listened to their conversation. I wanted to ask Max who this Jasper person was—if he even were a person—but I wasn't sure if I should. I wasn't sure of the role I played here or what part I was expected to play. Max wanted these people to think I traveled with him, and that meant I was supposed to know more than I actually did. That was a tough act to play with a million questions running around in my head.

"Well then," Oman said with a sigh, "I'd say the alignment can't come soon enough."

"Indeed," Max said and lifted his mug from the table.

Oman did the same as he said, "For tonight you

and your friend are our guests, so drink up and forget your worries." Oman shot me an expectant look as Max tapped his foot against mine underneath the table. Oman and Max were still holding their mugs in the air, and I realized they were waiting for me. I grabbed the mug that Oman had handed me before and raised it.

"To the order of things," Oman said.

His words echoed from both women on the other side of the room. They, too, held mugs in the air as they said, "To the order of things."

Juni did not have a mug, but she also murmured the words. As Max and Oman drank, I followed their example and lifted the mug to my mouth.

Fortunately, I noticed the strong smell of the substance inside the mug and only sipped. The liquid nearly burned my throat as it trailed down to my stomach and forced me to cough. Oman laughed as he watched me struggle to hold down the drink.

"It seems your friend has much to learn about drinking," he said. I guessed I probably shouldn't tell him that I usually did not drink at all.

As soon as the toast had passed, Lana neared the table holding two bowls and set them down. Cora followed hauling a tray as she walked over with her cane. Oman busied himself with Juni, and I took the opportunity to nudge Max.

"This Jasper character," I asked in a whisper, "is he who did that to your room back at the Grain?"

Max eyed me thoughtfully for a moment, as if he hadn't anticipated me putting the two together before he nodded, but as I waited, he apparently didn't intend to add anything to that. His attention seemed riveted on Oman and the small child. A quick glance told me that Juni had pulled Oman into a vivid conversation about her drawings, so we weren't in any danger of being overheard. I wasn't going to let Max off this easily, and I poked him in the ribs.

"What?" he said in a whiny voice.

I raised an eyebrow and, for a second, wondered if he'd regressed to a teenager.

"Jasper?"

Max blinked a few times as if he'd been miles away from this place before his eyes settled on mine. He grabbed his mug and drank a few gulps.

"Please don't tell me that's for courage," I whispered as I watched him drink. He grinned as he placed the mug on the table and shook his head.

"Yes, Jasper was the one responsible," he said. "I was just trying to buy some time. It's difficult to explain, and I don't want you to think I'm not willing to tell you."

"He wasn't that burned-to-a-crisp statue back home, was he?"

"No, that was one of my demons, and even though Jasper controls the Inanis, he is unlike anything you've encountered before," Max replied.

"Hold up," I said, shaking my head, "the Ina...what?"

"The Inanis," Max repeated. "The creature that showed up in my room is called an Inanis."

I blinked as I tried to get my head wrapped around

this. "And this Jasper controls these things." Max nodded as I added, "And they're after you?"

Max nodded again. "He's adamant to stop the alignments from happening."

"Why?"

"Because order stops him from invading the realms."

I opened my mouth, ready to utter my next question, but then hesitated, unsure of which one to ask first. The more I thought about it, the more questions popped into my head. *These realms Max had mentioned, were these the realms of existence that he'd mentioned before, including Earth? Was this Jasper character an alien like Max? Must be, so that would have been a stupid question. Wait, had he said one of* my *demons?*

Through the haze of questions that racked my brain, that last one resonated. I was just about to utter it as I noticed Cora approach with another bowl. Oman patted Juni on the head and stood before he followed Cora back toward the kitchen.

"So, these things, these Inanis, whatever they are, they can travel to Earth?" I asked at a whisper.

Max shook his head. "Not exactly," he said and hesitated. "It's more like...they appear." Max winced as if the words hurt.

"Appear," I said, sounding incredulous.

Max cleared his throat and shifted on his seat. He leaned in closer as he whispered, "That's the part that's kind of hard to explain, but I guess it's more or less like the way we came here."

I had no idea how I'd gotten here, and I was pretty sure I wouldn't understand it if Max explained.

"So, what happened to your room? I mean, presuming that thing didn't kill itself," I asked, hoping to veer the conversation back to what had happened back home.

"No, it didn't kill itself," he said. "I might be an old man back on Earth, but I know a few tricks."

"But you told me you weren't even there..." My voice faded at the wink Max shot me. He had lied to me and had probably lied to the police too. What had me troubled even worse was the way that Max's room, including the Inanis, had looked. Had it been the creature or Max himself who had destroyed the place and how?

"I know what you're thinking," Max said with a smile that was probably supposed to reassure me, but it didn't work. "I can handle the Inanis, especially on Earth. So don't worry." There was a sincerity in his eyes that seemed to falter the longer I watched him, and he quickly added, "I mean, one at a time, they are no problem, none at all."

My eyebrows rose at the added confession. *How big was the problem if there were more than one?* It seemed Max had finally started to open up, and I had hoped for the chance to ask more questions, but as Oman returned to the table, the opportunity was taken away from me. The moment had passed, and I would have to find another time to have my questions answered.

Not raised to let a limping old woman set the entire table, I stood, grabbed my basket and bowl, and took them to the kitchen. There, I allowed Lana to fill up my arms and helped set the table.

"Juni," Lana called out from the kitchen, "it is time for dinner. Clear your things." I'd just placed a plate on the table and was standing next to the small child as she frowned and muttered that she wasn't quite finished yet.

I bent down to glance at her work and felt surprised at the detail in her drawing. I'd never seen a young girl able to create such lifelike pictures. I wouldn't be able to draw like that if my life depended on it, but it was the subject of the drawings that kept my eyes fixed on them.

With the fence as a backdrop, the girl, who couldn't have been more than four or five years old, had drawn a vivid battle between figures dressed in armor similar to that of the men guarding the fence and something more ominous. The picture depicted what I could only describe as dark silhouettes with relatively human-shaped bodies. They looked like the dead risen from the grave after they had dragged their skeletal remains through a pool of thick, heavy oil and the substance had stuck to their forms. Juni hadn't drawn any eyes or noses, but they did have mouths. An extended lower jaw held sharp teeth inherent to a vicious predator.

The creature reminded me of the statue I'd seen inside Max's room back at the Grain, and from what I could tell of the drawing, Officer Klein had been right —the things did resemble the xenomorph from the *Alien* movies.

I was about to ask Juni about her drawing as Lana spoke in a warning tone, "Juni!" The girl flinched before she shuffled her pages into a pile. The disappointment on her face was evident, but she still shot me a thin smile as I helped gather her pencils. As she slid from her seat, I followed her to a cupboard that stood in the corner of the room.

She opened a drawer and placed her drawings inside.

"Thank you," she said as I added her pencils. My fingers brushed one of her small hands, and I felt a jolt of electricity run up my arm. I flinched and stared down at the girl. She seemed as surprised as me as she peered up at me with those big blue eyes of hers. Her hand rose and reached for mine. I hesitated, not sure if I wanted to experience that again. It must have been some form of static electricity, but it had felt like more than that because my hand still tingled.

The look of curiosity on Juni's face piqued my own, and I offered her my hand. This time as our fingers touched, it didn't feel like a swift charge, but more like a slow build up, and the tingle in my hand intensified. Juni narrowed her eyes at our clasped hands before her gaze shifted toward the table. She was looking at Max, who had his hand wrapped around the gem secured by a necklace around his neck. Max had his eyes closed as if he were praying.

As the tingling sensation in my hand grew painful, I jerked it away from Juni's grasp. She gave me an apologetic look before her eyes traveled back to Max.

He was staring at her or us now with a look I couldn't decipher.

A knock on the door broke the moment, and I shifted my gaze across the room. Without further notice, the front door opened, and Cyril entered with a broad smile on his face. A sturdy-looking woman I hadn't met stepped in after him. Oman and Max both rose to greet the tall man with the bald head.

"I hope you haven't started without us," Cyril said. His loud voice drew Lana and Cora away from the kitchen area.

"We wouldn't dare," the old woman said as she hurried to intercept the big man. It seemed her cane barely touched the ground as she made her way to him, and Cora appeared years younger as she opened her arms to hug him. Without hesitation, she moved to the woman at Cyril's side. "Moira, my dear," she said with apparent relief in her voice. "Thank goodness you are all right."

Moira stood a few inches shorter than Cyril but was still taller than most women I'd met. Dressed in similar armor, she looked just as impressive as Cyril. Her long dark hair sat tugged behind her ears, revealing a strong jawline with deep-set eyes, and the warm light inside the room made her bronze complexion look almost golden.

"Welcome, my friend," Oman said. "Lana, more drinks please." As he spoke, he shook Cyril's hand and then moved to Moira. They briefly hugged before Oman gestured at the table. "You are right on time."

"Thank you for having us," Moira said.

Cyril moved to Max, and they grabbed each other's forearms. "Finally we'll have time for you to tell me about your adventures," Cyril said.

"My adventures," Max replied mockingly. "It'll probably be next season before anyone can get in a word once you start blabbing."

Lana returned with two extra mugs and placed them on the table. "Sit. You must be famished," she said.

Cyril found his seat beside Oman and reached for a plate. Despite the formal pleasantries of the welcome and the invitation, it seemed that Cyril felt right at home, but Moira, on the other hand, acted a bit more reserved. She waited for everyone else to sit down before she moved along the side of the long table. As she did, she shot Max a nervous glance.

"Maximus," she said in greeting.

"Moira, good to see you're all right," Max replied. Having vacated my seat to help set the table, it appeared Lana had arranged it so she could sit across from Juni. Cora took a seat at the head of the table, which left me to sit across from Moira. She pulled her chair away from the table but didn't sit down as her eyes fell on me.

Moira shot me a look that hinted at recognition before she said in a soft voice, "You're the one who carried me from the battlefield."

I looked at her in surprise, not having realized that it had been her. She'd worn a helmet that had obscured her face. Considering the shape of the armor, it hadn't even occurred to me that the body could have belonged to a woman, not until Cyril had mentioned it. It wasn't as if her breastplate had actual breasts.

"Well, fortunately, I'd gotten some help, or else I don't think I'd have been strong enough," I said and glanced at Max.

Moira followed my gaze and offered Max another nod. As she shifted her eyes back to me, she said, "Still, I owe you my life and my thanks." She reached a hand out across the table, and with only a moment's hesitation, I returned the gesture to intercept. Instead of taking my hand, she grasped my lower arm in a firm grip. "Thank you."

Not sure what else to say I managed, "You're welcome, and the name's Sam, by the way."

"Cyril told me," she said as she tightened her grip on my arm. "I am Moira." With a nod, she released my arm and took her seat across from me.

As I registered that most of the guests sitting around the table had their eyes fixed on me, I started to feel uncomfortable, and I felt my face flush.

"Sam, my dear," Cora said, "you are most welcome at our table."

I nodded my thanks and watched as the distributing of food commenced.

CHAPTER NINE

Cyril was still laughing aloud at something Max had said. The deep baritone sound along with the broad smile and the twinkle in his eyes worked infectiously. It showed on the smiling faces all around the table, and I felt delight combined with a sense of unease at the same time to be part of it. I wasn't used to be around a lot of people for long stretches of time, and today it seemed endless. On any normal day, entertaining the elderly at the retirement home and my confrontations with Trish would have been enough to get me to go to bed early, but that wasn't an option right now. On the other hand, I wondered if anyone would notice if I'd snuck out of the room and hide in a dark corner.

None of the people sitting around the table held any similarities to each other, and it seemed obvious that there wasn't any blood relation going on here, but that didn't stop them from acting like a family.

Oman was in the middle of telling a very animated story. With grand gestures, he waved his hands in the air, while Cyril seemed to have trouble catching his breath, as if he couldn't stop himself from laughing. The big man clapped a hand on the table, and I even witnessed a tear at the corner of his eye. Max leaned with his elbows on the table, unable to suppress a smile as he listened and occasionally participated in the conversation.

At my side, Juni kept us all busy by asking questions. I'd just spent several minutes explaining why my hair was so short. She'd never seen a woman with short hair, and she seemed intrigued. At the moment, it was Moira's turn. With her athletic build and intense gaze, I could only describe her as some warrior woman that reminded me of an old TV show, although it was obvious that she was the total opposite of Cyril. Like Cyril, Moira was friendly, and from the way Juni looked at her, it was clear that the young child adored her, but she was much more of a quiet type. Like Lana, she had a well of patience as she listened to the little girl, who tried to convince Moira that she should cut her hair, too.

With Juni occupied, I took a deep breath as I let my eyes roam across the people sitting here at the table. While feeling exhausted, I also enjoyed the atmosphere, but couldn't help but feel like a bit of an intruder, intruding on what I could only describe as a family gathering. These kinds of get-togethers weren't something I had a lot of experience with. My mom had been an only child, so there were no aunts or

uncles or cousins to play with. My dad had two brothers, but I'd never met them. He'd severed all connec-
tions with his family ever since I'd been a small child.
I'd often wondered what it would've felt like to grow
up with the cousins that I knew I had but had
never met.

Once in a while, I caught Max glancing my way,
and he'd nod with raised eyebrows as if to check if I
were all right. Each time he did, I'd smile at him,
because even though these circumstances were too
strange to comprehend, I didn't want him to worry
about me. It should've been impossible not to be okay
sitting at a table, eating food that wasn't that different
from what I was used to and listening to friendly
conversation, and I didn't want these people to think I
was ungrateful. Cora and Lana had outdone themselves, although for all I knew this was how they dined
every day. The roots that I'd cut didn't just *look* like
potatoes; they also tasted like them. The same applied
to all the other different kinds of vegetable or fruits.
They might have had a different color or a different
shape, but they shared a distinct, familiar taste that
reminded me of Mom's cooking.

Mom and I hadn't dined together in a while, but
when we did, she'd make these elaborate menus with
at least three types of vegetables and a salad. Both of
us weren't that keen on meat, but Mom made a mean
grilled chicken.

As the laughter around me faded to the recesses of
my mind, I wondered what my mom was doing. *Was
she still out, having fun with her friend?* She'd been doing

that a lot more these days. To be honest, I didn't mind, not even if she had to borrow my car every day to do it. It wasn't as if I could provide her with an evening filled with entertainment—I never had.

She was my mom, and I loved her, and I knew she'd do anything for me. We'd just never connected in a way that one could describe as being close. Still, even with the inability to contribute myself, the warmth that radiated from the people sitting around me felt like a blanket, and I wished Mom was here, despite the absurdity of the situation. I could already imagine her throwing her charm at Oman, and it was only because of the hand touching my forearm that I was able to pull my attention back to the room.

I glanced down at the long, wrinkled fingers wrapped around my wrist. I looked up into eyes that might have held some ancient knowledge.

"Are you enjoying yourself, my dear?" Cora said in a soft voice. "For a moment there, it seemed as if you were miles away in some distant place." I wondered if the old woman knew how right she was. As it was, I didn't think it to be my place to explain.

"You have a great..." I started to say but then hesitated. I'd figured these people weren't blood-related, but they seemed more than mere friends. Deciding it didn't matter, I added, "Family." Turning away from her, I briefly glanced at the smiling faces, and as I faced her again, I said, "Thank you for having me." She patted my wrist before releasing me and removing the napkin from her lap. She pressed it to her mouth and then placed it next to her plate.

"Maximus has been a long-term and dear friend, and we've always been able to count on him," she said. "I'm sure he must be to you, too."

I cleared my throat not so much because something was stuck there but because I needed time to think of a reply. In one way, I felt as if I didn't know Max at all. After all, we'd spent a lot of time together over the past year, and I'd had no idea that he was an alien, although I could imagine why he wouldn't share information like that over lunch.

What I did know were countless stories which I should now probably consider fabricated. As it were, I couldn't grasp them not being true. The elaborate story of how Max had slipped in shallow water while fishing as he'd struggled to pull the animal from the depth of its natural environment. He'd fallen on his butt, and somehow the fish he'd been trying to catch had landed on his chest. The way Max had explained how the fish had looked at him with such disdain had been so elaborate and endearing that it couldn't be made up. He'd finished his story with a pointed look at my tuna fish sandwich and had claimed never to have eaten fish again.

Max had told me dozens of those stories, and perhaps I knew him better than I thought.

"He, eh..." I started to say, "we sort of met at this place where I would go to have a quiet lunch." The old woman looked at me intently as she waited for more. "He is good company and doesn't push a person to talk but listens if needed...you know."

During our lunches Max did most of the talking

while I listened. Of course, over time I'd divulged some aspects of my life. A complaint or two about my mom might have come up, but mostly I'd kept things to myself.

I looked up at Cora feeling embarrassed. Strangely enough, it felt as if I'd kept more secrets from Max than the other way around.

The old woman smiled as she said, "I do know, and he has been a blessing to us all."

"How so?" The words fell from my mouth before I could think about them. If she'd been surprised by my question, Cora didn't lead on.

"Well, for one, he has helped us build the fence to keep the Anguis from destroying our crops." Moira, who had pried away from Juni's grasp, had heard my question.

"Shouldn't you know these things if you travel with Maximus?" Her sharp gaze met mine as I quickly searched for a reply.

"Well, eh..." I started to say and reached for my mug. After a few sips, I managed, "He isn't that forthcoming with his accomplishments. I guess he's shy about that."

Seemingly satisfied, Moira shot me a knowing smile.

"That's our Maximus," Cora said.

As the evening progressed, I felt more at ease, and I found the stories I heard fascinating. Most of them involved Max as if he were an everlasting presence among them. This seemed odd to me because I'd gotten the impression that he never stayed around for long. Besides, since I'd worked at the Grain, I'd never known him to leave for longer than an afternoon. I didn't want to dwell on these details. I was becoming fascinated with the aspects of this world and focused on the tail end of Cora's telling of how the fence had come to be.

"As Max had suggested, a group of the villagers secluded themselves within a new settlement to come up with a solution," she said. "These were mostly men and women with very keen analytical minds, and with the guidance of Danara, a dear friend of Max's, they designed the fence."

"Ah, yes, the settlement is called Laeva, right," I said and hoped to sound convincing. I remembered Max mentioning it as we walked up to the village, and he'd said something about it being a place to go if the residents wanted to get away from all this. It seemed like a good way to indicate to Cora that indeed I had some idea of what Max did.

"It is," Lana said. "It's a place that some people find pleasant to go if they want to work on tasks with more complex analytical aspects or just want to read or write."

"Like a resort," I said.

Lana frowned and shook her head. "I do not know that word."

"Oh, it's..." I started to say, but then thought the better of it, because I didn't really feel like going into the semantics of things, "what we call back home what you just described."

"Anyway, it took us a long time, but we managed to finish the fence," Moira said. "Since then the number of casualties has dropped considerably." I sensed a shift in her voice, and her downcast gaze told me she was thinking about earlier today.

"I'm sorry for your loss," I said in a voice that barely rose above a whisper.

Moira looked up, and I recognized gratitude in her eyes.

"There is honor in sacrificing oneself for others," she said, "but that doesn't make it any easier."

I didn't know what to say to that; I'd never suffered a loss in that way. Kay had a cousin who had been with the army and had lost his life overseas, but I hadn't really talked to her about that. I'd been too busy dealing with my own misery. Great friend I turned out to be.

In an attempt to learn from past mistakes, I asked, "Were you close?"

Moira raised an eyebrow and shot me a look as if I'd said something inappropriate.

"I have trained and bled with these men and women," she said. "Of course, we are close."

"Oh, no," I quickly added, "I wasn't applying that you weren't. I just meant if..." My voice faded as our eyes met. She watched me expectantly, and I huffed out a breath. This was another reason why I should keep my interaction with people to a bare minimum. It seemed my words never came out the way I wanted them to and I always ended up insulting or hurting people in the process. Hoping to better explain myself, I said, "I meant, did you lose someone special, like someone you knew really well or maybe family?"

Moira shook her head before she glanced around the room.

"The Ora guards are my brothers and sisters in arms. This my family," she said with a faint smile on her lips. She watched the ongoing conversation at the other end of the table for a moment, and a mischievous grin curved her mouth. "Unfortunately, this family comes with an obnoxious bald guy."

I followed her gaze to where Cyril sat and watched him shove a spoonful of something into his mouth while he tried to keep talking.

Cora drew our attention back to her side of the table as she playfully slapped Moira on the wrist.

"You hush," she said, sounding stern, but the twinkle in her eye told me she wasn't serious. "Everyone is welcome at this table." Turning to me, she added, "Those two have been bickering ever since they've been youngsters and Oman took them under his wing."

"And once we'd tasted Cora's cooking, they never managed to get rid of us again," Moira said. The look she gave Cora combined with the smile that lit up Moira's face told enough about the appreciation she had for the old woman.

"So, you adopted both of them?" I asked turning to Cora. Despite the kind smile, the old woman offered me a funny look as if she didn't know what I was talking about. I must have stumbled upon another word that didn't make sense to these people and rephrased my question. "I mean did you take them in while Moira and Cyril were still young? Did you raise them?"

Her smile widened, and her eyes grew bright as understanding dawned. Straitening her shoulders, she said, "Here in Ora, we all do our part, and we take care of our own. If parents can't care for their children either because of sickness or whatever else might be going on then, we must help, and that's what we did." Cora turned to Moira before she added, "Sometimes, that means a more permanent stay, but we do what we can."

Something seemed to come over the old woman as she said those last words and the expression on her face revealed sorrow. For a moment, Cora's eyes shot in Cyril's direction before they returned to Moira. "I just hope that we–"

Moira placed a hand on Cora's and stopped her from finishing her sentence. "Trust me, you did more than I will ever be able to repay you for," she said, "and I even forgive you for letting that brute into your home."

The mischief in Moira's eyes along with the smile that she showed as she nodded in Cyril's direction was enough to vanquish the sorrow on Cora's face and replace it by pride. Moira's hand lingered for another moment on Cora's before both women turned their attention back to me.

"Do you have a family back home?" Cora asked.

"It's just my mom and me," I replied and hesitated. My stomach churned at the thought of Mom coming home and not finding me there. It probably wouldn't be until morning though before she'd start wondering where I was at. I felt a sudden need to know the time and wished I'd brought my phone.

Perhaps Cora had read the concern on my face because she patted my arm, and before I could ask what time it was, she said, "Don't worry. Your mom won't even have the chance to miss you."

I raised an eyebrow, not sure what Cora had meant by that statement, but I hoped she was right. It didn't stop the knots from forming in my stomach, though.

Juni stepped in to change the subject as she suggested to Moira that they could both cut their hair as short as mine. The young girl had a knack for demanding your attention.

Fatigue announced itself with a yawn, and again I wondered what time it was. So much had happened today, and even though my day working at the Grain —which would usually have been enough to get me to bed early—might as well have happened years ago, I felt it in my bones.

I stretched my arms and felt a strange tingle that started at the back of my neck before running down my spine. I shivered at the ominous feeling, as if a low current of electricity hummed across my skin. Instinctively, I turned to Max, hoping to find an explanation.

Max hadn't noticed my discomfort, and why would he, sitting at the other end of the table? I opened my mouth with the intention of drawing his attention but stopped before a sound could exit. The conversation at the other end of the table had ceased, and both Cyril and Oman had pensive glares as they watched Max. Max, on the other hand, had his eyes fixed on the tabletop. His face had gone serious and withdrawn, while he sat with his back straight.

Without looking up from the table, he lifted a hand and placed it on his chest. Fingers clamped around the stone hanging from the chain around his neck. The room fell silent as Max closed his eyes as if he were sensing something he wouldn't be able to see.

I shivered again and felt Cora's hand return to my wrist.

"You feel it, too, don't you?" she asked. I looked at her and saw the concern on her face. Her eyes shifted toward the end of the table where Max sat, and Cora's hold on my wrist tightened. I followed her gaze in time to see Max releasing his grip on the gem, letting it rest on the palm of his hand. Silence fell all around us at the sudden change in the atmosphere. Grim-looking faces had their eyes fixed on the stone in Max's hand.

Unlike before, the stone's brightness had returned, but it flickered erratically. Instantly, Cyril stood and walked toward windows at the front of the house. His whole body tensed as he stared outside.

"Oman," he said in a commanding voice, "viewer, please."

Oman stood without a word and moved to the wall with the big screen and pressed a hand to a panel beside it. The screen flickered to life, revealing an image of the fence and its immediate surrounding area.

Chairs scraped the floor, and I sensed people standing all around me, but I remained frozen in my seat, with my eyes glued to the screen. The horror displayed on the screen could only have been described as unimaginable, and I probably wouldn't have believed what I was seeing if I hadn't seen it before. The creatures from Juni's drawings looked like something out of a nightmare as they appeared from out of nowhere and engaged the guards in battle.

"It's the Inanis," Max said with a slight tremor in his voice, "and they have come for me."

CHAPTER TEN

As I stood before the viewer and stared at it in horror, Max followed Cyril to an adjacent room, but not before he shot me a look that had apologies written all over his face. My first reaction came as, damn right, he should be sorry for getting me into this situation. The sorrow that accompanied the apologetic look had me doubt that initial reaction, though. It was easy to recognize the pain in Max's gaze as his eyes flickered over the people who had welcomed us into their homes.

"Lana, supplies," Moira said in an urgent tone. Lana did not hesitate as she moved toward a large chest on one side of the room. She yanked it open, and the lid thumped against the wall.

Oman joined Cora and took her by the arm while he guided her to the front door. With a fierceness in her eyes that took me aback. Moira stared at me. Her eyes seemed to scan me from head to toe before she shook her head. I must've looked like a damsel in distress through her eyes. I was nothing like the strong warrior woman that she appeared to be.

I still stood rooted to the ground as she stepped closer to me. She made sure that our eyes connected as she placed both hands on my shoulders.

"Listen to me," she said in an urgent tone. "I need you to do exactly as I say." My eyes went back to the screen.

The images displayed switched to a different angle and showed one of the Inanis advance on one of the guards. The creature did not appear to be armed while the Ora guard continuously fired his staff weapon, to not much avail. The energy weapon did nothing to the advancing creature. Other guards had made use of the swords they carried around, but this particular guard seemed to have forgotten that he carried one on his back. As if it was a last resort, the guard swung his staff like a baseball bat.

Just as the size of its enormous jaw would have predicted, the creature moved like a predator, toying with its victim until it found the right moment to strike. The Inanis jumped the guard, and to my surprise, it did not sink its teeth into the guard's neck —one of the few spots not protected by armor. As soon as the thing had its bony arms wrapped around the guard, it seemed as if the entire makeup of the creature, its texture, changed.

Juni had done the Inanis justice in her drawing. An oil-like substance transferred from the creature to the guard. As if it were a living entity, the thick black ooze slithered a path along the guard's arms. The helmet worn by the guard prevented me from seeing his face, but from the way his head snapped back, and his body went rigid, I could imagine the pain he must have felt. I shuddered as I watched the oil-like substance cover the guard from head to toe. As soon as the substance had covered every inch of the man's body, he seemed to disappear. The Inanis had swallowed him up, and the guard was gone—just gone.

"Jesus! What the hell just happened," I said in a loud voice that verged on the brink of panic. Moira raised an eyebrow at my exclamation and glanced over her shoulder at the screen. Realizing what I'd just witnessed, she squeezed my shoulders.

"The Inanis feed on the essence of life," she said, "and use the body's matter to sustain their own being."

"It just...he just..." I uttered as I pulled my attention away from the screen and met Moira's eyes. In those dark depths, I saw that she knew exactly what had happened.

"We have to go," she whispered. Every muscle inside my body seized up with tension, and I wasn't sure if words could get past my throat. I nodded, but Moira did not seem convinced.

"You do not know me," she said, "but know that I am in your debt, and I'll promise to keep you safe." She searched my eyes. "Please, I need you to trust me and do as I say."

At the front of the house, Oman opened the door, which allowed the distant shouts and screams to reach us. The sound of an explosion would've made me jump if hadn't been for Moira's hand on my shoulders to keep me grounded. The first signs of panic started to coil inside my body. I could feel my throat go dry, and my hands trembled as my heart raced in my chest.

"Sam," Max said. His voice pushed through the haze clouding my mind and forced me to look up. Max had donned his armor and stood at Moira's side while he handed her one of two staff weapons before he placed a hand on my upper arm. "Go with her, Sam," he said, "and do as she says."

I wavered on my feet, but between Moira's and Max's hands holding on to me, they kept me from falling.

"Sam, please," Max said, "don't think about it. Just do as she says." I registered Max and Moira exchanging words, and from the cold expression on her face, I imagined Moira doubting my sanity. It felt as if hours had passed since I'd first witnessed the attacks on the screen, but I knew it couldn't be more than a couple of minutes.

Trying to force down the roaring panic in my head, I took a deep breath and slowly exhaled. I repeated the action before I slowly met Max's gaze. I nodded and opened my mouth to say something, but no sounds came out. I drew in another breath and cleared my throat before I managed to repeat, "Don't' think and do as she says."

A glimpse of a smile appeared on Max's face as he placed his hand on my head. I glanced at Moira.

"Sorry," I said. "Freaking out a bit. I'll try not to

do that again." For a brief moment, the hardness in Moira's expression disappeared and was replaced by a gentle understanding. The moment passed, and she said, "See if you can help Lana."

I nodded before I turned to the chest and watched Lana pull out several bags that looked suspiciously like backpacks. I might've lingered on the weird likeness of the packs that were similar to the one I regularly used at home, but Cyril's booming voice pulled me out of my thoughts.

"Maximus, we need to go now."

Refusing to dwell on what those words meant, I walked over to Lana. I kept reminding myself not to think as I grabbed two of the bags, hauling one over my shoulder, and carried them to the front door.

I met Max's eyes just before he gave me an encouraging nod. The determination he exuded made him look even more like a warrior than the armor he wore ever could. His presence soothed the gut-wrenching feeling in my stomach as I noticed Juni rooted to her seat.

After dropping the two bags near the front door, I quickly returned and knelt before her.

"Hey, Juni," I said to the girl who'd remained unmoving. Her big eyes seemed bluer than before, but they didn't hold the terror that I'd expected to see. Over Juni's shoulder, I noticed Lana carry another two bags toward the front door. I'd already felt the heavy weight of the bags and, to save time, decided to take the girl.

"Come on, baby," I said in a hushed tone to the

little girl. "Hang on to me." Juni shot a nervous glance in Lana's direction but did not hesitate as I guided her arms around my neck to take hold of me. Triggered by Juni, I turned to face Lana to see if I were overstepping any boundaries, but she merely nodded in approval.

As soon as her tiny fingers brushed my skin, I felt a jolt of static electricity that raised the hairs on the back of my neck. Heat surged through my body, but ignoring it, I lifted her from the chair and moved to the front door. As I held Juni and settled her on my right hip, I grabbed one of the bags off the floor and shouldered it. Lana, Moira, and Oman did the same.

I couldn't help myself as I took one last glance at the screen and gasped.

"What is it?" Lana asked, and I pointed at the screen.

"How are they doing that?"

Lana turned to the screen just as one of the Inanis dissolved into thin air. It seemed as if the ground swallowed the creature whole, and it wasn't unlike the way I'd seen the Anguis disappear.

"Maximus," Lana said, sounding anxious, "they are on the move."

Both Max and Cyril looked alarmed as their eyes flickered to the screen.

"Moira, get them to the woods," Cyril said. "Keep them safe." He met Moira's gaze for confirmation. As she nodded, Cyril added, "Maximus, let's go."

Shock ran through me as Cyril's words registered.

Max shot me a quick look, but before I could utter a word, he stepped outside and into the darkness.

Moira didn't leave me much time to ponder Max's exit and the fact that he'd left me alone—alone in an alien world with strangers and horrific creatures. She ushered us through the door and outside, where the distant screams of villagers filled the night.

"Here," Lana said, and I turned her. It seemed she wanted Juni's attention as she slipped a small shoulder bag over the child's head. "Keep this with you, just in case."

"I will," Juni replied and tugged the small bag between my shoulder and her chest.

"Now you stay with Sam, and do as she says," Lana added. Juni nodded and grabbed me tightly around the neck.

"I..." I started to say. "Maybe it's better if you take her." I never had much experience with children, and even though Juni seemed like a nice kid, I wouldn't know what to do with her if anything happened. Lana shot me a stern look. She clearly had her mind made up, but I feared she might be placing faith in me that I could never render, and I couldn't just leave it at that. For all intents and purposes, Juni was Lana's daughter, and she was entrusting me with her safety. "Are you sure?"

Lana nodded as Moira shouted, "Let's go!"

"Maximus trusts you," Lana added, "and I trust him." Before I could reply, she quickly followed Moira. I swallowed hard and glanced down into Juni's big blue eyes. She gave me a look that convened a similar hard-headedness as the one Lana had given me moments ago as she said, "Let's go, Sam."

With a glance over my shoulder, it was as if I were looking at a distant memory where empty plates and bowls still stood on the large table and a fire burned in the hearth. Joyful memories that should've merited my appreciation a whole lot more than they had at the time were replaced by a nightmare as the door closed behind us.

CHAPTER ELEVEN

As I stepped outside, I felt the instant cold of night attack my skin, and I shivered. Darkness had fallen over us, and I glanced up to see that the deep blue sky had turned to pitch black. Similar to how the daylight sky lacked a sun, this night sky did not hold any signs of stars or a moon. It was as if a black hole had swallowed up the light.

Another shiver ran through my body although this one was not as a result of the chilling cold. The once peaceful village had transformed into a raging inferno. Buildings engulfed in flames created a trail straight into the central square, making it seem as if the maze had caught fire.

"Oh my God," I said as the full picture of what was going on formed before my eyes. The view screen on Oman's wall had depicted only a narrow area of the fence. It had shown us nothing of the creatures that had made it across the open fields and attacked the villagers. Screams of agony, shouts of despair, and the constant sound of weapons fire caused my blood to run cold. The reality of things was so much worse than I could have imagined.

Max and Cyril were already heading down the hill at a fast pace, running toward the danger. Unconsciously, I took a few steps, as if my brain had been programmed to follow Max. A hand on my shoulder stopped me, and I turned to see Moira.

"No," she said in an urgent tone, "we hide." As she spoke, her gaze shifted from me to the small child perched on my hip. The imminent battle was no place for a child, and it wasn't hard to understand Moira's reasoning. "This way," she added. She gestured in the direction Lana, Cora, and Oman were heading. Without hesitating, I followed, but not before I searched the darkness for Max. He and Cyril had already disappeared into the maze of structures, and even if I did run after them, I didn't think I would find them.

Moving quickly, I caught up with the others. Lana eased to my side and placed a hand on Juni's back. The girl had latched onto me and pressed her face into the crook of my neck as her tiny hands fisted my shirt. I wasn't sure if it had been the outside cold or something else, but I couldn't feel that strange heat that emanated from Juni's body anymore. This felt like a relief, because the longer I'd held her, the more painful the sensation had seemed to get.

"It's okay, Juni," Lana said in an attempt to comfort the child. "Don't worry. This is not your fault." It took me a second to register what Lana was saying. *How could what was happening be this child's fault, and why would Lana think that Juni would feel any form of guilt?*

An image of the drawings popped into my mind, and I wondered if they might have something to do with it. If I hadn't been so occupied with keeping on my feet while carrying a small child and by being scared out of my mind, I might've asked what Lana had meant. As it was, I just tried to keep pace with the others.

We ventured down the hill parallel to the village as Moira lead us through the dark. Cora and Oman kept a steady pace despite Cora's use of her cane. Lana seemed glued to my side, and I caught her sideways glances a couple of times as if she wanted to take the child from me. She was already carrying two of the packs, and although I felt as if I'd be able to manage another pack, knowing that its weight would be significantly more than a small child's, I didn't think it wise to exact a change at that point.

To my right, I could see the flames grow brighter as they rose high above the buildings, engulfing everything in their path. Once in a while, blue streaks of energy bolted across the skyline, illuminating our surroundings for the briefest of moments. I tried to force the sounds of cries and chaos from my mind, but I seemed to be doing a lousy job of it. My chest felt as if it were caving in on itself as the tightening sensation made it harder to breathe. I fought to control the tremors that ran through my limbs, and tried not to think about dropping Juni.

Hoping that focusing on our way would help, I glanced forward to where Moira had taken the lead. She, too, carried one of the packs, but dressed in her bulky armor, it looked almost like a small handbag.

It seemed she was guiding us to the edge of the forest. I imagined that she wanted to use the enormous trees and brush cover to disguise our retreat, but I hoped there would be someplace to go. Perhaps she'd be able to lead us to a shelter of some kind—a safe place to hide.

A loud explosion caused me to stop in my tracks. I turned to see that the fires had caught up with us. It took me a moment to realize that the inferno reaching for the sky emanated from Oman's house. The entire roof had become engulfed in flames within seconds.

Dark silhouettes rushed from the house and off the porch. The figures blurred as they gathered close together, and I could not determine how many of them there were. The blue flashes from several staff weapons forced the silhouettes to scatter. I could see several guards rush up the hill, illuminated by the fire of Oman's home. They fired their weapons at the black outlines as they charged them. The guards drew their swords and forced the dark figures to split up. Two or three of the creatures rushed down the hill to intercept their attackers. Another two figures watched patiently as their companions attacked the guards.

With their heavy armor and helmets on their heads so similar, I could not determine if Max or Cyril were among the advancing guards.

Lana grabbed me by the arm as she yelled, "Sam, let's go!" She dropped one of the packs to the ground with a thud and tugged on my arm again. "Come on, Sam. We need to go now."

I wasn't sure if Lana's yelling had attracted the two creatures or if they had sensed our presence, but all of a sudden, the two silhouetted figures turned.

Lights from the flames coming from the burning building shimmered across their faceless heads and made their teeth gleam. Except for the protruding teeth, the creatures did not have actual faces, at least no eyes and no noses; it made me wonder how they knew where they were going. Of course, there would be some explanation, but I wasn't going to find out just yet.

"Sam!" Breathing heavily, I turned to look at Lana, and I felt that rush of panic coursing through my veins again. My legs did not move even though Lana tugged at my arm. Somewhere through the haze of static fear that overwhelmed my brain, I heard Moira's voice. Gathering from her loud tone, she must've been close, but I still couldn't make myself move.

"It's okay, Sam," Juni said in her tiny voice. She'd lifted her head from my shoulder and whispered near my ear. "We just need to go with them, and everything will be all right." I shifted my head so that I could peer into her piercing blue eyes. Shadows flickered across her angelic face, and I felt silly for needing a child to comfort me.

Lana tugged on my arm again, and I reminded myself to stop thinking. I needed to act, and I forced my legs to move. It was a good thing, too, because before I turned, I could see the two creatures rush toward us. My legs picked up the pace, but the heavy bag strapped to my shoulder along with a small child perched on my hip made it hard to move freely.

Despite my luggage, Lana and I manage to overtake Oman and Cora. Having been an experienced runner for years, catching up with an elderly man and a woman of the same age supported by a cane didn't give me much reason to congratulate myself. Oman's and Cora's struggle to keep up was apparent, but I had a feeling that this wasn't the first time that they had to run for their lives. The determination written across the old couple's faces surpassed my own convictions, and I could only hope I'd be as strong as them someday.

Moira shouted for us to move faster. She must've been right behind me because I felt the weight of the pack lift from my shoulder.

"Drop it!" Moira shouted at my side. "It's slowing you down." I did as she asked and relaxed my shoulder. Within seconds, the added weight disappeared. I did not check if Moira had taken all the load herself or had just dropped it. Instead, I wrapped my now free arm around Juni and picked up the pace. I couldn't as much see or hear the creatures as I could sense them behind me, and I knew that they were close.

We had nearly reached the edge of the forest, but a loud scream behind me told me it might be too late. Lana had disappeared from my side, and I slowed as I glanced over my shoulder. She'd stopped and watched how Moira engaged one of the two creatures that had descended upon Cora and Oman.

Moira fired the staff weapon given to her by Max. I wasn't even sure why they had those things because they didn't seem to make a dent as the blue energy struck the Inanis in the head. The creature did appear to be disorientated, and Moira used the moment to twirl the staff above her head before crashing one end down on the creature. Bones snapped as the staff connected with the Inanis, and the thing howled. I could only hope that the entity felt some form of pain.

Juni's arms tightened around my neck as I watched Moira land another strike to the creature's body. Feeling helpless and utterly useless, my stomach churned as I realized that Moira was fighting only one of the creatures—*where had the other one gone?*

I found my answer and gasped as I saw a section of the ground disappear near Cora and Oman.

"Look out!" I yelled as the second Inanis rose from the ground. Oman noticed it and grabbed Cora's cane. He swung it at the creature while he used his body to shield the old woman. He struck once and then twice, but with his third strike, the Inanis grabbed hold of the cane. Unprepared for the move, Oman jolted forward and fell into the arms of the creature. Instantly, the oily substance latched onto Oman's form. It didn't take long for the black goo to engulf his entire body. Moments later, Oman was gone.

Unable to stop her from putting herself into harm's way, Lana rushed toward Cora, who stood face-to-face with the Inanis. The old woman straightened her shoulder as if she wanted to show this thing that she wasn't afraid. At the sound of Lana's unintelligible screams, Cora turned her head and yelled back, "Get her out of here!"

Cora had barely uttered the words before the Inanis wrapped its bony arms around the poor woman. The images on the screen inside Oman's home of the guard being swallowed up by these things could in no way compare to the horror as I witnessed it now. For one, there had been no sound, and the guard's face had been obscured by a helmet. The scream that erupted from Cora's throat cut through me like a sharp knife, and the sheer look of terror on her face caused my heart to ache.

Lana skidded to a stop not far from the creature that had snuffed out Cora's life. Her head turned to Moira, who had discarded her staff and switched to the blade she carried on her back. Just as Moira took her first steps to engage the Inanis, the ground between Lana and me shifted. A hole opened up, and a third Inanis appeared right in the middle, cutting me off from both women.

I froze as the newly arrived creature howled and homed in on Lana.

Even with the sword, Moira had enough trouble keeping that first creature at bay let alone two of them. With tears streaking down her face, Lana turned to me, and with her face contorted with pain at having lost Cora and Oman, she opened her mouth to scream.

"Run, Sam!"

I wanted to help them, but how could I? I didn't have any fighting skills like Moira did, not to mention that I had enough trouble even breathing. *How was I going to be any use to them?* Besides, I had Juni to think about. So, this time I did not hesitate, and I moved as fast as I could. I pressed a hand to Juni's head, forcing her face against my shoulder, hoping that she wouldn't see what was happening behind me. I made it to the tree line and kept going, even though I wasn't sure where I was heading. I could hear a rustle in the brush behind me and could only guess at who or what had made the sound. I stumbled as the ground shifted before me, and I veered sideways, barely able to avoid the Inanis as it appeared in front of me.

A breath of icy air made my skin shiver as I brushed past it, but I managed to stay on my feet. Unsure of the sensation, I kept moving. I didn't think it could have been the Inanis, because after having seen what they could do, I had a feeling that a single touch of their skeletal fingers would have brought me to my knees. So, I tried to ignore the cold as it traveled up my back and sidestepped trees as my feet pounded the uneven ground.

As I ventured deeper into the forest, the trees

behind blocked out any light emanating from the fires that had engulfed Oman's home and the village at the foot of the hill. I doubted that a moon or stars decorating the night sky would have helped me navigate my escape underneath the thick canopy of trees but at this point, I would have settled for anything, even a lit match. The lack of light and rough terrain forced me to slow down even though the eerie sound trailing behind me got louder.

"Sam, look out!" Juni shouted close to my ear. Her warning came too late as I felt something impact my left side. With the young child, still in my arms, I tried to shift midfall, hoping that my body wouldn't crush her. I mostly managed it as my shoulder hit the ground first before I landed flat on my back. I groaned as I felt my head connect with the ground.

For a moment, all the sounds around me disappeared, replaced by a sharp ringing in my head. Juni's face appeared before me, and even though her mouth was moving, I couldn't hear her words. I shook my head as if that would jump-start my fuzzy brain, but everything froze as the large shape of one of those creatures appeared above us.

I whipped my head around, trying to see if I could spot Lana or Moira, but I couldn't find them. *How was I to protect Juni from these creatures without them?* I didn't know how to fight, let alone protect a child. I hadn't even been able to protect myself when it came down to it. Despite my eyes frantically searching for help, Juni and I were alone with that thing as another of its kind appeared from behind a tree. I was on my own again, just like I was on that dreadful night when my life took a turn for the worse. No one was going to help me, and as the vague memories of that dark and dank alley gathered at the forefront of my mind, I could feel the fear that came with them cripple my body.

Moving quickly, the second creature snatched Juni from my arms. The sounds around me returned with a vengeance, as Juni's cries pierced the night sky bringing me back before the full extent of those painful moments could fully immerge. Not that I even could remember what had happened, but I liked to keep it that way. I never wanted to go through that again.

"No!" I shouted out as the memories of what being touched by one of those things would do resurfaced. I couldn't let that happen to Juni, and I pushed myself up on my elbows. Juni was calling out to me, and I felt relieved to hear her voice even if they were cries for help. The creature held her in a tight grip that made it impossible for her to move, but she wasn't screaming in pain as I'd seen with Cora, and the black oily substance wasn't latching on to her. The relief that realization elicited was briefly lived as the second Inanis reached for me.

My feet fought to find traction in the dirt as I tried to push myself away from the creature and an inevitable fate. The Inanis's skeletal appearance, looking all ancient and dead, as if it had just crawled out of a grave, might have given the impression it would move slowly, but it did anything but that.

In one swift move, I felt its bony fingers wrap around my throat, and with a display of strength, it hoisted me to my feet. The sudden rush of cold that hit me as the creature pulled me against its body caused my body to tremble. My heart raced, and I couldn't breathe as the fear of what was to come overwhelmed me. I closed my eyes and prayed for it to be over with quickly.

I couldn't decide on gratitude or dread when it turned out that it wasn't over as quickly as I had hoped. Cold seeped into me where the length of the creature's body pressed against mine, chilling me to the bone, but there was no pain. At least none of the pain that I had witnessed on the faces of the likes of Cora and Oman. The only pain I felt came from the creature tightening its grip around my neck, squeezing until I couldn't catch my breath. There was no oily substance creeping up my skin and draining me of my life essence.

Unsure of how long the creature had held me within its grasp, I felt it shudder, and I gasped as I was flung to the ground. My hands dug into the ground as I caught myself. The soft soil got under my fingernails as I fought to get air into my lungs. A coughing fit made it even harder to breathe as I felt my stomach stir and I was unable to stop myself from throwing up.

Perhaps I should've been mortified by staring down at the content of my stomach, and I was, but there was also something else. Anger veered up inside me as I remembered how much effort Cora had made in preparing the meal that had ended up in the dirt. It seemed ridiculous, but she and Oman had placed so much care in making sure that everyone felt welcome at their table and now both of them were gone. I couldn't just let their deaths go in vain.

Pushing myself up, I turned to see what was going on. The two Inanis just stood there, one holding Juni and the other empty-handed. Seeing the two creatures with their massive teeth taking up most of their faces, it seemed that spark of defiance lit by Cora and Oman's memory quickly snuffed out as bile rose in my throat. Panting hard, I lowered my head in the hope that would keep me from throwing up again.

The Inanis didn't move except for their heads as they turned from me to each other and back again. Unable to read their expressions, I couldn't be sure, but they appeared to be confused. A cold shiver ran through me as I realized that I should have been dead. I'd witnessed not an ounce of hesitation on their part as the Inanis had latched on to Cora and Oman and had fed on their life essence. *Why hadn't they fed on me like that?*

As the nausea subsided, I maneuvered into a sitting position and noticed how my hands shook uncontrollably. Apparently, my revelation had been short-lived. I looked up, wondering what was going on, when one of the faceless monsters standing over me knelt, grabbed the front of my shirt, jerked me up, and then slammed me back down. As my head struck the ground, the world around me faded into nothingness.

CHAPTER TWELVE

The brightness of the deep blue sky hurting my eyes seemed nothing compared to the agony and strain I felt in my left arm. Also, my back and butt felt like sandpaper as the hand with an iron hold on my wrist dragged me across the desert. I managed to look up at the Inanis that tugged me along by my arm. Its oily skin glistened as it reflected the blue sky, which gave its bony build a metallic glint. My eyes trailed from Inanis's back up to where the neck seamlessly merged with its head and edged over into its strong jaw with its massive teeth.

Pain shot through my arm and down my back as I tried to reach the hand clamped around my wrist with my free arm.

"Please," I managed to say. My voice sounded as hoarse as my throat felt, and my words were barely audible. "Please," I repeated. The word came out a bit stronger, but despite my efforts, the Inanis ignored me.

My fingers clawed at the hand as I tried to get a handle on what was going on. Several of the faceless creatures surrounded me as they moved at an agonizingly fast pace. Shifting my gaze from one to the other, I could recognize the shape of a human head, but they had no eyes and no noses.

With a groan, I pleaded for the Inanis to stop, but it showed no intention of doing that. In fact, it showed no sign that it had heard me at all.

"Stop. Please stop," I said as a dizzying haze clouded my mind. My stomach started to revolt. I had already lost most of its content, but still bile rose in my throat. I did not want to puke on myself, and I tried to breathe evenly, but it felt as if air refused to reach my lungs.

Before my eyes forced themselves closed, I noticed Juni in the arms of one of those things. The girl rested her head on the shoulder of a faceless creature, but her eyes held mine. I blinked, amazed at the lack fear on the young child's face before the blissful darkness grabbed me once again.

The next time I opened my eyes, I had to blink to check if my lids actually worked. I stared into blackness as I lay on my back. A small fire burned brightly somewhere to my right, and I realized that the day must have turned into night again.

Coldness made my body shiver, but I kept myself from moving. My back and bottom felt as if they were on fire, and I feared any movement would increase the painful pinpricks that ran up and down my body.

A small hand pressed to my forehead, and as she leaned forward, I looked into Juni's eyes. Like before I did not detect any fear in her gaze, but the concern behind her eyes seemed apparent.

"Hey, Sam," she said. Her voice sounded small but filled with relief. With care, I eased my head sideways and saw one of the Inanis standing several feet away with its back turned to us. "You should come sit closer to the fire," Juni added. "It'll warm you up."

Unsure if I should move, but pretty confident that staying flat on my back wouldn't help me anything either, I shifted to my side. I groaned as pain shot up my arm left arm, and I was glad I'd chosen to turn to my right. Pushing myself up into a sitting position, the cold air that sliced through the thin fabric of my shirt felt like a relief. It numbed the burning sensation on my back and even took my mind away from the pain in my butt as I sat. The moment lasted only for a few seconds before the discomfort returned and an uncontrollable shiver ran through my body. My teeth chattered as I took in my surroundings.

Except for the small fire illuminating the Inanis's oily skin as they surrounded us it seemed as if we'd found ourselves inside a black hole. The skeletal men stood unmoving as they surrounded Juni and me standing in a circle with their backs turned to us. Beyond the boundaries of the wall constructed of their bodies, I could only see blackness.

Juni grabbed my right arm and tugged on it to get

me to sit closer to the fire. I managed to shift along the ground and instantly felt the heat where it warmed my body. I ignored the sand that had found its way underneath my clothes as Juni guided me to sit near her. I was probably carrying around tons of sand by now.

"What happened?" I asked. I felt out of sorts having to ask this young child to tell me what was going on. Being the grown-up, I felt an urge to protect her. Juni's eyes did not waver as she held mine. She didn't look as if she needed my protection until she shifted closer and leaned into me while placing her hand on my leg. Perhaps I'd been wrong in assuming that she didn't need protecting.

I glanced down at my shaking hands. They've been doing that a lot lately, although at the moment I didn't feel that tightening sensation in my chest or had trouble breathing, which would usually be telltale signs that I'd wind up embarrassing myself. Max had been right before when he'd suggested that something else was going on. The therapist who I'd spoken to a couple of times during my stay at the hospital had called it PTSD, but I could never bring myself to admit that I suffered from a post-traumatic stress disorder. It wasn't as if I'd witnessed the atrocities that one would after having been sent to fight a war like soldiers had. My traumatic event had lasted mere minutes, and I didn't think I deserved to compare my experience to that of people who had gone through real issues.

Intellectually, of course, I knew this to be horse-shit. None of us were the same, and we might all react differently to specific situations, which shouldn't diminish the perception or the impact of what had happened.

I just couldn't help feeling like an idiot when the inability to breathe and the sudden rush of fear left my body in a state where I couldn't stop shaking and wasn't able to move after some asshole had cursed me out because I'd crossed the street without noticing his car heading for me. Confrontation always rattled my nerves and triggered my brain in such a way that I had to fight to keep control over my body.

It seemed odd that this situation that would probably have been the biggest confrontation in my life—well, except for the one that kept tormenting me in my sleep and flashed across my mind at the most inconvenient times—had me sitting here next to a fire in an alien desert with only my shaking hands as a reminder.

Still not willing to worry Juni, I shoved one hand under my leg to hide my trembling fingers, wrapped my free arm around the child's tiny frame, and pulled her closer.

"I think the Inanis are taking us to King Danara," she said.

"King Danara," I exclaimed.

"Shhhh," Juni hissed and pressed a finger to her lips while she shot me look as if I'd lost it. That, coming from, what, a five-year-old, had me feeling a bit disconcerted.

I'd heard the name mentioned several times before now and had learned that he and a bunch of brainiacs had secluded themselves within the confines of a small settlement that they had built. *But hadn't Cora mentioned that Danara had been a dear friend of Max's?* I hadn't gotten the impression that Danara was a bad or violent man, a bit eccentric if I would have guessed based on what Max had told me. Glancing around, I noticed none of the Inanis paid any attention to us. Still, I moved my mouth closer to Juni's ear.

"I thought the Inanis worked for Jasper." Saying Jasper's name made my stomach drop as Juni nodded.

"They do."

From what Max had told me, this guy was adamant to stop the alignment, but what would he want with us?

"Then why would the Inanis take us to King Danara?" I asked.

"I don't know," Juni replied with a shrug, "but the only place out here that they might take us to is Laeva."

Max had been the first to mention Laeva to me as the settlement some of the residents go to if they wanted to get away from all that Ora had to offer. After witnessing all the activity that occurred on the streets of Ora, I'd imagined Laeva as a place filled with a bunch of introverts sitting around, reading books, and talking philosophy.

"Do you think this king might be working together with Jasper?"

Juni shrugged again. "I don't know."

We sat in silence for a while, and it started to weigh on me. Time might as well have stopped.

Nothing around us moved, not even the Inanis. It seemed as if Juni and I were the only people left on the planet.

"Do you think Lana is okay?" Juni whispered. I'd expected the question, but that didn't mean I had an answer ready. At least not one that would sound convincing. From what I'd seen, the Inanis were relentless, and even with Moira at Lana's side, who had proven herself to be a formidable warrior, I'd feared the worst from the moment we'd gotten separated. *How would I tell a child that one of the monsters keeping us captive probably swallowed up her mom?* I couldn't voice that to Juni, but I didn't want to lie to her either. This was precisely the reason why I didn't want kids of my own. I had enough trouble conversing with grown-ups, and I wasn't equipped to handle these heartbreaking situations, let alone deal with a grieving child. Taking a deep breath, I gathered my nerves and faced Juni.

"Well, last I saw her," I said, "she was with Moira, and I'd bet she'd do anything to keep Lana safe." Juni nodded her head almost imperceptibly.

"Moira will keep her safe," she said with a small sigh. I wasn't sure if I should bring it up, but I felt curious about the child's relationship with Lana, who, with her exotic beauty, looked nothing like the fair-skinned child with her deep blue eyes, sitting next to me. Besides, it wasn't as if we had anything else to do as we sat here in the desert, and I didn't think sleep would come easily tonight.

"So...Lana, she takes care of you?" I asked.

"Yep," she replied, sounding a bit more perky, "ever since Maximus found me." As if the mention of Lana had triggered some memory, Juni sat up straight and tugged at the strap that ran across her chest. She produced the bag Lana had given her and stuck her hand inside.

"He found you?" I couldn't hide the shock that resonated within my voice, but Juni either didn't notice or didn't care. Her attention was riveted on the bag as she rummaged inside it.

"I don't remember much about it, but he brought me to Lana." I had to swallow past the lump that stuck in my throat before I could reply.

"Lana is pretty lucky to have you."

"And I'm lucky to have her," she said, "and so are you." She looked up at me and smiled. She raised her hand and held out a package wrapped in a handkerchief. She opened it and revealed something that, despite its green color, looked suspiciously like an oversized granola bar.

Juni severed a piece and handed it to me. For a moment, I eyed the sticky, unidentifiable mass suspiciously, but after a growl from my stomach, I decided to take a chance and took a bite. Besides, I had thrown up most of my dinner, and I could use something to help me get rid of the awful taste that lingered in my mouth. It took some chewing before I could swallow the dry, sticky substance, but it tasted sweet, and my stomach demanded more.

"That we are," I said and without even thinking about it, I kissed the top of Juni's head. "I'm sure you'll be back with her before you know it." Juni remained quiet as she munched on her piece. She seemed to be contemplating something.

"What are you thinking about?" I asked as I stabbed with a finger at a piece of goo stuck between my teeth.

"I just hope Lana won't be mad because I didn't tell her." Something in her voice changed, and I shifted so I could get a better look at her.

"Tell her what?"

"About the Inanis," she said in a small voice. "I've been dreaming about them." I shuddered. Those things would have anyone waking up in a cold sweat.

"Is that why you were drawing them?"

Juni nodded. "Maximus once told me that they might show up and that I shouldn't worry about them, that they couldn't hurt me, but..." Her voice trailed off, and she lifted her head to look at the skeletal men surrounding us. Then she whispered, "They're very scary."

"Has Maximus told you what they want?"

Juni shook her head before she snuggled against me again. "No."

This conversation was quickly turning into the previous one I'd had with her only moments before when she hadn't been able to answer any of my questions either. She was just a child thrust into the middle of this. I didn't want to come across as if I were interrogating her, so I squeezed her shoulder and let the questions rest for a while.

Juni revealed a small flask from her bag, and I took

a few sips before I handed it back. I'd finished half of my alien granola bar, and I felt strangely satisfied by the small piece that I'd eaten. Considering that I had no idea how long this trip was going to be, I decided to make it last and wrapped it in the handkerchief.

Juni had just finished her piece as I tucked my left-over back in her bag.

"Thank you," I said. "That was great." Juni looked up with a smile and seemed pleased, but I could tell she was still bothered by the idea that Lana could be mad at her. I patted her arm as I said, "You know, I haven't known Lana that long, but I'm one hundred percent sure that she won't be mad." She didn't look up and stayed tucked at my side as she asked with a full mouth,

"How'd you know?"

"Because I'm really smart," I said, "and I know these things." Juni chuckled and the sound made me smile. "Besides, Oman has seen your drawings, and he must have told Lana. Remember how she said this wasn't your fault before we left the house?"

Juni tilted her head as she mulled over my words before she nodded.

"I guess..." she said but didn't sound convinced.

"Remember: I know these things," I managed to say with a smile and tickled her tummy. Juni giggled like she had when Max had teased her. Hoping to have eased her mind, I added, "Close your eyes and try to get some sleep."

∾

With every second that passed, it became harder to place one foot in front of the other. It felt as if the sand that had accumulated in my sneakers had turned to lead, making each step a struggle. I'd tried to sleep but had seemed unable to find a comfortable position because my back still felt as if it were on fire and my arm ached. Peering up at the blue sky, it was hard to imagine that the heat terrorizing my body did not emanate from a sun hovering over our heads. My shirt was soaked, and the fabric could not hold any more of the sweat that trickled down my back.

My left arm felt numb, and I shifted Juni to my right. Fortunately, the little girl seemed aware of my struggle and did not protest as I moved her for what might have been the fiftieth time. She even held a tight grip around my neck to ease some of her weight.

After a restless night, one of the Inanis had grabbed my arm and pulled me to my feet. Without a word, he kept shoving me until I got the gist and started to walk. At first, Juni had tried to walk on her own, but her tiny legs weren't able to keep up the strenuous pace held by the Inanis.

At this point, I didn't know how long we'd walked. The fence that had loomed at our backs for the longest time had disappeared below the horizon a while ago, and now all I could see around me was the desert sand and the deep blue sky.

I chanced a peek behind me but could only see more of the same. *How were Max and the others ever going to find us? Were they even looking?* I glanced down at Juni and had to believe that they wouldn't just abandon her

—at least not as long as they were alive. Juni had mentioned that there wasn't anything else out here except for Laeva, so maybe it wouldn't be so hard for Max to find us after all—I just hoped he'd be able to.

The five Inanis formed an enclosure around us with their bodies, which would easily prevent any form of escape. Not that I had any hope of escape. There was nowhere for us to run except in some unknown direction that would probably leave us dead in this godforsaken desert.

"Don't worry," Juni said. "We'll be there soon." Even though it felt odd that this little girl I carried in my arms tried to ease my worries, I felt glad for her effort. I hadn't been able to calm my racing heart ever since we'd started this gruesome walk, and it took all my effort to focus on not hyperventilating. I tried to keep my breathing steadily by following the Inanis's rhythm as they walked and that seemed to work. Although, as we trotted on and fatigue settled in my limbs, it became harder to keep my eyes open, and my focus began to waver. The heat and the uneven ground beneath my feet did not seem to affect the creatures' pace, although that didn't surprise me.

My hand started to stroke Juni's back in a similar rhythm to my breathing. I refused to close my eyes even for a second, because if I did, I feared, I might drop to my knees and curl up in the sand. I had a feeling the Inanis would not condone such action. Unfortunately, I appeared to have lost control of my eyelids, and I briefly closed my eyes. It couldn't have been more than two seconds as Juni spoke up, "Look out."

She'd barely uttered the words when I hit something solid and icy cold. My eyes shot open as a shiver ran through me, and I realized that I'd walked into one of the skeletal men. I glanced around and noticed all five of them had stopped. There did not appear any reason for the abrupt halt, and I took a few steps back. Then I felt it.

A slight tremor reverberated through the soles of my sneakers, and I held my breath. I turned in a circle as my eyes searched the desert. I'd felt this tremor before, and I could only pray this to be something else. A cloud of desert sand sprung up like a fountain into the distant sky, and my heart sank.

"Oh no," I uttered. Juni lifted her head from my shoulder and followed my gaze.

"Uh-oh," she said, and I glanced into her big blue eyes as I replayed her reaction in my head. *Was that all she had to say?*

The tremble underneath my feet increased, and another burst of sand flew into the sky closer than the one before. I looked around to gage the reaction of our travel companions.

None of them moved, and I stepped closer until I found myself standing face-to-face with one of them. Unsure of how to connect with it, I waved a hand in front of the Inanis's head. It wasn't as if they had eyes I could look into.

"Do you see that?" I asked as I pointed in the direction of the dust cloud that dissipated as quickly as it had shot from the ground. "We need to get out of here." The Inanis did not move and did not give any indication that had it had even heard me.

The ground started to shake, and I shifted on my feet to keep my balance. Another spurt of sand burst into the sky only several yards away from us. That triggered the Inanis, and they moved to stand in a circle around us.

"That's the Anguis," Juni whispered near my ear. "He's always in a bad mood."

I glared at the girl. "You call that a *bad mood*?"

"Yeah, it's just a mean old, grumpy Anguis," she added. I shook my head amazed at the fact that the girl did not appear to be afraid. *How could that be?* It occurred to me that Max and Cyril had talked about this thing as if it were a domestic animal. Perhaps Juni saw it in the same light—like some pet that, instead of chasing a mouse, could swallow a human whole. I shivered at the thought.

Closer than I would've liked, the ground opened up like some sinkhole. I stepped further away from it but bumped into one of the Inanis, who were using their bodies to enclose us fully.

"Jesus, do something!" I yelled and slammed an elbow into one of the skeletal men. Not that I'd expected that that would help—and I could've spared myself the cold shiver along with pain in my elbow. I swallowed hard as the snakelike creature poked its head from the hole and rose to tower over us. It looked just as impressive as it had the day before with its dragon-shaped head. Massive teeth looked ready to take someone's head off as the creature flexed its jaw and its scaled skin bristled.

The Inanis surrounding Juni and me did not seem impressed and didn't even move as the Anguis bent its head closer to us. The snake opened its mouth and hissed, and I could feel its warm, stinky breath waft over us. One of our five captors took a step forward, arms raised at its side.

For a moment, the two creatures just stared at each other, although the Anguis twitched and bobbed its head as if it were ready to pounce. The Inanis opened its jaw and released a howling sound similar to what I'd heard the night before after Moira had struck one of them.

The Anguis visibly flinched before snapping its teeth. As I watched the standoff, tension built inside me, and I felt uneasy on my legs. All of my instincts screamed at me to run, but where would I go? Besides, four Inanis surrounded me, effectively blocking my exit. And then there was Juni I had to think of.

Another one of the Inanis stepped forward and howled just as the first one had done. The sound appeared to be a source of agitation for the Anguis.

"What are they doing?" I whispered.

"They think that the Anguis wants to eat us," Juni replied, "and the Inanis want to stop it."

"It what?" I said and glared at Juni. "How do you know that?"

"Because that's what the Anguis does," she replied. "It gets hungry, and other than us, there is nothing else out here."

"And that doesn't bother you?"

She just shrugged and giggled like only a little girl could. "No, because I know a secret," she whispered in my ear. "Want to know?"

I nodded. At this point I'd take any glimmer of hope I could find.

"The Anguis can't eat me."

"Really," I said a bit dumbfounded.

"Uh-huh," Juni said, "Maximus told me."

Well, if Max had told her, then it must be true, but I tried to keep the sarcasm from my voice as I asked, "Why not?"

Juni moved closer to my ear and whispered so I could barely hear, "Because I'm the Sapphire Twin."

My eyebrows rose, and my mouth unhinged as I stared at her. *Were these the imaginary tales of a five-year-old, or was she telling the truth?* Max had told me that the gemstone he carried around his neck had a twin, but I just assumed it was another rock. *Had he mentioned it was another rock?* I couldn't remember. *But would it even matter?* If the Anguis couldn't eat Juni, then that would be great, but I still had myself to worry about.

The snake hissed, and the noise pulled me from my thoughts. A third Inanis stepped forward, and this time they howled simultaneously. The sound was about three times as annoying, but it had nowhere near the effect on me that it had on the Anguis. The snake shook its head vigorously and snapped its teeth. It rose to its full height, but then seemed to think better of it and disappeared back into its hole.

The ground started to tremble again, but from the

spurts of desert sand shooting into the sky, I could tell the Anguis was backing off.

"You can breathe now," Juni said as the tremors faded. Until she'd uttered the words, I hadn't even realized that I'd stopped breathing. I drew in a breath and felt my body shake as adrenaline pumped through my veins. This whole situation was getting to be too much.

As if nothing had happened, the Inanis returned to their previous position and started walking again. Terror-struck, I stared at the hole until I felt an icy hand on my back shoving me forward. Without any choice, I forced my legs to move and matched the Inanis's stride.

"This is all just too weird," I muttered. Juni shifted in my arms to look at me.

"How so?" she asked. She gave me a funny look that translated into "this is as normal as it comes," and I wasn't sure how to reply to that.

"I'm not exactly from here, remember?" I said.

"I know," Juni said, looking thoughtful, "but surely, you've seen the Anguis before?"

I chuckled humorlessly as I replied, "Indeed, I have." I didn't tell her that the last time I'd seen that thing, it had almost killed Moira.

The memory of the tall warrior woman showing up at Oman's place triggered a replay of what had set out to be an enjoyable evening among new friends. Now I didn't even know what had become of them.

"It's just a big old Anguis," Juni said as she patted my back. "That's all."

"If you say so," I managed to reply with a thin smile.

It wasn't just the Anguis that had me worried. From what I'd gathered so far, the Inanis worked for Jasper, and Jasper was the one desperate to stop the alignment. If what Juni had told me was the truth and she was the Sapphire Twin, then Jasper might get what he wanted. *The realms of existence will fall.* That was what Max had said what would happen if the sapphire stone wasn't aligned. *What if the plan was to get Juni all along to stop the alignment from happening?*

The thought racked my brain as I fell back in stride with the Inanis and managed to refocus on my breathing, so I could adapt it to their pace. I couldn't allow myself to think—not even for a second. If Juni had been the Inanis's target from the start, then right now, I was the only one that might be able to help. Lana had entrusted her to me, and I refused to let her or Max down. I couldn't break down, and therefore, I focused on getting air in and out of my lungs at a steady rate.

CHAPTER THIRTEEN

E ven though it felt as if I'd been walking for days, it was probably closer to hours when I noticed something large and black loom on the horizon. I shifted Juni in my arms again, so I could wipe at the sand that must have gathered in my eyes because I couldn't be seeing what I thought I was seeing. I blinked, but the image did not disappear. I figured it must have been exhaustion that had caused my vision to blur. It took me a while to believe what I saw as we closed in on the object.

"What the..." I muttered under my breath. Juni stirred and lifted her head from my shoulder.

"We're almost there," she said. I shot her a look and then returned to scrutinize the structure.

"Is that what I think it is?" I said.

"How should I know what you're thinking?" Juni replied.

I grinned at the child's remark before adding, "I mean, it looks like a castle."

Juni's gaze shifted toward the medieval-looking structure.

"That is Laeva," she said before asking, "What's a castle?" I pointed a finger at the stone structure. Large blocks of concrete, blackened by some form of erosion, had been meticulously stacked and formed huge outer walls. Two towers loomed on the left and right side of the structure. A colossal gate that kept intruders out sat at the center of the wall.

The structure resembled castles that I'd seen in old movies and seemed totally out of place in the middle of a desert.

"That is a castle," I said in answer to Juni.

The sand that had battered my feet during our strenuous walk soon became solid ground, and the feeling took some getting used to. The Inanis stopped before the gate, and we had to wait until it started to lift off the ground. Metal clanked, what I could only imagine being chains on man-sized pulleys that worked to retract the gate. The Inanis in the lead did not wait for the gate to fully lift, and as soon as the lowest metal bar cleared his head, he started walking again.

I wasn't sure if it was fear or some perverted excitement at the prospect of finally getting to rest that rushed through my veins as we crossed the threshold.

"What do you think this King Danara wants from us?" I asked. From the unsteadiness of which the words left my mouth, I rethought my previous notion and determined fear would be the right answer.

"I'm not sure," Juni replied. "He's never done this before."

"Do you mean the kidnapping, or attacking the village?" I asked.

"What's kidnapping?" My eyes shot to Juni's before I glanced around to take in our new surroundings.

"It's when you take a person against their will," I said.

The faceless Inanis guided us onto a small square set within the enormous walls. The ground was layered with cobblestones, and for some reason, they felt slippery beneath my sneakers. Water glistened on the stones, and as I stepped into a puddle, it felt as if the air shifted around me. The desert heat dissipated, and was replaced by a cold mist. I instantly shivered as minuscule droplets of water clung to my face and body. My shirt along with the rest of my clothes were still wet from sweating, and as the temperature dropped, I could feel the goose bumps rise on my skin.

"Well," Juni said, "I guess then he's never done either before."

"So, who is he?" I asked.

"All I know is that he built this place." Juni replied. "And Oman usually says nice things about him." I could only hope that would be the case. Perhaps this was just some big misunderstanding, and this King Danara would let us go home. Although from the undeterred movement of the Inanis I couldn't imagine this could just be some mix-up. They had taken us, and I figured whoever lived inside this enormous brick structure wanted them to bring us here.

The Inanis guided us up some stairs past a set of doors that looked as if the structure held a giant inside. I clung to Juni as if my life depended on it as the Inanis led us along a deserted hallway.

Torches mounted on the walls illuminated cold, undecorated bricks. Solid-looking wooden doors lined the walls every twenty feet or so. The temperature inside felt even colder than it had outside, and as we walked, it became harder to keep my teeth from chattering while my sneakers squeaked on the glistening tiled floor.

At the end of the hall, the Inanis leading our group opened a set of doors and stepped aside so we could enter the large chamber that lay beyond. Columns evenly spaced rose high above us to support a curved ceiling. The columns divided the area into three aisles with the middle one being the widest. Colored glass set in the vast windows depicted violent battlefields containing strange creatures. If something like a sun would fall upon the decorated windows, I'd bet they would have looked beautiful if it weren't for the horrific scenes portrayed within the glass.

In fact, the battle scenes displayed reminded me of Juni's drawings. I hadn't asked her about the picture she'd drawn. Back in the desert, Juni had mentioned that she'd dreamed about the Inanis before they showed up and that she'd regretted not telling Lana or Max about them. Seeing these depictions in the glass, I wondered if she might have seen them before and conjured the Inanis up in her dreams subconsciously. *Maybe this was all just some weird coincidence?* The reality of our situation reduced the inner workings of my mind to mere futile thoughts as we were guided to the far end of the space.

With its curved ceiling and massive columns along with the colorful windows, the place reminded me of a church of some kind. Except instead of an altar and benches, this church had a big hearth.

The footsteps of the Inanis were loud and echoed inside the open space as they lead us down the center aisle. They stopped several feet away from the enormous hearth that stood about as tall as I and had a fire burning within. A wooden chair and a sturdy table stood in front of it, while large bookcases covered the surrounding walls. I felt grateful for the heat that emanated from the flames and had to resist the urge to move closer.

The five Inanis formed a half circle around the hearth, encasing Juni and me within its confines. Afraid to move, I searched their shapeless faces but, as expected, found no answers.

"You can put me down now," Juni said.

"It's okay. I can carry you," I replied.

"You look like you're about to fall over, and I can walk," Juni said. I didn't doubt her observation skills. I could feel it in my bones; my entire body felt as if I were about to collapse.

Time had escaped me while walking through that desert, but my feet ached, and I hadn't been able to catch a lot of sleep the night before. My back still hurt from when the Inanis had dragged me across the rough sand, and the burning sensation on my skin had kept me awake most of the night.

I let Juni slide down the front of my body until her feet touched the ground. As soon as she found her footing, she gripped my hand and held it tight. She shifted her head to take in the impersonal space for a moment before she looked up and our eyes met.

For the first time, I could read uncertainty within those big blue eyes. For a child as young as Juni, I had to admit that she'd taken being kidnapped by faceless creatures that looked as if they had crawled out of a grave better than I had. Although I knew she missed Lana. Worse than that, Juni must be worried because we had no idea of what had happened to Lana or Moira—I just hoped she hadn't seen how the Inanis had taken Cora and Oman.

An involuntary shiver ran through my body at the memory of their screams, and I pushed the thought from my mind as I glanced around the room. The occasional torch mounted to the stone columns provided some light within the darkened space. The large bookcases had momentarily rekindled my hope that we were dealing with a bunch of knowledge nerds who'd come to Laeva to replenish their minds. That's how I'd imagined this place after hearing Cora and

Max talk about it, but to me, this didn't seem like a place I'd come to do anything, let alone think.

I hadn't noticed anyone enter, and I jumped at the sound of a strange voice.

"It is about time."

I jerked my head around and noticed a person standing before the hearth, with his back turned to us. My mouth fell open as I observed the tall figure. He looked as if he might have been twice the size of me. I'd bet he'd even tower over Cyril. A piece of fabric circled his broad hips to reach his knees. A wide belt held the skirt in place while he wore nothing else except for a pair of sandals. Muscles that looked to have been carved out of granite bulged along his back, shoulders, and arms. He resembled an oversized David that would've made Michelangelo proud.

"I was afraid you wouldn't make it in time," the tall figure said.

I looked down at Juni as she tugged at my arm. Without making a sound, she moved her mouth and formed the words *King Danara*. I glanced back at the tall figure and wondered why he wasn't wearing more clothes. I guessed the fire would feel nice, but the room was chilly, and frankly, I felt cold.

King Danara turned, and I thought I detected surprise in his reaction. As his eyes shifted from Juni to me, he said, "Why did you bring that one?"

One of the Inanis stepped forward until he came face-to-face with Danara or, well, maybe faceless-to-chest. It bowed before the creature raised its head. The Inanis did not speak, and neither did Danara, but it appeared as if some sort of communication took place as the King nodded before waving his hand at his apparent servant. The Inanis moved backward until it reached its previous spot and stood at attention.

"I see," King Danara said. He stepped away from the hearth and rounded table until he stood before us. "Who are you?" he asked. "And how is it that you managed to circumvent the Inanis's might?"

His eyes did not veer from mine, and I figured the question was addressed to me, although I didn't quite understand what he meant by me circumventing the Inanis's might.

"Sam," I said, but for a three-letter name, the word came out strained.

"That phrase does not mean anything to me. What is your name?" he asked again. I swallowed hard as I felt my throat close up.

His eyes held mine, and his chiseled jaw flexed as he ground his teeth while his bald head gleamed in the firelight. In fact, his whole body shimmered as if oil saturated his skin, although it wasn't as gooey looking as it was with the Inanis.

"Samantha Judd," I said. I hardly ever used my full first name, and it felt off to say it.

I could not read the expression on Danara's face as he clasped his hands behind his back and stared at me.

"My Inanis tell me that their powers had no effect on you," he said. "How is that possible?"

As if his tall frame hadn't been intimidating enough, his voice sounded deep and hollow at the same time, and it felt as if God himself were speaking to me.

"I'm not..." I started to say and hesitated. A sudden rush of terror washed over me as if saying the wrong thing would cost me dearly. "I don't know." It was all I could say because I wasn't sure if the Inanis had even used their powers on me. Although they had grabbed me as they had done with Cora and Oman. I remembered the chilly feeling that had run down my body as if someone had shoved me inside a freezer, but that might have been the effect of my fear of dying.

As it were, it seemed as if Danara was as much in the dark about me still being alive as I was. The thought that I wasn't supposed to be here, that the Inanis had tried to kill me, should've rendered my body useless and gasping for breath, but it hadn't. The mere notion that those creatures hadn't been able to swallow me up and feed off my essence kept me upright. Danara's servants couldn't hurt me. Well, they could hurt me plenty, but at least they couldn't do to me what they had done to Cora and Oman. The idea was only a minor relief, but I wasn't going to complain.

I clung to that tiny inkling of a blessing and tried to control my breathing as King Danara's gaze shifted to Juni and he asked, "Do you know?"

Juni vehemently shook her head.

"I don't know, King."

He seemed pleased with her using his title. He

lowered himself down onto a knee as he peered into Juni's eyes.

"It's about time, isn't it?" he said.

Juni's nod was barely perceptible. I figured they might be talking about the alignment, although I couldn't be sure. It didn't stop a gut-wrenching feeling from stirring inside me. "You will help me break down the walls between the realms and join Jasper as he——"

"You can't align the stones. Only Maximus can," Juni said, unbothered about cutting Danara off midsentence. And she sounded pretty confident for a five-year-old. Danara raised an eyebrow, and for a brief second, it looked as if he might have been a bit shocked by the child's statement. He recovered quickly as he chuckled.

"It seems Maximus has fed you the same lies he has fed to us all," Danara said, "but even you, little one, shall abide by Jasper's will——"

"No, he hasn't," Juni said in the same tone she'd used before. "And, no, I won't. I don't wanna cross the realms. I like it just fine here."

This time, it didn't look as if Danara was willing to laugh this one off. His brow furrowed as Danara fixed his gaze on Juni.

"Silence!" His voice boomed inside the huge space and bounced off the walls. Juni visibly flinched and pressed her small frame against my leg as Danara added, "You think you can defy me." It didn't sound as if he'd finished yet, and my actions came forth more out of reflex than an act of bravery, but I couldn't let this brute scare Juni like that. With Juni's hand in mine, I pulled her behind me and blocked her from Danara's view.

With him still kneeling on the ground, I had some height advantage and stared down at him. That might have been the reason that made me brave enough to speak up.

"Stop scaring her." With his eyes locked on mine, Danara rose to his full height in a slow and deliberate move. By the time he stood, I had to crane my neck, and I instantly regretted my decision to say anything. The look on his face either meant *Who the hell do you think you are?* or *You'll pay for this.* I felt Juni's pull at the fabric of my running pants as she pressed against my leg, but I couldn't look down to see how she was doing.

Danara still had his eyes fixed on me, and I felt afraid to break eye contact. All I wanted to do was to crawl into a corner of the room and disappear. Unfortunately, that wasn't an option. I didn't care if Danara thought of me as a coward, and diverting my gaze would surely do that. He would've decided already that I wasn't worth his attention, but I wanted to be strong for Juni. Despite the fact that she'd taken all of this a lot better than I had, she was still a little girl who was all alone and didn't even know what had happened to her family. This was the least I could do.

With his eyes locked on mine, Danara bent forward until I could feel his breath on my face. His eyes were as dark as the night sky, but as I stared into them, I could see red-golden flecks within his irises that looked like burning cinder. They reminded me of the sparks of fire that had danced inside the dark veil that had tried to engulf Max and me right before the sapphire stone had transported us here.

"You think you can tell me what to do inside my own home?" Danara said in a menacing tone. "You think you can come in here and defy me?" His voice grew louder, even though he kept his face close to mine. Tiny specks of saliva landed on my cheeks as he spoke. I swallowed hard but forced myself not to move or even flinch. That wasn't easy, considering that I could feel the tremor that raged through my body worsen. Remembering that I was holding Juni's hand, I balled my other hand into a fist and squeezed so hard that my nails dug painfully into my skin.

"Just leave her alone," I said. It wasn't as strong a sentence as I'd conjured up in my mind, and my shaky voice didn't help either, but those few words left me feeling a bit more confident. I squared my shoulders and managed to hold the tall man's gaze.

"You are of no consequence to me," Danara said after a moment and straightened. "Take that one to the dungeons."

"Wait. What—" I uttered. But I had no chance to say anything else as I felt bony fingers clamp on my shoulders.

"No, Sam has to stay," Juni said as she clung to my hand. One of the Inanis jerked my shoulder, and I lost my grip on Juni's hand. The young girl did not hesitate as she fought to grab it again. She managed to grasp my fingers and turned to face Danara.

"Please, Sam has to stay. Please let her stay."

Danara flicked his wrist, and another one of the Inanis stepped forward. Two of the creatures held my arms, and I felt the cold of their touch seep through my bones. I struggled against their grip, but they wouldn't relent.

A third Inanis reached for Juni and grabbed her. For the first time since our journey together had started, I could see despair written across the young girl's face. She was scared. As I felt her hand forcefully removed from my grip, I called out to her, "It's okay, Juni. I'll be back soon." I doubted it, but I had to say something. It tore at my heart to see the fear in the small child. I wanted to comfort her even though at this point the chance of us seeing each other soon again would be slim. "It's okay. You have to be brave. All right?" Uttering the words made me feel like a moron. My hands shook uncontrollably, and it wouldn't be long before my entire body would shut down. There was no way I could be any kind of support to this child, not as the fear was about to consume me.

"Silence," Danara said in a loud voice that reverberated through the spacious room.

"Your time will come soon enough," he said as he looked at Juni.

"What are you doing? She's just a child." I pleaded. "Please don't take me away from her." Nothing that I said seemed to matter as the Inanis dragged me from the room.

CHAPTER FOURTEEN

I kept my eyes shut and focused on my breathing as the Inanis led me by the arms. That probably wasn't the brightest thing to do as I stumbled over steps leading down. Fortunately, the two creatures had a firm grip on my arms and kept me upright as they let me down the staircase. I could feel the temperature drop even further, to a point where I could not discern if my chattering teeth were a result of fear or the cold.

We exited the staircase into a darkened hallway, not unlike the one I'd seen up top before we had entered King Danara's domain. The only difference seemed to be the fewer number of torches, and the lack of light gave the hallway a creepy and dingy atmosphere.

The two Inanis pulled me to a halt in front of a wooden door with a little hatch at eye level. One of them knocked, and the sound echoed down the hall behind me. We waited as silence fell until I recognized the muffled sound of footsteps behind the door. The small hatch opened quickly, and to my relief, a normal-looking face appeared. As soon as the hatch had opened, it slammed shut, and the lock clicked before the door opened. Hinges creaked loudly, making me cringe. A lanky figure stood in the shadows, and revealed itself to be a young man as he stepped into the faint light.

Surprise was etched on his kind face, and his green eyes were wide as he stared back at us. He pulled a hand through this messy dark-blond hair that nearly reached his shoulders.

"Eh..." he said and hesitated, "welcome." It sounded like a question, as if he had no idea what we were doing down here. He shot me a brief glance before his eyes trailed to my companions. The moment turned into an awkward silence, and the young man nervously scratched the back of his head. "Can I help you?" he asked just as I felt the silence become unbearable.

Without further notice, the Inanis shoved me forward, and I stumbled through the door opening. If the young man hadn't caught me, I feared I would've fallen flat on my face.

"Okay," he said, elongating the word as he steadied me.

I turned just in time to see one of the Inanis close the door behind us, and it clanged shut. The young man still had his hands on me for support, and I quickly pulled away from him. Feeling like my legs were about to collapse, I reached for the wall to steady myself. As I looked up, I caught the young man staring at me for a while until he seemed to remember to lock the door, and he turned to secure the latch. Then he returned to staring at me.

I took that moment to glance around, and it wasn't hard to determine where I'd ended up. The place was no more than a continuation to the hallway outside except for the fact that the doors lining the wall all had bars in front of them. I swallowed at the lump that formed in my throat, but I couldn't clear it.

At that point, my legs did collapse, and I sagged down along the wall until my butt hit the ground. My breath seemed stuck somewhere halfway down my lungs, and my head felt woozy. Hoping to stop my vision from tunneling, I closed my eyes; I pulled my legs up and lowered my head as I struggled to breathe. The memory of sitting with Max in the grass, surrounded by sheep, popped into my mind, and I held on to it. As if he were sitting by my side, I could hear his deep, soothing voice counting off a rhythm that helped me get air into my lungs again.

I wasn't sure how much time had passed before my breathing evened out, but as I looked up, the young man stood leaning against the opposite wall, patiently watching me.

"Eh...are you all right?" he asked, sounding uncertain. I nodded that I was, and eased my head back against the wall.

I tilted my head to the left and took in the doors with the bars.

"Are you sure you're all right?" the young man repeated. "Because you don't look fine."

Glancing back at him, I noticed his pale complexion. He looked as if he'd just seen a ghost, and a look of concern edged across his face. He didn't resemble anything that I would have imagined a guard working in a dungeon would look like. He seemed more like the kind of guy who would help an old lady with her groceries. Hoping that my instincts were correct, I took a deep breath and pushed myself up.

I flinched as he stepped closer, but then I realized he was just holding out his hand to help me. With his help, I got to my feet but immediately had to reach out for the wall to steady myself. It seemed my legs weren't as ready as I'd thought.

"Easy," he said as he grasped my arm. On pure reflex, I pulled away from him, but as I met his wide gaze, I could tell he was only trying to help.

"Sorry," I said, "but I'm fine." I wasn't sure why I was apologizing to the man who held me captive, and I shook my head.

"What now?" I asked in an unsteady voice.

The young man shrugged as if he had no clue. "Not exactly sure," he said. "No one has ever been brought down since I started working here." I glared at him for a moment and then shifted my attention back to the prison cells before returning my eyes to him.

"We're alone down here?" I asked. I couldn't stop the tremble in my voice, and I wondered if I even should've asked the question. I wasn't sure if I should be glad no one was down here or if I should be afraid of it.

"Yeah, well, this hasn't been the most exciting job I've had," the young man said as he brushed by me and ambled down the hall. He stopped at a table and chair about halfway down the space. He reached for a cup that stood next to a pitcher and drank from it before setting it down again.

I glanced around again, not sure what to do. A streak of light filtered inside through a high window at the end of the hall. Four torches evenly divided along the narrow space provided light to see. I shivered, feeling cold, and I crossed my arms around my waist, trying to keep warm.

"So, where did you come from, and why did Danara send you down here?" the young man asked. I looked at him in surprise. This was not what I'd expected from a dungeon in a medieval castle.

"Eh..." I said and hesitated. It was a valid question, but the absurdity of it hit me nonetheless. I glanced down at my shoes as if the answer might be written on them. It seemed ages ago that I'd tied those sneakers and stepped outside my apartment building for a quick run to clear my mind. *What the hell did I do to get here?* I realized the young man was staring at me as he waited for my reply.

"I'm not sure," I said. The young man placed his hands on his hips and cocked his head.

"You're not from Ora because I think I would have remembered seeing you," he said as his eyes trailed up and down my body. "You seem different."

I glanced down to look at my black running clothes and sneakers. They didn't look anything like his tunic-like garb, which seemed way too cold for this place, although different from what I'd seen in Ora. His garments had long sleeves. I shook my head without a reply. *What was I supposed to tell him?* He shrugged and then took a few steps until he stood in front of me.

"My name's Deyo," he said as he offered me his hand. His name rang familiar, but I couldn't place it. The smile on his face, though, was warm and inviting, and I figured this was probably better than being chained to the wall by some brutish, bad-smelling prison guard.

"I'm Sam," I replied as I shook his hand.

"Sam, welcome to the dungeon," Deyo said as he gestured around the room.

I felt a bit lost as I stood there in that dingy hallway surrounded by empty jail cells. My body shivered, and goose bumps trailed up my arms, but my throat felt as dry as the desert we had walked through, and I couldn't help eyeing the pitcher standing on the table.

Deyo's eyebrow raised as he figured out what had caught my attention before turning back to me.

"You walked through the dunes, didn't you?" he asked.

I nodded, not sure if my throat would even be able to conjure up a sound. He moved to the table and poured another cup from the pitcher. I reached for it with a trembling hand as he held out to me. Afraid to drop the cup and spill its contents, I grasped it with both hands and eagerly drained it. It wasn't nearly enough to quench my thirst, but I didn't dare to ask for a second cup. Deyo seemed like a nice guy, but he probably wasn't assigned guard duty for that reason. I didn't want to push my luck.

I moved closer to one of the open doors and glanced inside. The two-by-four room did not look inviting, even though it appeared clean. Except for a small cot shoved into a corner, there wasn't much to see, not even a window.

"So...why is this place so empty?" I asked, hoping to get some conversation going. Interacting with others wasn't normally my strong suit, but I'd grab at straws if it meant keeping my mind focused and, if lucky, keeping him from locking me in one of those cells. I couldn't let myself get sucked into my own head right now, not again, and I tried to steady my breathing. Deyo shrugged before answering.

"I don't think anyone's ever been down here," he said as he led his eyes roamed over the open cell doors. "Except for me." My eyebrows rose at his admission. "I used to work as a cook in the kitchen upstairs." He shoved his hands into the pockets of his loose pants that came with the tunic before he continued. "This used to be a fun place to work," Deyo said, "even if it did mean that I had to travel the dunes every fortnight." I glared at him I couldn't help it.

"You're from Ora." A frown formed on Deyo's face as if I'd said something stupid.

"Of course," he replied.

"Wait...you're Deyo," I said as if he didn't know that already. "You had gone home with the others, but Cyril sent you back." Deyo's frown deepened as he glared at me.

"You know Cyril?" A jolt of hope surged inside me.

"And Max..." I said, but at the questioning look he gave me, I corrected myself. "I mean Maximus."

The following just tumbled from my mouth, and I even forgot to breathe.

"You've got to help me. I need to get out of here. This King Danara is up to something. He has these creatures...I mean, you've seen them, and I think he might be trying to stop the alignment, and from what Max—I mean Maximus—has told me, the man is crazy for trying—"

"Don't talk like that about King Danara," Deyo interjected and even sounded offended. "He has built this place so we could come here and expand our way of thinking. Ora has never flourished so well since he and Maximus helped us to focus on our own abilities."

My heart rate picked up as I felt anger replace the remaining fragments of hope as it surged through my veins. The memories of a pleasant get-together viciously disturbed by faceless skeletal men sat edged at the forefront of my mind, and my back still burned from being dragged through the desert.

"You think attacking the village and kidnapping

Juni and me is flourishing!" Deyo flinched at my harsh tone, but that didn't stop me from continuing. "Why don't you ask Cora or Oman if Danara is such a nice guy—oh wait, you can't because the Inanis ate them. The same Inanis that report to your king."

Wide-eyed, Deyo stared at me as if he couldn't comprehend what he'd just heard.

"What you mean, attacked the village?" he said.

"The Inanis, they attacked Ora," I said.

Deyo shook his head. "The Inanis don't work for King!"

"Well, they do," I said. My voice held the anger building inside me, and the image of Juni pleading with the king only fueled it. The young girl was all alone up there with that giant of a man.

As if he couldn't comprehend what I was saying, Deyo kept shaking his head. "It doesn't make sense," he said. "There is no reason to think King has anything to do with this."

"Well, the fact that the Inanis brought us here should ring a bell." I nearly shouted the words at him, and I threw up my arms in despair. *How was I going to convince this guy?* "After they destroyed the village!"

Deyo searched my eyes as if he were trying to discern if I were telling the truth or not. A moment later, he raised a hand to his mouth as if my words had only just then registered.

"How bad...I mean...my parents," he said and started to sound incoherent as he struggled to catch his breath. He seemed to be in genuine distress. I instantly regretted my outburst. I hadn't considered that he might have family back there, but I couldn't take it back now.

"I'm not sure," I said in a softer tone. "The village was in flames, but I passed out after they captured us, so I..."

I shook my head and, for a moment, caught Deyo staring into nothingness. I gathered my nerves and moved closer to him. As I placed a hand on his arm, his eyes met mine. His eyebrows rose as if he'd just remembered something.

"You said Juni."

"Yeah, they took both of us." As soon as the words had left my mouth, Deyo grabbed my shoulders. On instinct, I stepped back and pulled away from his grasp.

"But the alignment is tonight, and Juni needs to be with..." he said seemingly oblivious to my reaction, which was just as well. Deyo acted frantically, and he started to scare me. "You said you know Maximus. Where is he? He has to align the stones or else Ora might be lost. Juni needs to be there."

I was sort of aware of the importance of the alignment. *"Realms of existence will fall"* and all that, although my mind tried very hard to ignore the implications of what those words meant. Deyo's mention of Juni did strike me. The little girl had revealed her importance concerning the alignment, but I'd pretty much dismissed it as being a child's fairy tale. What kind of an insane place was this where a child would be made responsible for this entire world.

"So, it's true," I said. "Juni is the Sapphire Twin."

"Juni is the key to a successful alignment," he said. His voice rose an octave as his hands grabbed hold of my shoulders again. This time, I let him as he rambled on. "King would never allow this."

"Deyo," I said in a loud voice hoping to regain his attention. Terror reflected in the young man's eyes, and I wondered if I looked like him when I had one of my episodes. As soon as the thought entered my head, I banished it, afraid it would trigger something I wasn't equipped to handle right now.

"I have to talk to him," Deyo said and pushed past me. He strode in the direction of the door, and I quickly ran after him. I caught up with him just as he unlatched the lock.

I kept my distance as he paused with his hand resting on the latch. It wouldn't be in my best interest if he viewed me as a threat and left me behind in this dungeon. If I wanted to get to Juni, then I needed to get out of here.

Deyo shot me a questioning look as if he wasn't sure what to make of me. I figured I'd get him to talk; that might relieve some of the tension, and besides, I still knew too little of what was going on.

"This alignment, how does it work?" He gave me that look again, as if I'd said something utterly stupid.

"Juni needs to be in close vicinity to Maximus for the alignment to happen before the end of the day."

Deyo opened the door and stepped into the adjoining hallway.

"Wait," I said as I followed. "What are you planning to do?"

"I have to talk to him."

I overtook Deyo and, forgetting about wanting to come across as nonthreatening, I stopped him by grabbing his shoulders.

"You can't just walk up to him. He has Inanis guards. They will...take you."

"There is no way that King is working with the Inanis. He wouldn't do that," Deyo said, "because that would mean he'd be aiding Jasper, and King knows what will happen if the realms fall."

"And what was it that you thought the Inanis were doing when they brought me to the dungeon? Take me for a tour of the property?" I said with a considered amount of cynicism, "Who do you think told them to do that?"

It wasn't hard to read the despair in Deyo's eyes. He'd known Danara a lot longer than I had, and he seemed adamant that the tall man had nothing to do with it. Maybe there was a different explanation. I took a breath to calm myself. Shouting wasn't going to help me convince Deyo that Danara had turned to the dark side.

"What if they'd done something to him?" I said as I released his shoulders. "He might not be acting like himself, and if he isn't, you can't just walk up to him."

Deyo lowered his chin and lifted a hand to squeeze the bridge of his nose.

"I should've stayed up there," he said under his breath. Not sure if I'd heard correctly, I asked, "What do you mean?"

He shook his head as if nothing were wrong, but I

wasn't buying it. I was about to pose a question, but Deyo beat me to it. "Then what do you suggest?"

Time wasn't on our side, and I didn't think this would be the right moment to get into all the details. At least I had made it past the dungeon door. Now all I had to do was find Juni, get her away from Danara and back to Max. I swallowed hard at the thought of the impossible task ahead and glanced over my shoulder down the empty hallway. Only a handful of torches that were barely enough to see by lit the way that I needed to go. The flames reflected on the wet surface of the stone floors, adding to the dingy atmosphere.

A shiver ran through my body, and I quickly released Deyo's shoulders, so he wouldn't notice the tremor in my hands and balled my fists at my side. There had to be a way inside Danara's chambers.

"I have to find a way to sneak in there," I said, taking a deep breath as I took my first determined step.

"Wait," Deyo called after me, but I ignored him as I ran down the hall.

My sneakers squeaked as I sprinted down the hallway. As I passed several wooden doors, I cursed myself for not paying better attention when the Inanis had brought me down here.

"Just keep your eyes closed," I muttered to myself. "How stupid is that?" I slowed my pace in the hope of finding some clue that would tell me where to go. Thinking back on it, I felt pretty sure that we had exited a door on my left side.

"Sam!" Deyo shouted after me. "Where are you going?"

Walking now at a speedy pace, I glanced over my shoulder. Deyo stood about halfway down the hall from me, seemingly without any intention of catching up with me, and so I stopped.

"I need to get to Juni," I shouted back him. "I'm not going to leave her in the hands of Danara." I pointed an accusing finger at Deyo as I added, "And if you think of ratting me out to Danara—"

"I'm not," Deyo replied as he threw his hands up in the air in exasperation, "but if you want to get up there, then you need to go through here." Deyo pointed at a doorway.

I took a quick look around and had to curse myself again for running past the only door that had stood open. I jogged back to where Deyo was standing but slowed and eventually stopped several feet in front of him. I did not feel afraid of the young man. His lanky features and boyish good looks made him appear harmless, but I wanted to be on my guard.

He must have noticed my hesitation because he lifted his arms with his palms up as if to reassure me that he wasn't a threat to me.

"I can help," he said. Uncertainty caused me to shift my feet as I held Deyo's gaze. *His eyes held determination, but for what? Determined to help Danara, Juni…me? Maybe he just wanted what was best for his people, but how could I be sure of that?* It wasn't in my nature to ask for help. I preferred to do things on my own and keep the rest of the world as far at bay as I could.

Taking a step closer, I glanced past the open door and noticed the stairwell leading up. Deyo certainly knew his way around the castle. If I wanted to find a way inside Danara's chamber without being caught and rescue Juni, then I would need his help.

"Thanks," I said, hoping my decision wouldn't haunt me in the end and started up the stairs. The sound of footsteps echoing behind me inside the hollow space told me that Deyo had to be close on my heels.

"I just don't understand what King Danara would want with Juni," he said in between his heavy breathing. "He knows the stones have to be aligned. If not, it will hurt him as much as the people of Ora."

I sensed my breathing getting labored as well as I sprinted up the rounding stairs.

"Maybe he lost his mind."

I stopped at a landing and peeked out the door. Nothing looked familiar, but that wasn't a surprise.

"One more," Deyo said as he stopped behind me. I glanced at him as he bent forward and braced his hands on his knees. It seemed Deyo wasn't in such great shape. I wasn't feeling in the best shape of my life either, but then these past few days had been exhausting.

"I should've gone up there," Deyo said as he fought to catch his breath. One of my feet already rested on the next step, but I paused to look back at him. He'd mentioned that before, and I'd been intrigued then, so this time I wasn't going to let him get away with it.

"What are you talking about?"

Deyo shook his head. "Cyril. He asked me to keep an eye on things, but after I came back, King sent me down there."

"And you didn't think that was strange?"

"Not really," he said with a shrug. "I often went down there if I needed time to think or wanted to read in silence."

I glanced down the steps and raised an eyebrow. "In a dungeon?" I must have sounded incredulous to him as I added, "For days?"

"I don't enjoy being around people," he said unapologetically. "It's just who I am." It seemed Deyo and I had more in common than I thought. "About two days ago, I went upstairs to make myself something to eat when I saw one of the Inanis venture down the hall—it scared the wits out of me."

"I'd bet," I said.

"I was about to make a run for it when I bumped into King, and he told me he'd sought contact with Jasper's demons to see if he could open up a dialog."

"And you believed him?" My voice rose an octave and cleared my throat.

"I had no reason not to," he said as he looked up to meet my gaze. "With every day that passes, Jasper is getting closer to stop Maximus from aligning the stones, and if there is one person in this world who wants to prevent that, then it's King."

I placed my hands on my hips and blew out a breath. This thing was getting more complicated by the minute.

As I resumed my climb up the stairs I kept a slower pace.

"So foolish of me. I should have gone back to Ora and told Cyril. Then we wouldn't be in this mess."

"Well, I should've stayed home last night," I whispered.

"What?" Deyo asked. I looked over my shoulder and noticed a look on Deyo's face that told me that he hadn't understood, and I quickly added, "Danara is your friend, so don't be too hard on yourself, although I don't think we can risk thinking he's on our side."

From everything people kept telling me about Danara, it seemed he was a decent person. Well, used to be a decent person, because there was nothing decent about the man I'd met upstairs. *Maybe this Jasper I kept hearing about had decided that he wasn't in the mood for talking and had done something to Danara.*

"Do you think Jasper could have done something to Danara?" I asked. "You know, to make him go all psycho and stuff."

"I don't understand," Deyo said from behind me.

I squelched a groan and sought a better phrase to explain Deyo what I meant.

"I mean, like, eh...to change him, to make Danara do things that he normally wouldn't do," I said. "Could Jasper control him somehow?" When no answer came, I glanced over my shoulder and noticed

Deyo had stopped. His face had turned pale as he vehemently shook his head.

"But then he would have to be here...he can't be here." His voice trembled as he uttered the words. I took a few steps down and reached a hand out to touch his shoulder.

"I didn't say Jasper was here," I said in the hope of calming him down. "Maybe his Inanis have done it for him. No one said anything about Jasper being here, okay?"

Deyo nodded and took a deep breath. "Okay."

I squeezed his shoulder before I returned my attention to the last few steps that let us up to the next landing. It felt a bit unreal to me to be the one trying to calm a person's nerves. Usually, I would be the one getting that treatment. I couldn't help feeling a little invigorated knowing that, even though I knew damn well how troublesome it must be for Deyo.

I poked my head out the door and noticed that we had ended up in the hall that had brought us to King Danara's chambers. Before I could enter the hallway, Deyo grabbed my arm.

"We should wait for Maximus. He would know what to do," he said. "Maximus is a warrior trained to protect us and to make sure the alignment happens as planned."

I shook off Deyo's hand as I thought of my new old friend. The old Max, who was in his eighties, did not at all resemble the warrior Deyo described, but the new Max might've stepped right out of a story told by

Homer himself. Both seemed alien to me, and I had to smile at my internal pun.

"What?" Deyo eyed me curiously, and I wiped the smile from my face.

"Maximus isn't here right now," I said. The words had barely left my mouth before a knot formed in my stomach. A sudden rush of feeling alone threatened to overwhelm me, and I had to remind myself that I wasn't alone. Deyo was here, although I had my doubt how useful he'd be in a tight spot—couldn't be worse than me, though. I shook my head and forced the feeling aside. A sensation like that would only add to my already existing fears and could easily morph into panic. I couldn't let that happen, not now. I had to find Juni.

I poked my head through the door opening again and glanced around. The hall was empty, and everything just seemed a bit too quiet.

"Let's go," I told Deyo, despite the ominous feeling brewing in my gut, and stepped into the hallway.

CHAPTER FIFTEEN

I'd only taken a few steps down the hallway when I saw the Inanis standing guard in front of Danara's chamber. There were two of them, and I froze on the spot.

"This way," Deyo whispered. In the same instance, he tugged at my arm and pulled me down an adjacent corridor. Deyo made a right turn and then headed left before he slowed his pace.

All of these hallways looked the same, with their dampened floors and flaming torches bolted to the walls, and I had no idea where Deyo was taking me, but considering that he'd stayed here for long periods of time, I hoped he knew where he was going.

Deyo lifted a hand and halted before he glanced over his shoulder. I could not decipher the look on his face as he tilted his head.

"Something is wrong," he said. I almost exclaimed that of course there was something wrong. We wouldn't be scurrying down darkened hallways afraid of being caught by skeletal men if it weren't. He edged forward before poking his head around another corner. Then he stepped out into plain view and just stood there. I glanced around to see if no one were around before I joined him.

An enormous kitchen loomed before us. It wasn't the squeaky-clean retirement home-type of kitchen, but it was impressive nonetheless. Large counters lined every wall and surrounded an enormous firepit in the center of the room. Pots and pans hung from hooks, and fruits and vegetables similar to what I'd seen in Oman's home covered every surface. A small fire burned within a stove, but otherwise, nothing inside the room moved. There wasn't anyone there.

For a kitchen of this size that seemed odd. I would've expected at least one cook preparing some kind of meal. I had a feeling that same observation had stopped Deyo in his tracks.

"Where is everyone?" I asked.

Deyo shook his head. "Most have gone back to Ora, but Canton and Vera were here this morning when I came up to fetch some breakfast, although I haven't seen them since."

"Were they the only ones who had stayed?"

Deyo shook his head again turned and walked over to a window. Apparently unsatisfied, he craned his neck to widen his view. Getting curious, I followed his example and looked out the window. I let my eyes roam over a beautiful garden that, despite the depressingly thick fog, seemed to flourish. It seemed this place didn't always suffer from this kind of doom-and-gloom weather. I couldn't be sure because of the lacking-a-sun bit, but it seemed nightfall was upon us.

"No one is out there," Deyo said, stating the obvious. He looked thoughtful as he added, "Marcus is always out there tending the garden. He's kind of obsessed with it. Martha is usually out and about mopping the floors. We all do our bit to help out our community. I mostly help out right here in the kitchen."

"Maybe they changed their minds and have gone back to Ora." I watched Deyo carefully hoping for a confirmation, but the grimace on his face told me he wasn't convinced. The sinking feeling that I knew what had happened to these people washed over me, but I didn't want to say it out loud. With the Inanis around, it seemed obvious, and from the look on Deyo's face, I had a feeling that he was thinking the same.

An awkward silence followed, and I let my gaze roam around the spacious kitchen. Except for Deyo and the Inanis, I hadn't seen anyone else within King Danara's court. It seemed odd to call oneself a king if he let his servants get swallowed up by the Inanis.

"What is he a king of, anyway?" I asked more to myself than Deyo as I walked to the center of the room. With only the two of us inside this quiet space, it wasn't surprising that he'd heard me.

"What do you mean?"

I leaned against one of the counters and lifted my hands to gesture at our surroundings.

"He calls himself a king, but a king of what—an empty castle?"

Deyo raised an eyebrow that clearly told me he had no idea what I was talking about.

To clarify what I meant, I added, "You know, king of the castle. He's like the leader, right?"

Deyo shook his head, and as he did, I remembered Juni's reaction to the word *castle*. He must not have known what it meant either.

"We all live and exist here as equals. King Danara is his name," Deyo said as he stepped closer.

I glared at him, feeling a bit nonplussed. "So, what are you saying...he's not 'a king'?" I used air quotes to emphasize my point before I gathered there was probably no use to doing so.

"He is just...King," Deyo replied with a shrug. "Like I said, King Danara is his name." The look he gave me told me Deyo was doubting my sanity, and by this point, I couldn't blame him.

I shook my head and raised a hand to wave him off. "Never mind."

Having decided that we must have lingered long enough inside this room, Deyo headed for the exit. Following, I nearly bumped into him as he suddenly stopped. The sound of footsteps on the stone floor made my blood run cold.

"Maybe that's one of the cooks," I said with a hopeful note in my voice.

A soft growl and the clack, clack sound of bones on the stone floor dissipated that hope. This could only be an Inanis approaching the kitchen. Deyo turned, and his eyes were as wide as mine most have been. He took my hand and pulled toward the closest counter. With a hand on my neck, he forced me down to the ground after he shifted several sacks that smelled like spoiled food to make room. He pushed me into the shallow space before he squeezed in beside me and used the sacks to hide us from view.

The footsteps grew louder as I fought to keep my breathing steady, which wasn't easy considering the foul smell that surrounded us. Besides, this space felt too cramped. I squeezed my eyes shut, but the darkness behind my lids and the body pressed against me caused memories to resurface at the forefront of my mind that I didn't want to revisit—certainly not now. Not with an Inanis so close and the possibility of being discovered. *Not now, not now.* The words played on repeat in my mind as the sound of the Inanis's tread grew louder.

Deyo must have sensed my discomfort, because he reached for my hand and squeezed it lightly. His simple touch distracted me enough to shift my train of thought, and Max's voice popped into my head. I focused on his words as he recited the numbers in my head just like he had while I was sitting in the grass with my head between my knees. A moment later, I forgot all about breathing as the Inanis entered the kitchen. I clamped my jaw shut to keep my teeth from chattering and felt my entire body tremble.

I kept my eyes closed and tried not to think about the Inanis as it rustled through some of the stuff on one of the counters. Max's voice, deep and rich, filled my head, and I wished he was here with me. He'd promised me that he'd get me home, and he'd better not have been killed during that attack on the village because I was going to hold him to that promise. I wanted to go home. I missed my mom and Kay. Even the prospect of having to go back to work and face Trish was better than this.

It felt as if I'd been sitting here for hours waiting for the creature to leave, but in reality, it might only have been seconds.

"He's gone," Deyo whispered. I didn't feel as sure about that as Deyo, and I sat unmoving for another minute or so until Deyo tapped my shoulder. "Come on, Sam."

I opened my eyes and remembered to breathe, taking in deep gulps of air. Spots flashed before my eyes from either squeezing my eyes shut so tight or lack of oxygen. Either way, I took a moment to even out my ragged breathing.

Deyo had already climbed out from under the counter and held out his hand for me.

"This way," he said as I took his hand. Deyo was the only one who could help me find Juni, and I needed to trust that he was truly convinced that Danara wasn't his friend anymore and that Deyo wouldn't sell me out. I had to stop myself from over-thinking, and I figured reacting would probably the best way to achieve that. Therefore, I blindly followed Deyo to the kitchen exit.

As I let him lead me through the kitchen, I thought about grabbing one of the sharp-looking knives or the small hatchet lying on one of the counters. The Inanis's powers apparently didn't work on me and arming myself might give me an advantage, although having seen their strength, I couldn't see myself successfully using it against them. They'd probably take it from me and kill me with it, so I decided against it. Deyo picked up the pace as he skirted down another hallway. After a couple of turns, he stopped at a narrow door tucked away behind a curtain. He grasped the doorknob, and the door squeaked as he pushed it open. I grabbed his shoulder, unnerved by the sound and afraid of being found out.

"It's okay. They won't hear," he whispered. "No one ever comes this way, except for Martha when she's cleaning, and we're not close enough to the chamber yet."

"Then why are you whispering?" Deyo shrugged without giving me an answer as he entered another narrow corridor. The space was just wide enough to hold one person, and I didn't think that it would fit someone overweight. I closed the door behind us, and we were instantly bathed in darkness.

"Oh shit," I said as I braced myself with a hand on either side of the enclosure. I wasn't sure if it was the darkness or the claustrophobic size of the space that had me freaking out this time, but I cursed myself as I felt a shift in my breathing.

"You okay?" Deyo asked. I shook my head but then realized they would not be able to see me because I couldn't see him either. "Sam," Deyo added in a questioning voice.

"I'm...fine," I managed to reply, but felt anything but fine. A hand slapped me in the face, and I yelped.

"Sorry," Deyo whispered after making an elaborate shushing sound. His fingers trailed to my shoulder and then grabbed my right hand. "I've got you."

Figuring that standing here in the dark wouldn't help me one bit, I forced my feet to move as Deyo tugged at my hand. "We're almost there."

My breathing sounded labored, and I tried to control it, but our slow progress moving through the blinding darkness made it impossible for me to compose myself. To my relief, I noticed a shimmer of light at the end of the tunnel and did not want to think of the irony of that.

"Shh," Deyo hissed as we neared the end of the corridor. I could barely see him move a finger to his lips. He placed a hand on the wall and pushed it. That particular section of the wall did not look any different from any of the other brick walls, but I heard the softest of clicks. A panel shifted, and Deyo slid it open just enough for me to see the evenly spaced columns inside Danara's chamber beyond the opening.

"Now what?" I asked at the barest of whispers as I peered into the large room. My mind had been set on getting here, but I hadn't actually thought about what to do once we got here.

"Move to your right and hide behind the first column," Deyo whispered. "I'll be right behind you after I close up."

I hesitated, not sure if I could do this. I wasn't a trained warrior like Max, and there was no chance in hell that I could do anything to stop Danara. Compared to me the man was a giant and, with his muscular body, as strong as an ox.

"Sam," Deyo said so quietly that I barely heard him. Ignoring him, I forced myself to think of Juni and the way the young child had looked at me after Danara had ordered for me to be taken away. The way she had grasped for my hand and had refused to let it go until an Inanis had snatched her off the ground. Lana had entrusted her to me to keep her safe. Admittedly, that was a questionable choice, but I had committed to it, and now it was up to me to honor that task. Questioningly, Deyo repeated my name.

Steeling myself, I took a deep breath and nodded. The only light that reached us from inside Danara's chamber came from a couple of torches, and I doubted Deyo had seen my muted reply, but my first step past the hidden doorway would be a big enough clue to my answer.

Determined not to make a sound, I eased myself through the opening and noticed that we'd exited near the entrance of the chamber on the left side of the center aisle. I did as Deyo said and moved behind the large column closest to the panel. The door Juni and I had used to enter the chamber the first time wasn't that far off to my right. There was ample space between the massive stone pillars, but from this angle, they almost acted like a wall hiding us from view. It also worked like that the other way around, and I couldn't see what was happening at the far end of the chamber. I imagined Danara sitting in front of his fireplace.

Standing there concealed behind the first of many columns, I had to force myself to stay hidden as Juni's voice reached me from beyond the depth of the vast space.

~

"No," Juni said in her tiny voice, but she sounded determined.

"Sit still," a deep voice that could only have been Danara's said.

"No, you don't even know how it works," Juni said. I glanced to my left, willing Deyo to move faster. Of course, I had no idea what to do or if I could even help Juni, but I couldn't just keep standing here.

With my body pressed against the column, I shifted to my right and peeked around the massive stone pillar. At some distance, I could see Juni sitting on the table in front of the hearth. Except for Danara pacing the width of the chamber, the place seemed empty; no Inanis were present. Danara groaned out of frustration as he turned to face Juni again.

With two strides of his incredibly long legs, he stepped closer and knelt before the young child.

"This should work," he said. "Why doesn't it work? It has to work." He started to sound desperate. The way he seemingly stared at the child sitting on the table, it looked as if she were his last and only hope.

"It's not supposed to," Juni replied. "Only

Maximus can make it work." Danara lowered his head and shook it as he placed his hands on the table on either side of Juni. The young girl dangled her legs, either nervously or playfully, I couldn't tell.

"Hush, little one, and let me think," Danara said. He just stood there for a long moment staring at Juni. I could barely hear him as he started to speak again as if he were talking to himself. "Jasper will know what to do."

A hand on my shoulder made me jump, but my teeth digging into my lower lip kept me from screaming out. Deyo stood next to me with a finger to his lips. His head shifted from left to right in a frantic manner, searching the large chamber for anything out of place.

"So now what?" he asked. He barely made a sound, and I had to pay close attention to his mouth to decipher what he was saying. I shrugged my reply. I'd not thought this through.

At the moment, there weren't any Inanis around, and maybe that could work to our advantage. Most people I'd encountered, including Max, had mentioned Danara to be a good person. The arrival of the Inanis might have provoked a change in him. So maybe trying to talk to him without those creatures around would make a difference.

"Maybe you can talk some sense into him," I whispered. Deyo had mentioned before that he wanted to talk to Danara, but that had been down below in the dungeon. As I looked at him now with his eyes wide and mouth hanging open in shock, it seemed he wasn't so eager anymore. *What if I were to talk to him?* Although I didn't think I'd made a great first impression, I had to try something.

Peeking around the column again, I saw Danara still kneeling before Juni as if he were praying or something. A loud crash beyond the doors made his head snap up and me flinch. There was another loud noise as if someone had stepped on a branch in an otherwise empty forest. The sound was muffled by the door, but loud enough that it reached us with ease.

Danara stood and slowly turned to face the door just as it flung open, and I gasped as I watched Max standing in the opening. My heart jumped into my throat at the sight of Max. He'd made it out okay, despite the seemingly hopeless situation I'd witnessed at the village, and he hadn't forgotten about us. Max was right here, and he'd come for us. Barely perceptibly, Max tilted his head in my direction. He didn't acknowledge or indicate my presence, but I clasped a hand over my mouth when I realized he must have heard me. Fortunately, Danara was too far off to have heard it as well.

"What is this!" Danara exclaimed as he saw Max, who ignored the question. His heavy boots clanked on the stone floor as Max strode toward the center of the chamber. His eyes never left Danara as he stopped in front of him, and Max had to tilt his head to look up at the tall man who loomed over him. Max's armor gleamed as it reflected the flames from the hearth, and even though Danara towered over him, his posture gave a promise that he wouldn't back down.

"What are you doing?" Max asked. "How could you betray your own people?"

Danara flexed the muscles in his shoulder and pushed his chest out as he gazed down at Max.

"You were the one who gave the Inanis the key to the fence," Max continued. "You gave them access and let them kill so many."

"It is time for a change," Danara said, undeterred by Max's accusation. His deep voice sent a chill down my spine as his words echoed inside the hollow space. Danara hadn't argued Max's accusation, and in a way, it made sense. Danara had helped build the fence so it wouldn't be far-fetched to think he might have had a hand in allowing the Inanis to breach it. Could this be the reason that Lana and Oman had chosen not to act upon Juni's drawings that, in hindsight, could be seen as a warning? They thought that they were safe behind the fence. They'd assumed Danara to be their friend and couldn't have imagined that he would betray them.

"That is not your choice to make," Max replied. His hands were balled into fists as he stood in defiance in front of the tall man.

"You are right, the choice is not mine, but it has been made nonetheless," Danara said.

It occurred to me that this standoff might just be the distraction I needed, and I glanced at Deyo, whose skin had turned even paler than it had been inside the stairwell. I grabbed his shoulder and pressed his back against the column as I maneuvered my body around him as silently as I could. Careful to keep my body from view with the help of the neighboring column, I eased back until I could see out the open doors. Nothing seemed to move, and I wondered where Danara's Inanis had run off, too. *Were they getting ready to strike, or had Max dealt with them already?* I wanted to give Max credit for taking them out, but I'd seen those creatures fight on the screen that hung inside Oman's home, and I'd witnessed firsthand what they could do. They were vicious warriors, and although I did not doubt Max's abilities, I couldn't imagine him taking them down all on his own.

On the other hand, it might be possible that the Inanis couldn't hurt Max. At least not in the way they had disintegrated Cora and Oman along with so many others. They hadn't hurt Juni, but then why would they if they'd been after her in the first place. *Maybe they needed Max to be here, too?* The only anomaly in all of this was me. Sure, they hadn't been able to kill me with their powers. *But why had the Inanis brought me along? Curiosity?* From the moment the creature reached for me, I'd felt sure I was going to die, but then I hadn't. *Maybe it had something to do with the fact that I wasn't from around here?*

Still, the entrance appeared abandoned, and I moved back to my previous position, so I could see the two men standing before the young child sitting on a table.

"What are you doing?" Deyo asked. I didn't think it would be a good idea to tell Deyo that I had no clue.

"I'm going after Juni," I replied. To my surprise, the words sounded more confident than I felt. From what I could see, Max took a different approach. Since he was dressed in his armor and unable to see his face, it was difficult to read his intentions, but the hands that had previously been balled into fists flexed and relaxed.

"King," Max said, apparently referring to Danara's first name, "my friend, you cannot interfere with what is meant to be. You know this."

With the men in conversation and Danara having his back turned to Juni, who still sat on the table, I figured I had to take my chance.

"Stay here," I whispered and squeezed Deyo's shoulder. Before he could reply or I could change my mind, I tiptoed along the length of the chamber to hide behind the next column and prayed my sneakers wouldn't squeak on the stone floor. Taking my time, I bridged the spaces in between columns, and at the last one, I peeked around the massive stone pillar, where Juni caught my gaze. She lifted her hand and waved. I waved back at her and then pressed my finger to my lips until the young girl nodded in understanding. Her eyes returned to the two men, and I couldn't decipher the look on her face. I'd expected her eyes to be filled with fear as one would expect from a small child, but she appeared calm. From this position, I only stood a few feet away from the hearth and the table with Juni on it.

"Things will change, my old friend," Danara said, "and as soon as Jasper arrives, you will know the truth of it."

Juni sat with her tiny fingers clasped around the

edge of the table. She audibly gasped, and this time her expression did change to a look of fear. Her reaction made me flinch, but the two men ignored her.

The name *Jasper* and the notion that he was coming had elicited the same effect on Juni as it had on Deyo. He'd turned ghostly white, and for a moment, I'd even feared he might throw up. I shifted behind the column until Juni could see me, but kept myself hidden from the two men.

"You are stronger than this," Max said. "It does not have to be this way."

"You have no idea of my strength," Danara said, raising his voice, and I felt his words reverberate in my bones. "And like me, you will bow to Jasper."

Without warning, Danara struck his fist into the center of Max's chest. The force of the blow lifted Max off his feet and threw him back. I gasped as Max landed hard on his back, and his metal armor clanked on the stone floor.

Danara spread his arms at his side, and his muscles bulged along his back as he lifted his head up to roar at the ceiling. The sound made me shiver, but his words made my blood run cold.

"He is coming!"

The words had barely left his mouth when Danara charged Max, who had clambered back onto his feet. This time, Max was ready for him, and he blocked several punches before landing one of his own. Danara stepped back as he placed a hand on his lower rib cage.

"You cannot win this," Max said. "If Jasper wants

to destroy the realms by aligning the stones himself, then he'll need at least two stones, and mine is in a safe place."

Even from where I hid behind the column, I could see the fine chain that ran around Max's neck, and I had a feeling he was bluffing. Danara turned to Juni for just a second, and he started to laugh before he returned his attention to Max.

"I can't argue with that," he said as the grin on his face faded. Danara's hands moved to a small pouch secured on his broad belt, and retrieved something. As he opened his hand, I saw a sapphire stone, not unlike the one Max carried around. "Jasper promised me it would work. I guess he's not all-knowing after all."

Max shot Juni a concerned look. The little girl's knuckles had turned white from gripping the table edge, and her legs had stopped swinging. She shrugged as she met Max's gaze, and I noticed a look of surprise in Max's eyes.

I had no way of knowing what this was all about, but I had a feeling I wouldn't like it when I found out.

"All there is for me to do now," Danara continued, "is to keep you from aligning the stones and wait for Jasper to arrive."

I remembered Juni mentioning that the stones had to be aligned before the end of the day and I glanced at the large windows with the colorful glass. The gray sky hadn't allowed a lot of light to enter the chamber through the windows to begin with, but now all I could see was blackness.

The day had turned to night, but I didn't know

what time it was. Not that I had any concept of how they calculated time in this place.

The only thing I could think of doing was to get Juni, which had been the plan all along. I had to trust Max that he could take care of Danara, and once he did, he'd be able to align the stones with Juni's help, whatever that meant.

Danara charged again, and I couldn't bear to look as he slammed Max's body into one of the columns. I had to focus on Juni, and I quickly made my way to her as Danara and Max grappled.

As soon as she saw me, she opened her arms in invitation. She wrapped her arms around my neck, and I froze as an electric charge ran down my spine.

"Jesus," I whispered as I felt a tingle run through my skin. It felt similar to what I'd experienced as my hand had skimmed Juni's fingers after we'd put away her drawings.

"Who?" Juni asked.

I shook my head unable to answer her, and I almost pulled away, but Juni tightened her grip on my neck.

"You can do it, Sam," she whispered near my ear. I lifted her off the table, and she seemed heavier than before. Her legs wrapped around my waist, and I could feel the heat radiate from everywhere her body touched mine.

"What is this?" I asked in a shaky voice.

"You're the reason Danara couldn't make it work," Juni said. Behind me, the clank of metal made me jump, and I turned around. Danara had Max pinned to the ground with a knee planted on his chest.

Max's eyes glowed bright blue as his met mine. Heat flared through my body, and it intensified the longer I held Max's gaze. Everywhere the girl touched me, it felt as if my skin caught fire. Forcing down the urge to drop Juni, I started to move back to hide behind the column.

Danara still had his back to us, and I figured he hadn't seen us. With Juni in my arms, I swiftly moved to the next column, and the hope of escape grew with every step, but that hope faded as I heard Danara's booming voice echo inside his chamber.

"Inanis!"

Within seconds the sound of footsteps reverberated down the hall, and the Inanis entered the room.

I'd just made it to hide behind the third column as Danara stood, leaving Max lying at his feet. Max didn't move as Danara hovered over him with a smirk plastered on his face. We only had four or five columns to go, but I didn't dare move.

"Did you really think you'd get passed my Inanis so easily," Danara said. "If it were up to me you would feel their wrath."

Max tilted his head to look at the Inanis as they filed into the chamber. I counted six of them as they flanked the room on either side. I lost track of the creatures as they moved behind the massive columns but then reappeared as they stepped out from behind them.

One of them held Deyo by his neck and pushed him out in front of him as if he were holding a rag doll. I held my breath as I expected Deyo to be swallowed up at any second by the faceless creature with its skeletal body. Instead, the Inanis, including the one holding Deyo, took a position in front of each column. It didn't stop the fear from washing over me as I kept myself from being seen.

I pressed my head against the cool stone of the column as I struggled to hold Juni. The uncomfortable heat started to take its toll, and I felt my head go woozy. Focused on my breathing, I hardly noticed the conversation between Max and Danara carry on.

"But then they aren't yours, are they?" Max said as he pushed up to lean on his elbows. "They're Jasper's to command. You're just his puppet, just like the Inanis are."

"Do you think you can upset my resolve with your petty comments?" Danara replied. "I could kill you within the blink of an eye." His words didn't suggest that Max was getting to him, but his tone did, and the smirk had disappeared from Danara's face.

"But you won't because Jasper has ordered you not too," Max said. Danara did not have a retort to that and stood there grinding his teeth. Max seemed convinced that Jasper wanted him alive, and even dared to show Danara a hint of a smile.

"You can wipe that smug of your face," Danara

said. "Jasper only wishes for you to witness the fall of the realms."

"Jasper will never kill me," Max said, "because if he did that, he'd never be able to enter the main realm."

"Although I doubt that. Jasper will have his reasons," Danara replied, "and despite not having the pleasure to squeeze the life from you, I must admit, I'm looking forward to seeing the look on your face once you realize you have lost everything."

"What is it that he has promised you?" Max continued. "Did he promise you access to the main realm—my realm?" The mention of the main realm being Max's realm piqued my interest even though my body felt as if it were on the brink of collapse, and I shifted to get a better look.

Danara lowered his head to fix Max with stone cold eyes. "He has, hasn't he?" Max added.

I must have missed the funny part, but something had to be funny because Max started to laugh. The bitter sound wasn't anything like I'd heard coming from Max before. "Jasper can barely cross the other realms. What makes you think he'll ever be able to cross into mine?"

"But he does cross the realms, and I'm told he has even breached yours," Danara said. "I know one of the Inanis has paid you a visit." Max stopped laughing, but his eyes never wavered from Danara.

"And it paid with its life." Max's voice came out cold and harsh, but it wasn't the way he said it that caused my body to shiver. Sitting at Oman's table,

Max had told me that the statue inside his room back at the Grain had been an Inanis. Perhaps that information hadn't sunk in yet, or maybe it was just unimaginable for my earthbound brain to comprehend that one of those things could show up at the place where I work. *But what did that mean?* Danara had mentioned one of the Inanis had breached Max's realm—did that mean Max's realm was Earth? *Were Jasper and Danara trying to cross over to Earth?*

Too engrossed in the conversation, I barely noticed Danara's sudden shift as he looked over his shoulder. I froze as our eyes met. Danara's eyes narrowed for a moment before they grew wide. As if realization dawned on him, he stepped away from Max and turned to face Juni and me.

Max clambered onto his knees as he glanced our way, and the concerned look he gave me didn't boost my confidence. I'd hoped he might be able to defeat Danara, but with the addition of the Inanis, that seemed impossible.

I held on to Juni even though the tingle of electricity her touch elicited started to become painful. In turn, Juni tightened her grip around my neck as I took an instinctive step back.

Danara narrowed his eyes at me again, and I held his gaze as he started to laugh.

"I don't believe it," he said as he looked back at Max. "You've entered another one into the equation."

Max did not react and kept his expression neutral as he got to his feet. A faint blue glow reached his neck and chin from where I knew he kept the sapphire stone hidden behind his breastplate. The secured location wasn't able to hide the stone as it glowed so brightly. Juni's previous words came back to me as I focused on the blue light: *You're the reason Danara couldn't make it work.*

Danara had tried to align the stones. The reason for that eluded me. Perhaps if they aligned with one of their own stones instead with the one Max carried around, it would be easier for Danara and this Jasper to cross over. Something I had no knowledge of was playing out here, and it seemed I'd become one of the variables.

"Did you really think this deception would stop us?" Danara asked. He returned his attention to Juni and me, and the ominous grin on his face made my stomach churn.

"You cannot interfere with the alignment!" Max shouted as Danara moved toward us.

"Watch me," Danara called over his shoulder.

With Danara blocking my exit, I had no choice but to run back to the hearth. As Danara approached, I moved behind the table as if this simple wooden piece of furniture would stop a man of Danara's size. I felt the heat of the fire burning inside the hearth as I stopped in front of it. Across the chamber, I caught a glimpse of Deyo who stood frozen as if he didn't dare to move. I couldn't blame him for that, considering the claws of the Inanis wrapped around his throat. One wrong move and the Inanis might decide to kill him, but that didn't keep him from showing the concern that radiated of his face. Still, Deyo's concern was of no use to me right now, because I had nowhere to go as the giant mass of a man closed the distance between us.

"I will not!" Max shouted as he ran toward us. He slammed into Danara's back, and the table legs scratched along the floor. I had to jump out of the way or else Juni and I might have ended up inside the hearth. Max repeatedly pounded his fist into Danara's side, and the tall man groaned as he braced himself on the table.

"Enough," Danara shouted, and he swung his bulky arm to strike Max in the face. Max stumbled backward but caught himself and gathered his strength to face Danara again.

The large man was quick, but his movements weren't as fluid as Max's. Max dodged and side-stepped Danara's wide swings before landing several punches to the taller man's lower body.

Max fought like the warrior his appearance made him out to be, but I feared it wouldn't be enough against Danara. That man seemed to be made of concrete. With Juni in my arms, I stayed close to the hearth as the fight between Max and Danara returned to the center of the chamber.

The Inanis might not have had eyes, but I knew they were watching me somehow. I didn't think making a run for it would be in my best interest right about now, but then, waiting for Danara to defeat Max and have him do whatever he wanted to didn't seem like a viable option either. I felt trapped and unable to move, just as I had when I was grabbed and dragged down that alley.

"I don't know what to do," I whispered more to myself than to anyone else.

Juni raised her head from my shoulder. Her eyes glowed as bright as Max's as she said, "I'm sorry."

Tears threatened to overflow the young girl's eyes, and I felt my heart break. *How could this child feel such a responsibility for something she could not control?* I internally cursed myself for being so self-absorbed that I kept slipping back into my own personal misery and wasn't present of mind enough to console a child or, more importantly, keep her safe.

"It'll be—" I started to say, but right at that moment Danara snaked his arm around Max's torso and threw him across the chamber. He landed hard, and his body skidded across the floor. Before he could manage to move, Danara was on him again.

He wrapped an arm around Max's throat and pulled him to his feet. Max gasped and clutched at Danara's arms, but I could see his strength fade as he struggled for air.

"Now witness the change about to come," Danara said. "Seize them."

CHAPTER SIXTEEN

The Inanis who up until then had stood like statues turned their faceless heads in my direction. They howled in unison, and except for the one holding Deyo in a tight grip, they all took a step forward.

"Oh shit," I muttered under my breath. I glanced at Max, who still struggled against Danara's hold but could not muster enough strength to get free. I shuddered as five of the six Inanis took another simultaneous step toward me. My eyes frantically searched the chamber for a way out as a sense of hopelessness washed over me.

At the other side of the room the doors had remained open, but with six Inanis between me and the exit, there was no way for me to reach it. There was also the hidden passageway that Deyo and I had used, although I wasn't quite sure if I'd be able to find it again. There wasn't much choice, and as the Inanis closed in, I clamped Juni harder to my chest. Ignoring the painful tingle that ignited my skin, I bolted to my right.

My sneakers squeaked on the floor as I dodged the outstretched arms of the Inanis reaching for me. The creatures might've been formidable warriors, but with their oil-caked skeletal forms, they weren't that swift on their feet. I moved behind one of the columns to stay out of the reach of the first Inanis, but another one quickly closed in. It howled as it lashed out at me, and on instinct, I turned to shield Juni.

It struck me in the back, and I stumbled forward as I felt a slash of cold streak down my spine. As if my body wasn't able to handle the contrast between the burning sensation that came with holding Juni and the icy cold touch from the Inanis, it intensified the pain, and I felt as if someone had jabbed a blade into my back.

I groaned and fell to one knee as I braced myself on an arm while holding onto Juni. The girl strained to hold on to my neck, and the urge to protect her forced me back to my feet. I ran along the length of the wall of the outer aisle. The remaining Inanis had taken positions in the open spaces between the columns and blocked my view from the center of the chamber.

I scanned the wall and the wooden panels along its lower half, hoping to find the hidden passageway, but everything looked the same—nothing was out of place. I knew it had to be somewhere near the first pillar from where Deyo and I had first stepped out, but

I didn't know what to look for. As it was, it seemed hopeless.

In a desperate attempt to find a way out I patted wooden panels with the palm of my hand and then started to slam my fist into them, hoping to hear the hollow space behind it. Unfortunately, each time I struck a panel a solid thud came back to me.

"Sam," Juni whispered close to my ear. Her warm breath tickled my skin and set my nerves on fire. I wouldn't be able to keep this up for long. My body ached from the constant burning sensation, and I would have to put Juni down soon.

"Sam," Juni said again as I pounded my fist on the wall. The urgency in her voice made me stop pounding, and I paused to listen. The room around me had fallen silent as the girl added, "It's okay."

I slowly turned to find the Inanis standing around me in a half circle. I drew in a shaky breath, aware that there wasn't anything I could do as one of them stepped forward and grasped Juni's small form. He jerked at her body and grabbed her tiny arm to disentangle her from my neck, and I felt a strange combination of fear and relief. The cold air inside the chamber doused the fires that traveled up and down my skin, and I felt as if I could breathe again. On the other hand, the dire expression on the young girl's face caused a different kind of pain deep inside my chest, and my hands grasped at her legs in a desperate attempt keep her close.

Two Inanis stepped in to grab my arms and stopped me from reaching for the child. Their cold, bony fingers dug into my skin, and their strength made it impossible for me to move. I felt my breathing quicken as they let me back to the center of the chamber where Danara still had his arm wrapped around Max's throat.

The two Inanis pulled me to a stop in front of the hearth and turned me to face Danara. Heat from the flames prickled the back of my neck, but it couldn't stop a shiver running through my body at the sight of Danara holding Max.

Sweat coated Max's skin, and his eyes didn't seem able to focus. It appeared as if all the strength had been drained from him, and he looked nothing like the strong warrior I'd come to know.

"Now," Danara said close to Max's ear, "if you even twitch, my Inanis will tear them apart." Max gave a slight nod, which was all that Danara's arm wrapped around his neck allowed.

My gaze drifted to my left where the Inanis holding Juni stood. He awkwardly held her in his arms, and I could see the girl squirm against his grip. Danara released Max from his hold and shoved him forward. Max fell to his knees, and Danara knelt beside him. Even in a kneeling position, Danara looked impressive as he held out his hand. He turned his wrist as he opened his fist to reveal the blue stone.

"This, my friend, will be your undoing," he said in

his deep voice. Danara stood and gestured at the Inanis.

"Secure him," he said and took a couple of steps toward me. Two Inanis stepped forward and made their way to where Max still sat on his knees. As Danara came closer he effectively blocked my view of Max, and for some reason, I felt abandoned.

My mind raced as I tried to make sense of all of this. *How had I gotten myself into this? Why had I ever decided to go on a run after my conversation on the phone with Kay?* Our talk about her visit and us going on a hiking trip along with the eventful day at the retirement home had triggered the stupid urge to clear my mind. Running would usually do that, but this time I wished I'd chosen differently. The hiking trip had sounded intimidating, but compared to this, it would've been a breeze, and I wished I could've been a person that would gladly accept such an invitation. *Who wouldn't want to spend time with a friend?* Kay wasn't just a friend; she was my best friend. And if I somehow made it out of here, I promised myself that I would tell her. Not to mention the things I needed to tell my mom. There were only two people who had mattered in my life, and I couldn't even talk to them about the things that mattered. Now I'd probably never get the chance.

Danara held the stone out in front of him, and the sight of it alone made my skin tingle. Every time I came too close to a stone like that, my body heated up. I'd felt that strange sensation when I came in contact with Juni's fingers as we put her drawings away. Max had been sitting at the table but at about the same distance as Danara stood from me now. Max, too, carried one of those stones although I hadn't felt the tingle standing next to him. It only occurred in Juni's presence, and as a matter of fact, it only occurred with Juni in Max's proximity. Something must've happened that connected me to the stone.

As soon as the thought crossed my mind, I could see the stones lying in the grass after I'd spilled the content of Max's bag. Touching Juni's hand as we'd put her drawings away hadn't been the first time I'd sensed this strange sensation. I'd felt it after picking up the stones and holding them in my hand back home at the small clearing. Touching the gemstones must have triggered all of this.

"Set the child on the table," Danara said. The words had barely left his mouth when the Inanis carrying Juni moved her to the table that stood in front of the hearth. As the creature stepped away from her, Juni rubbed her arms where it had held her. The young girl had been resilient through all of this and was probably even stronger than me, but right now she looked vulnerable as her blue eyes strayed from Danara to me.

Danara grabbed her chin and forced Juni to look at him. He grinned as he stared into her eyes before he shifted his attention to me.

"This is quite a trick you managed to pull off," he said. "I hadn't even noticed at first. Must be the approaching alignment." He moved closer to me, and this time he grabbed my jaw and forced me to look at him. Fascination was written all over his face as he stared into my eyes. "How did he do it?" He muttered the words in a way that I wasn't sure if he were talking to himself or to me. Questioning eyes searched my face as if I could give him the answer that he was looking for, but I had no idea what he was talking about.

"Why are you doing this?" Max's voice startled me, and I wasn't the only one. Danara released my jaw and spun on his heel to face Max.

"You have to ask?"

Max shook his head. "Jasper has gotten to you. You know that, right?"

Danara laughed, and the sound made me shudder. It reminded me of all the evil laughs produced by villains in the movies that would generally have me laughing in disbelief. I never would've thought I'd actually experience it.

"You are endangering this world," Max said, undeterred by Danara's reaction, "if you continue to let Jasper control you."

"And what is it that this world has done for me?" Danara said, spreading his arms. With slow, deliberate steps he moved closer to Max as Danara lifted his gaze toward the ceiling. "After everything that I have given these people, what have they ever done for me?"

Max looked surprised by Danara's reply. "You live the life you always wanted to live—"

"The life that was chosen for me," Danara retorted in a loud voice as he stood before Max. It seemed Max had struck a nerve with the tall man.

"You exiled me from Ora just because I was different."

"You were the one who did not want to live in the village because you felt out of place, and you created a safe haven for others who felt the same," Max said. "You created a haven for them, but all of them, including you, know that you are always welcome in Ora."

My attention shifted toward Deyo, who stood unmoving at the side of one of the Inanis. His slender figure and rigid posture made him look like a wooden plank, but I figured that had something to do with the hand clamped at the back of his neck. He'd told me that he, too, had come from Ora and that his parents still lived there—at least I hoped they still did. He'd also mentioned that he went home every fortnight. Everything he'd told me and everything else I'd learned about this place suggested that people had come here to seek refuge once in a while from a place that for all intents and purposes might be too noisy for them to think.

I hadn't met any of the others who had come here, but nothing that Danara had said rang true to me. I wondered if Jasper might have something to do with this shift in Danara's perception.

Danara was done talking as he came toward me with a couple of firm strides. His hand wrapped around my neck with ease before he shouted an order at his Inanis holding me.

"Release her."

As soon as the Inanis dropped their holds on my arms, I instinctively wrapped my hands around Danara's wrist, trying to break his grip. He tightened his fingers around my neck, and I gasped for air.

"Danara!" Max shouted. I couldn't see him, but it wasn't hard to hear the anger that resonated in Max's voice.

As if I were some puppet, Danara jerked me closer to the table and pushed my hips into it. My legs buckled and forced my butt to rest on the table. My vision blurred as tears trailed down my cheek. I barely registered Juni close by my side as she scrambled on the top of the table to get away from Danara.

"Let's see how it will work now." Juni squealed as Danara grabbed her by the ankle to pull her closer before he deposited her in my lap. If the large man could handle me like a rag doll, I did not want to imagine what he could do to a little girl. As soon as Danara touched Juni's fragile frame, a jolt of electricity scrambled all of my brain functions.

"Don't do this." Somewhere I registered Max's voice in the back of my mind, but my nerves were too busy processing the flaring heat that made me feel as if I were on fire to produce a coherent thought.

Danara's eyes shift from black to the bright blue, and for a fraction of a second, I thought I might have been looking into Max's intense gaze. Then I noticed the flecks of smoldering cinder, and the longer I stared, the more red-gold flakes accumulated within his eyes.

He released Juni and held out the stone he'd been carrying around. It, too, appeared different now that I could see it from up close. The stone held the same red-gold flakes, which seemed odd for a sapphire. I didn't know much about gemstones, and I wasn't sure if a sapphire could hold multiple colors, but apparently it couldn't be red.

A while back, I'd bought a birthday gift for my mom, a necklace with a tiny red stone embedded in the pendant. The guy who had sold it to me had insisted that it was called a ruby and that there was no such thing as a red sapphire. I hadn't checked if any of that were true, and it wasn't as if any of that mattered. My pain-ravaged mind started to stray, and I fought to focus.

With Danara holding the stone on the flat of his hand, it occurred to me that he wouldn't be able to hold Juni, and my eyes shifted to the young girl perched on my lap. She clung to me as if her life depended on it. The thought of pushing her away tore at my heart. Even though I wouldn't be much use at it, I wanted to comfort her. The last thing I wanted was to push her away, but the searing pain running through my body caused my brain to scream for release.

The only thing that I could think of was that Danara was using our direct contact to align the stones. I'd learned that somehow Juni was the Sapphire Twin. Danara held the other one, and I figured he must want me to act as some kind of conduit, and this was causing me to feel this awful. Only a small fragment of my brain considered the fact that Danara aligning the stones was bad for this place. Most of my concern sadly fell on my own well-being. Considering the fact that breaking the bond would benefit both causes, I forced Juni from my lap.

The girl did not struggle, as if she knew what I was trying to do, but it wasn't as if she was helping me.

"Sam," she managed to say between sobs. My vision started to waver as it became harder for me to breathe, but I sensed some of the burning feeling fade, and I hoped it had to do with distancing myself from Juni's frame and not with the fact that I was losing consciousness.

"Not yet," Danara said with a low growl. He wrapped his fingers around the sapphire stone and pressed his fist to Juni's torso. The girl fell onto her back on the table, and the heat within my body flared up again. Just as I thought that Danara's terrifying gaze would be the last thing for me to see, I heard a loud crash behind him.

"It's about time you showed up," a voice said, and I wondered if it was Max. I couldn't tell anymore. The edges of my vision started to blur, and I could feel the darkness creep up on me. It occurred to me that I'd been doing this a lot lately, but my consciousness faded before I could finish my train of thought.

CHAPTER SEVENTEEN

Someone was shaking my shoulders, and I wanted it to stop. My body felt like it did after I'd gone running and had pushed myself too hard. I just wanted to lay still and rest.

"Come on, Sam. Wake up!" A voice grazed at my consciousness, and I felt my shoulders being shaken again.

Despite my reluctance, I opened my eyes, and I had to blink a couple of times before Deyo's face came into focus. The memories of where I was came rushing back, and I pushed up into a sitting position.

"Take it easy," Deyo said as he pressed a supportive hand to my back. I was sitting on the floor and actually felt comforted by the cold trailing up my butt and spine. A quick glance to my side confirmed Juni was sitting close by, with the fabric of my pants clutched in her tiny fists.

One of the Inanis also lay on the ground not that far from us, and besides faceless, this one appeared to be headless. The sight caused my focus to shift to the center of the chamber, and I gasped. The remaining Inanis fought with several Ora guards. Metal clanked, and energy blasts exploded as the Ora guards struggled to gain the upper hand.

Among the clashing bodies, I noticed Cyril and Moira fighting back to back as their swords whooshed through the air. At the sight of them, relief washed over me, and although I was glad they were all right, it seemed they had gotten themselves into another uncertain situation.

Max stood in the middle of the room in an apparent face-off with Danara. They stood motionless, like a pair of gunslingers waiting for the clock to strike noon, and they appeared oblivious of the fighting that occurred around them.

"Come on. We have to go," Deyo said as he tugged at my arm to pull me to my feet. I managed to comply, but I had to brace myself on the table to keep myself from toppling over again. Deyo's grip never wavered, though, and he helped me to stay upright. Juni stood as well and looked up with a plea in her eyes. Taking a couple of deep breaths, I bent down to put my hands on her tiny waist. Automatically her arms wrapped around my neck and with Deyo's help, I managed to lift her. My skin tingled where she touched it, but it didn't seem as bad as it had before. Maybe I'd built up some resistance against the agonizing sensation.

"I can carry her," Deyo said as he held onto my free arm.

"I got it." I didn't imagine the girl would let me hand her over anyway.

"I've just had about enough of you." Cyril's voice drew my attention to the fighting, and I was just in time to see him launch one of the Inanis against a stone column. The creature came to a stop with a loud crack, and before it could move again, Cyril hovered over it with his sword in hand. He swung it over his head once before he launched it at the Inanis. With a loud clank, the metal of the sword hit the solid rock of the column. It was impossible to gage the faceless creature's reaction, as its head wobbled for a second and then tumbled to the ground.

Cyril motioned to Moira who had a tight hold on one of the other Inanis. The creature struggled to get its bearing, but then grasped on to Moira's arms. Instantly, the Inanis's oily skin started to latch on to Moira. She screamed in pain, but Moira wasn't one to give up easily. She met Cyril's gaze before she shifted her body and threw the Inanis to the ground. Cyril swung his sword again and struck the creature in the head. With a crack, its skull split in two, and the oily substance that made up the creature's skin seeped out from where I would have expected its brain to be.

Apparently, the Inanis weren't as formidable as I had thought, or at least not as formidable as Moira and Cyril. It must've been the surprise attack that had allowed the creatures to roam through the village. If it hadn't been for Danara, who had helped the Inanis to breach the fence, and for the way they managed to disappear into the ground and pop up anywhere, I had a feeling that Cyril and his Ora guards might have been able to stop them.

Deyo tugged on my arm, and I followed him to the side of the chamber until we found relative safety behind one of the massive columns. Deyo seemed nervous as he glanced in my direction. I wouldn't have blamed him for that. We'd managed to get ourselves situated in the middle of a battle, but for some reason, I had a feeling that his fidgeting had to do with something else.

"What?" I asked as his eyes kept shifting away from mine. He hesitated for a moment, and I was about to ask again as he said,

"Nothing, but..." His hesitation started to unnerve me. It wasn't as if I didn't have enough to worry about. I had a scared little girl in my arms whose touch started to feel like acid burning my skin while a war raged around us.

"What is it?"

"It's just that your eyes...they..." Deyo started to say, but a loud crash drowned out his words. One of the Inanis lay on top of the table, but just as the Ora guard was about to swing his sword, Deyo nudged me forward. "Go!"

There was no time to fret about Deyo's reluctance and, had I been back home, an encounter like this might have had my mind reeling. I had always hated the looks given to me by my coworkers. I had hoped that going back to work after my stay at the hospital would get my mind off things, but it only took me a couple of days to realize that all I wanted to do was to get away from those people. I couldn't handle the questioning looks asking, *"Is that her?"* and *"What happened?"* or *"What is wrong with her?"*

Dwelling on such things seemed futile now because running away wasn't an option. I needed Deyo's help to get out of here, and we had to find a way to get Juni and Max together so that he could align the stones.

Hoping to avoid any attention from the Inanis, we moved from one column to another, as Deyo was trying to lead us to the hidden exit that we had used come here in the first place. I had no intention of leaving, but I let him guide me until we reached the column closest to Max and Danara.

The Ora guards had taken care of most of the Inanis, although I could still hear fighting beyond the doors and further down the hallway. Deyo tugged at my arm again, ready to move to the next column, but I refused to let him lead me. He shot me an urgent glance.

"Come on. We have to get out of here." He whispered the words, but I wasn't going to sneak out of here—I couldn't. We were running out of time, and Max needed to align the stones. Because of that, we needed to stay close. For a moment, I considered whether I should hand Juni over to Deyo as I felt her touch rekindle the burning sensation on my skin. Our proximity to Max or even Danara probably had caused it. But even knowing how uncomfortable her touch made me feel, Juni was a part of this, and though I wasn't sure how this was going to pan out, I feared she would have to face it along with me.

I shifted to glance around the column to find Max and Danara standing in the same position. This time, though, there weren't any Inanis to protect Danara. This time, along with Cyril and Moira, several other Ora guards had gathered a position behind Max ready to defend him.

Moira looked paler than usual, but considering the nasty abrasions on her arms, that was understandable. Her left arm hung limp as blood trickled to the floor, but she held her sword firmly in her right hand and had taken a fighting stance. Some of the other Ora guards were in even worse shape, and all looked haggard. Cyril, on the other hand, had a wicked grin plastered on his face and a dangerous glint in his eyes. All of them stood as one with Max.

I heard shouts coming from the hallway, and I felt relieved as even more Ora guards rushed through the door. They all took what I imagined to be strategic positions around Max, but Danara did not seem impressed.

"He knows now," Danara said. "He has felt the beginnings of the alignment, and he knows it is not finished. He will come."

I gathered that Danara was talking about this Jasper person again, and my eyes shifted to the door as if the Ora guards might have overlooked him and he would appear there somehow. Max stood motionless with his eyes fixed on Danara.

As if someone had taken a deep breath and expelled the air to blow out birthday candles, all the torches snuffed out, bathing the room in semidarkness. The fire inside the hearth still burned brightly, and it flickered shadows cross Max's dark skin.

"Uh-oh," Juni said, and I followed her gaze up toward the ceiling. Black clouds that reminded me of that moment in the clearing when I'd first spotted Max there on that crazy night started to fill the room. That night had seemed so long ago, but now the memories of the murky cloud felt as clear as day as they penetrated the forefront of my mind. Flashes of red light like fire shot through the blackness as the cloud descended upon the chamber.

Pain ripped through me, and I had to stifle a scream as I shifted back behind the column to hide from view. Unable to tolerate her, I had to lower Juni to the ground. The girl looked dazed as she peered up at me but didn't complain. I had a feeling she understood what was happening, but I didn't think that she felt the same pain as I did while our bodies connected, and I could only be grateful for that.

"He is coming," Danara said in his deep voice.

Taking a couple of deep breaths, I fought to regain my bearing. Deyo shot me a concerned look. "We should get out of here." The urgency was clear in his voice, but I shook my head. "Seriously, Sam, you don't look so good, and I promise we'll stay close."

"I'm okay." I didn't recognize the croaky sound that exited my throat. To emphasize that I was okay, I squeezed Deyo's shoulder before I turned away from him.

I slowly etched around the column until I could see Max and Danara facing off in the middle of the chamber. Cyril, Moira, and the rest of the Ora guards might as well go home because I doubted if Danara even realized they were there. He had his head tilted back as he stared up at the cloud while it formed above their heads. To my surprise, Max had his eyes locked on mine. *Had he seen us hide behind the column, or had he rather sensed us being there?*

He inclined his head before refocusing on Danara just as the tall man lowered his head to face Max again.

"Can you feel it?" Danara said. "You must've known it would always end like this one day."

Max shook his head as he took a step back. "I have no intention of ending it here." Max took another step back. "Cyril, I'll be needing a little time."

Instead of replying, Cyril stepped forward until he stood at Max's side. On Max's other side, Moira did the same, and so did the other Ora guards. Max, on the other hand, took another step back, his eyes still locked on Danara. The big man had returned his attention upward and seemed fixated by the brewing storm above his head.

The view was quite stunning, I had to admit. I

didn't know what kind of technology or perhaps even magic would be able to create such a whirlwind of blackness etched with fire and flecked with gold. The whole thing looked like Danara's eyes had looked as he'd held me down on that table, holding the sapphire stone in his hand.

I was still gazing up at the cloud, just like Danara, as I heard Max's voice loud and sharp.

"Now!"

Within a fraction of a second, both Cyril and Moira charged Danara. I could just register the surprise in Danara's gaze before both of them knocked him down. In the same instance, Max bolted to his left, heading our way as the remaining Ora guards took a stance around the three bodies flailing on the ground. I caught a glimpse of Cyril and Moira's struggle to keep Danara on the ground before Max blocked my view.

Above our heads, the cloud grew thicker and doubled in size. Lights flared, similar to a lightning bolt, but instead of white, the light flashed blood red. I flinched as another flash made it seem as if the ceiling were on fire.

"The alignment needs to happen," he said in an urgent voice, "now."

"Let's go," I said as I looked first at Deyo and then down at Juni. The girl looked up at me with pleading eyes, but I could not help my hesitation. I hoped she wouldn't register the fear in my eyes. I didn't want to face the pain it would cause if I were to pick her up, especially with Max standing so close. Frozen to the spot, I just stood there with my eyes riveted on the young child.

Max must have noticed, because before I had a chance to do anything, he knelt beside the girl and picked her up. He turned toward the exit doors but stopped midstride. I bumped into him, and a jolt of electricity shot through my arm. With a yelp, I jumped back, but Max didn't seem to notice. His eyes were fixed on the door and on the Inanis that were making their way through the opening.

"Where the hell did they come from?" I hadn't meant to shout, but the words tore from my throat before I could think about it. Although not all of them, some of the Inanis were drawn to us by my words and I felt like kicking myself at my own stupidity. The sound of their bony feet clacking on the stone floor made my skin crawl and the memories of them holding me against their ooze-dripping bodies sent an icy shiver down my spine. I'd stopped counting after five, and I knew we'd never make it that way.

"Deyo, we need the other exit!" I said and felt that tightening feeling in my chest acting up again. *Why did this keep happening at the most inopportune times?* Couldn't this stupid anxiety crap hold off just for once because I'd be sure there'd be plenty to freak out about after we made it out of here alive. I mean, *if* we made it out here alive. I rolled my eyes at the stupidity of my internal musings. I must have lost my mind.

"Show us," Max said to Deyo. The urgency in Max's voice snapped me out of my daze. I stepped out of his way and shot a wary look in Juni's direction.

As if he knew what I'd been thinking, Max shifted Juni to his left arm and moved the girl further away from me. Making sure not to touch me, Max gestured after Deyo, who had set off in the direction of the hidden entrance.

Within seconds, Deyo had slid the panel to a side and ushered me inside. I froze as soon as I'd passed the threshold. Darkness loomed before me, and if it weren't for the sliver of light that penetrated from within the chamber, I wouldn't have been able to see a hand in front of my face.

"Get in there," Max said. *Who was he talking to? I was already in there, right?* I felt as if I'd lost the ability to think, and my hands trembled as they grazed at the rough wall.

Static ran up my spine as Max poked a finger into my back and forced me to take a few steps forward.

"It's okay, Sam," Deyo said. "Just feel your way along the wall." It sounded easy enough, the way Deyo explained it, and I'd done it before, but somehow, I couldn't get my limbs to move. The Inanis were right on our heels, and I couldn't get myself to move. I didn't have to internally debate the issue; the logic was there. When chased by evil creatures intend on sucking the life out of you—you run. *Why was that so hard for my limbs to understand?* The electrical pinpricks that assaulted my body whenever I came in too close a proximity to Max and Juni finally forced me to move, although the tightness in my chest worsened as I heard the panel slide into place, leaving us in utter darkness.

"It's okay, Sam. Just remember to breathe," Max

said before I heard a rustle. Remembering to breathe seemed like a good idea, but thinking it and getting my lungs to work at the same time felt like a stretch at this point.

A flash of blue flashed across my eyes, and I realized what the rustle I'd heard before had been. I turned to see Max fiddle with the chain that hung around his neck. The necklace with the sapphire stone clinked softly against the metal of Max's armor as he pulled the gem from beneath the protection of his breastplate. The stone glowed bright blue and lit up the dark space. Relief washed over me, and lucky for me, I remembered how to breathe.

Soon enough that memory was interrupted by a loud banging on the other side of the wall. I yelped at the sound, and my heart shot into my throat. Juni and Deyo had a similar reaction, and even Max must have flinched because I felt a brief brush of static run up my arm. Having seen us, the Inanis now knew about the hidden passageway and were trying to get it to open.

"Go," Max whispered. Fortunately, the light that emanated from the stone allowed me to see, and with the Inanis banging on the wall, it seemed that I had found enough incentive to get my legs to move.

Haunted by a nagging fear that the light around Max's neck would snuff out, I couldn't stop my hands from trailing the surface of the rough walls, just in case. At the end of the narrow passageway, I pressed myself against the wall as Deyo scooted his way first past Max and then overtook me. It was probably a good thing that Deyo wasn't built like the rest of the Ora guards, or else he probably would've gotten himself stuck. Deyo led us out of the passageway, and after we waited for him to close it up, we followed him back to the kitchen.

CHAPTER EIGHTEEN

As soon as we entered the kitchen, Max unceremoniously sat Juni down on one of the counters. One of the pots hanging from a hook slightly swayed above her head, and someone had lit two torches that, along with the small fire still burning within the stove, cast a yellow glow over the counter-tops. The enormous firepit in the center of the room looked to be untouched, and I didn't think someone would be cooking a meal here anytime soon. Fortu-nately, the still empty kitchen gave me a moment's respite to catch my breath.

Max pushed a couple of strands of blond hair from Juni's face before he cupped her jaw and tilted her head until she faced him. Their gazes connected, and he stared into Juni's big blue eyes for the longest time. For a moment, I wondered if they were having a full-blown conversation without using their voices. It was Deyo who seemed unable to stop fidgeting and kept scratching his head who spoke first.

"We can't stay here. They'll find us." There was an urgency in his voice that was understandable. Danara was still out there, and even though he had several Ora guards occupying him, including Cyril and Moira, with the help of the newly arrived Inanis, I didn't think it would take him long to catch up with us. Max blew out a breath and closed his eyes before he lowered his chin to his chest.

"What's wrong?" I asked. I glanced a peek at the window that Deyo and I had used to search the garden for any sign of life, and I noticed the same darkness that I'd seen through the windows inside Danara's chamber. Juni had mentioned that the alignment had to occur before the end of the day, but when would that be? *Did this place have something like midnight where one day transitioned into the next?*

Max shot me a sideways glance, and I didn't like the mournful expression on his face.

"I am sorry, Sam," he said in a way that made my stomach churn. "You are now a piece of the puzzle."

"What does that mean?" As soon as the words fell from my mouth, I knew they were pointless. I already knew the answer. It was for the same reason that Danara had failed at his first attempts to align the stones. When he was trying with only Juni. Something had happened and had made me part of the equation.

"It seems you have become part of the alignment," Max said. He hesitated but then took my hand in his. I immediately felt the palm of my hand warm up to his touch and a static tingle run up my arm. It only took about a second for the burning sensation to become painful. I wanted to pull my hand away from Max, but that wouldn't solve our problem.

"You need me..." I said and hesitated, as if saying the words would seal my fate in something I wouldn't like and certainly wouldn't be able to control. "You need me to be a conduit."

Max nodded, and from his concerned expression, I could tell he didn't like it either.

"It'll be okay, Sam," Juni said as she held out her hand. Memories of pain that the touch of her skin had caused before send a cold shiver down my spine. The little girl was trying to comfort me, and even though she was only a child, I didn't seem able to show her my appreciation. I could just stare at her hand without feeling any compulsion to take it.

My chest heaved as my eyes switched to my own hand. It shook uncontrollably, and in my mind, I could already feel the pain as it raced up my arm. My stomach hurt as if someone had punched me, and I wanted to throw up. My vision wavered as if a switch had been flipped and all the lights had gone out. For a second, I imagined holding a brick in my hand. *What good was a brick gonna do me?*

"This is not good," Deyo said, voicing the direness of the situation. Deyo's words, but more likely the tone with which he'd said them, slowly lifted the fog in my head. If the thought of touching Juni had sent a cold shiver down my spine, the sound of Danara's voice turned my blood into ice.

"Max!" the tall man's voice sounded hollow as it echoed somewhere down the hallway. "He will find you, Max."

"We are running out of time, Sam," Max said. He kept his eyes on me as I felt a similar breath of wind as I'd experienced in Danara's chambers. The two torches lighting the room flickered, and the fire that burned inside the stove wavered within its enclosure. Another chill ran down my body.

Why was I stuck in my own thoughts with all this going on? Why was I risking these people's home? Why was I risking their lives? My gaze shifted back to Juni, and I stared into her big blue eyes. *I'd tried so hard to keep her safe, so what was stopping me now? And I wanted to go home, right?*

For a second, I looked up and gasped. The black haze of clouds billowed inside the kitchen close to the ceiling, as if they had decided to follow us from Danara's chambers. Bright flashes of red and gold illuminated our faces as the veil of darkness grew in size.

"Jasper is on his way," Deyo said. His mouth hung open as he stared up the swirling mist above our heads. From the heart of the black veil, a flash of lightning reflecting a color so crimson and dark, that looked as if it were painted by blood ripped through the air and struck the firepit in the center of the kitchen.

I hadn't noticed any wood in the pit before, but that didn't stop the flames from rising high above our heads. Looking up, I could see the red-gold flecks of smoldering cinder growing in intensity as the thick black cloud pushed them closer together. Instead of smoke billowing up, the dark veil descended upon the fire where it seemed to liquify. Perhaps it had something to do with the heat exuded by the flames, but somehow the dark veil transformed into an oily substance, not unlike the stuff that made up the Inanis. More and more of the dark veil gathered in the flames, where it grew in mass until it molded into what looked like a solid figure.

I risked a sideways glance, and the utter look of desperation on Max's face made me wish I hadn't. Juni sat unmoving on top of the counter while Deyo scurried backward until he bumped into a table. Like Max, I stood frozen in place as I watched the scene unfold.

"He is here!" Danara's voice sounded like a thunderclap that had accompanied the blood-red slash of lightning. I could only see the tall man's silhouette as he stepped into the room and stopped on the other side of the firepit. Instead of a storm, the room suddenly grew calm and so quiet that the rapid beating of my heart reminded me of the loud electronic music I played while running.

"Sam," Max shouted breaking the baseline in my head. It was hard tearing my eyes away from the pile of goo as it molded itself into shape. The urgency in Max's voice was palpable though, and as our gazes met, I noticed that so was the fear in his eyes. "We have to do this now!" Max held out his hand for me to take, but I couldn't help my hesitation. There was so much going on that I couldn't wrap my brain around. What was clear though, and edged into my mind, was the pain that I had felt when Danara had tried to align the stones.

"Please, Sam," Juni said, pleading for me to take her hand. As if her voice flipped a switch inside my brain telling me to get over myself, I knew what to do. Lifting my hand, I reached for Juni's, but before our fingers could touch, I froze again. My hand hung midair, and I was unable to move.

"You are too late." I didn't recognize the voice, and before I could even tell from which direction it had come, I felt something tug at me. A force similar to what I had experienced at the small clearing back home pulled at my body drawing me closer to the fire in the pit. I tried to call out to Max as his grip on my hand faltered, but I couldn't even manage to open my mouth. It didn't matter, I had failed them all. *Why would Max even bother to help me?* I had failed him, and I was going to be the reason that the realms would fall.

I wanted to scream as a hand grabbed my wrist and the cold touch turned my blood into a river of ice as it pumped through my veins. Turning to face the source of my discomfort, I expected to face something similar to the Inanis, and although this figure seemed to be made out of the same oily substance, with its cloak and a hood covering its face, it looked more human.

"Join me," it said just before the world around me shifted.

CHAPTER NINETEEN

Whipping my head from left to right, I searched for Max, Juni, and Deyo. I was still in Danara's kitchen, but something was off. Except for the figure dressed in a cloak and hood, I was all alone.

The fire in the pit and stove had gone out, and the temperature in the room around me had dropped significantly. I couldn't detect a light, but it wasn't dark either because of a bluish glow that had to come from somewhere.

The hooded figure had released my arm, and I tried to back away from him, but my movement seemed sluggish as if I were under water. It seemed fitting in combination with my surroundings, which made me feel as if I had gotten myself stranded on the bottom of the ocean. Although this could also have something to do with my inability to take a breath.

"Welcome," the figure said. I hadn't thought it to be possible, but the hooded figure's voice sounded even more menacing than Danara's. If I hadn't been standing still already, I would have frozen on the spot. "Finally, we get a chance to meet."

I had to work my throat to swallow before I was able to force any words out.

"You're...Jasper." His mere name had been a source of fear to the people of Ora. Deyo had almost jumped out of his skin after I had mentioned the name. As I stood in his presence, that notion didn't seem as foreign to me anymore. His entire being turned my body into a trembling mess, and I was about one second away of cowering down on the floor into a fetal position.

"I can only imagine what Maximus has told you about me," Jasper said, "but I can assure you that they are all lies."

I snorted out half a laugh that was accompanied by a strange sound that bordered on hysteria, and I quickly clamped my mouth shut. Just being in Jasper's presence would convince anyone that this guy was bad news. "Now, now, don't be such a hasty judge. We've only just met."

To his credit, he seemed to make an effort to sound less like an evil menace bent on letting the realms of existence fall.

"What do you what?" To my surprise, there was only the slightest of quivers in my voice.

"I can appreciate you taking the direct approach," he said with a chuckle, "although, I must say, I hadn't expected it." Because of the cloak, I couldn't see his feet move as he stepped out of the pit. Fortunately, he kept his distance as he circled around me. Wanting to keep him in my sight, I slowly turned on the spot along with him. "I had you more for the type to heel and sit as you are told," he added.

"You don't know anything about me," I said, feeling annoyed at the dog reference. Jasper might be some all-powerful alien who had separated me from my friends and sucked me into this blueish realm, but that didn't mean I was going to let him insult me. I cocked my head in an attempt to get a glimpse of his face, but with his hood pulled low it was as if looking at a faceless Inanis.

"I know everything there is to know about you," he said in a sharp tone, "and unlike some, I am not going to lie about it."

As fast as my surroundings had changed before leaving me alone with Jasper in an empty blue-lit kitchen, this time everything changed.

The kitchen was gone; no more counters, no more firepit. Instead, I was surrounded by walls—buildings in fact. A dumpster stood to my left, blocking my view of the street and the evening traffic. I stopped breathing as I realized that I wasn't just back on Earth, but I was back in that alley on that fateful night. My brain tried to tell me that this wasn't possible. Max had said to me that we hadn't traveled through time. Although that didn't mean that we couldn't or that Jasper couldn't.

Hands grabbed me from behind, holding me tight and pinning my arms to my body. I could feel the warm breath as it grazed my skin and closing my eyes shut, I screamed.

"Now, now, not so dramatic," Jasper said. His voice sounded as if it originated from inside my own head and it instantly cut off my scream. I couldn't feel the hands that had been wrapped around me only moments ago, but that didn't stop me from jerking out of the grasp that truly wasn't there anymore. Stumbling, I fell to my knees.

Tears blurred my vision as I opened my eyes, but I could tell that I wasn't in the alley anymore. Jasper had brought me back to the empty kitchen with its bluish light. My impaired vision made him look massive as his form moved closer. I wanted to shrink away, but Jasper wouldn't let me. He grabbed my arm and pulled me to my feet.

"Let me go," I said as I struggled against his grip, but Jasper wasn't going to relent. He pulled me close to him and just as I had with the Inanis, I could feel the cold of his touch penetrate my bones.

"Now," he said, elongating the word, "we can begin." Breathing heavily and still reeling from the experience of being back in that alley, I shut my eyes. I just wanted this to be over with. Jasper was too strong for me to do anything, and by not resisting this might all end fast. "Just breathe. I need you to be with me on this."

His words washed over me in a wave of calm, and

for a second, I could hear Max counting like he had in that field, helping to sooth my nerves. The grip on my arm disappeared, and for a fleeting moment I thought that it was over, but as I opened my eyes, he was there again.

Jasper stood before me with his arms spread as if he wanted to show me something. His head hung low, so I still couldn't see his face, which made me wonder what he was hiding. *Did he look like one of the Inanis underneath that hood?*

As he took a step back, I realized what it was that he wanted to show me. I couldn't even begin to fathom how Jasper did what he did. It wasn't as if I had an explanation of how Max had gotten me here in the first place or that I could pretend that I knew how these stones that Max wielded worked. Perhaps that was the reason that I didn't question the changes that in other circumstances would have caused me to doubt my sanity.

As before, the kitchen was gone, but I hadn't returned to the alley either. This place was something new, and unlike anything I had ever seen.

"I thought you might like to know the truth," Jasper said. "The truth Max was never going to tell you."

I heard Jasper's words. It was hard not to with that booming voice of his, but that wasn't what drew my attention. I might have been frightened out of my mind, but I wasn't that far gone that I couldn't tell the difference between right and wrong. Jasper had done nothing but bring misery to the people of Ora, and the only thing Max had wanted to do was to try and prevent it and protect his friends.

That notion made it easy to ignore Jasper's words. What wasn't easy, was to ignore the wonder of what I was seeing before me.

"What is this place?"

Jasper just stood there watching me as if he deliberately gave me time to take it all in. The room that lay before me must have been as big as a football field, but instead of green grass, the space was filled with sunbeds. Thousands of beds stood in long rows that reached as far as my eyes could see. They were the kind of sunbeds you'd find at the side of a pool, although these things looked a hell of a lot more comfortable.

It seemed that I wasn't the only one who thought that, because every last one of them was occupied. Pale-looking figures that had some resemblance to a human form, but clearly weren't, remained unmoving as I stood there watching them. Their skin looked paper thin and nearly see-through, giving me a clear idea of what their bone structure must be underneath it. Their faces were covered by masks with wires running to various machines surrounding the sunbeds, and tubes sat stuck down their throats. I couldn't detect any visual markers to discern a difference in sex despite the fact that they were all naked. These folks were definitely alien, even though the lifeforms before me looked sick and fragile and they reminded me of the elderly back at the retirement home.

"Welcome to Denuo," Jasper said. I flinched at his booming voice echoing in this massive room. He was still standing close by, and I kept my eyes diverted from him. Instead, I half turned and noticed a window. The window took up the entire length of this strange place, and the view was surreal. Despite the unfamiliar landscape, I instantly knew where I was.

It was Max himself who had made the dismissive comment about his home, and at the time I hadn't thought much of it, but as I stared at the sorrowful landscape that stretched as far as the eye could see, his words didn't seem that far out of place. Max had told me that he came from a place so bland that it looked like cream cheese spread on toast and in fact the empty plains that lay before me looked exactly like that.

"This is Max's home planet," I said in a whisper and more to myself than to the evil menace that had brought me here.

"It seems that you are not as dense as you look," Jasper said. "Now, let's get to business."

I heard him move behind me, but I was too afraid to turn and face him.

"Why did you bring me here?"

"Because I need your help." Jasper sounded calm and collected as if he had everything under control. That was a whole lot more than that I could say for myself.

"My help?" My voice quavered, and even though I

wanted to ask what the hell he was talking about, I couldn't get the words past my lips.

"This," he said with a long hissing sound, elongating the word as if he was waiting for me to turn. I closed my eyes for a second, blocking the empty stretch of land that for all I knew made up the entire surface of this planet and took a deep breath. I wasn't going to be able to run from this, just like I hadn't been able to outrun Max in that dessert. I had no choice but to listen to what Jasper had to say.

Balling my fists, I slowly turned around. As I faced Jasper, he made this soft humming sound, and even though I still couldn't see his face, I had the feeling that he was laughing at me.

"As I was beginning to say," he said, "this is the place Max abandoned a long time ago. These people needed him, and he just left them here to rot."

I wouldn't have described the alien figures lying on sunbeds as being in a state of decay, but they didn't look healthy either. The uneasiness that came with Jasper's accusation caused my feet to shift, and my sneakers squeaked on the slick floor. I had no intention of believing anything Jasper told me, but that didn't stop me from feeling sorry for these people. All I knew was that there had to be a different reason for them to be in this state. Max would not have left them like this if he'd had any choice.

"I see the doubt on your face, but soon you will learn," Jasper continued. "Once this world was thriving, but now look at them. They're just lying there waiting to die."

Jasper moved around me, and as he headed over to the first sunbed, I grimaced at the oily substance on the floor left behind by his cloak.

Everything looked so real, but I didn't think it possible for us to have traveled to another planet —*could it?* For one, I hadn't seen Jasper wield any stones and besides, Max had told me the gemstones weren't used for travel between planets.

Jasper let his black-clad hand run over one of the sleeping aliens. With his attention elsewhere, I turned around to get a better grasp of my surroundings. To my left, at the far end, I could make out what looked like a door, which might be a way out. I had a feeling I'd be able to outrun Jasper, but then what? Turning to the large window, I stared out at what only could be called a wasteland.

"Maximus did this," Jasper said. The shock of his words made me forget about the door and the waste-land behind me as I turned to face Jasper.

"What?" I croaked. My mouth had gone dry, and my throat refused to work as I tried to swallow.

"He did this. He left our people in ruin, and all I'm trying to do is to get back to them," Jasper said. "Bring Juni to me and help me save my people. Help me get back to them."

To his credit, he sounded convincing. Unfortunately for Jasper, his appearance and the lack of an actual face to look at as he spoke didn't much help his cause. He must have recognized the doubt from my expression, because he added, "If you help me align the stones, I will get you home, and you will never have to set foot in one of the realms again."

I wasn't sure what he was playing at; he must've known that Max would've told me that the realms would fall if Max weren't the one to align the stones. I sure as hell wasn't going to hand Juni over to him. *How dumb did he think I was?*

Straitening my shoulders in an attempt to add some resolve to my answer, I said, "No." My reply held a vote of confidence even though I didn't feel it myself.

For the longest time, Jasper didn't do or say anything. He just stared at me. His lack of eyes hidden by the hood helped to not divert my gaze, but it didn't take long for my nerves to wreak havoc inside me. Still, I wasn't going to give into him that easily. I clamped my jaw shut to keep my teeth from chattering out of fear and crossed my arms over my chest to hold my ground.

"You are willing to sacrifice these people," he said. "You can let them die just like that?" In a moment of weakness, I let my eyes divert to the rows of fragile looking aliens hooked up to all kinds of machines. As I turned back to Jasper, he added, "Their deaths will be on you."

I had no reason to believe anything that Jasper said although I could tell that something was seriously wrong with this world. Still, even if he were telling me the truth and all these aliens were doomed because of something Max had done, I had the people of Ora to consider. They had invited me into their home with open arms, and after the Inanis had taken us, Moira and Cyril had come to our aid. I had promised Lana to look after Juni. I couldn't just ignore all that just because Jasper, who was the cause of all the bad stuff that had happened these pasts few days, wanted to save a race of aliens that I knew nothing about. Despite my resolve, I feared I was about to let them all down.

Perhaps he had grown tired of waiting for my reply when Jasper approached me with large strides. Instantly, my eyes searched out the door on the far side of the room, but it wasn't any use. I couldn't move.

Grabbing my arm, he said, "Then I must find another way to convince you to set me free."

CHAPTER TWENTY

As soon as I felt Jasper's cold touch, it disappeared along with the alien world that had surrounded me. Like it had before, everything shifted and once again, I found myself standing in a dark alley.

"Perhaps this will help you change your mind." I could barely hear Jasper's voice, and as I looked around, he was nowhere to be seen. That didn't stop him from adding, "Just call my name if you change your mind."

Like before, I knew that on some intellectual level this had to be an illusion. Somehow Jasper had gotten inside my head, making me see the things he wanted me to see. Taking me back to a moment in time that I had worked so hard to forget was probably some cruel last attempt to convince me to help him.

The knowledge wasn't enough to stop my racing heart. This was too much. I couldn't go through this again. At the sight of the wet concrete ground and the bricks that made up the tall buildings enclosing me in the alley, images of what I'd worked so hard to forget along with the memories that I'd lost on that fateful night rushed back into the forefront of my mind. Hands grabbing me, pulling me into the dark, the taste of metal in my mouth. It was happening all over again. A harsh voice whispered near my ear, and the warm breath that grazed my skin spiraled my fear out of control so much that I didn't even register his words.

I never carried a purse, and except for my phone tucked into the front pocket of my jeans and a wallet in the back, I had nothing on me. *Why didn't he just take them?* The thought resonated as I was dragged further down a narrow alley.

"Just take it," I vaguely remembered shouting before his hand had clamped down on my mouth, but he didn't seem to hear me, or perhaps he hadn't cared. Tears ran down my face while I tried to make sense of what was going on. It wasn't that hard to conceive that this wasn't just another robbery, and the thought nearly stopped my heart.

In an act of sheer desperation, I wrenched an arm free and swung it out to clutch at the air. My fingers scraped the rough stone, and I felt the skin break as I hopelessly sought something that would stop him from dragging me further into the depths of the dark alley. Help came in the form of something cold and metallic that felt like a pipe. I grabbed it and managed to stop his progress.

My small victory was short-lived as I felt a blow that knocked the air out of my lungs. I fell to my knees as I gasped for air. As if at some considerable distance, I heard a voice, but it wasn't like the harsh whispered words spoken to me before. This wasn't the voice of my assailant, but more like a god-like voice that sent a chill down my spine.

"It is not that hard, Sam," Jasper said. "Bring Juni to me and help me align the stones and I will make it all go away. If you don't, I will let you relive your greatest fear over and over again."

I felt as if there were two persons residing in me; two versions of me. One who knew what Jasper wanted from me and one who was fighting for her life in some dark alley.

Someone else spoke, and this time it was my assailant's voice again, and while I recognized the anger within it, I couldn't recollect his words.

My life was spinning out of control, and my mind was going along for the ride. Words, sounds, and images collided with each other as if they weren't supposed to exist in the same realm. It was as if two worlds had been stuck into a blender stirring up time and space. *How was this possible?*

My fear of reliving what had happened that night kept me from remembering the details, but I knew the outcome. I couldn't give in to Jasper's demand; too many people were counting on me. All I could think of was to trust myself and let it happen. I had survived once; I could do it again.

"Help me, Sam, and I will make it all stop!"

Jasper's presence inside my head became more persistent, but it didn't matter, because I had made up my mind.

"No," I shouted to emphasize my resolve.

Obscured by darkness and tears, I couldn't see, but my hands roamed across the ground to find something I could defend myself with. Hopefully, someday I could reconcile the stupidity of what I was about to do as my fingers wrapped around a loose brick. My assailant must not have seen because he moved in closer and grabbed a fistful of my shoulder-length hair.

I lashed out, brick in hand, while I screamed like some animal in peril. I felt my blow connect. Unfortunately, I hadn't hit him hard enough, but apparently, I'd antagonized the bastard sufficiently for him to change his mind about dragging me off.

He cursed as he hit me again and again until for some reason, I couldn't feel the pain anymore. I vaguely remember someone shouting in the distance as I stared at the brick still clutched in my hand.

"Sam!" There was urgency in the voice that pulled me out of the dark. The brick wasn't in my hand anymore, but my fist was closed tightly as if my mind still thought the object was there.

"Sam, please," the voice repeated, and I felt grateful that it wasn't the harsh whisper of the man who had attacked me in that alley nor Jasper. I felt comforted by the voice that oddly enough reminded me of Darth Vader. Max was calling out to me.

As if thinking his name alone acted as electricity

jolting me awake, I realized I was back in the kitchen. The original kitchen along with the orange glow of the torches and with Max, Juni, and Deyo standing around me.

I was on my knees before Jasper while he held a tight grip on my wrist. Unsure of how I had ended up here down on the ground, my first instinct was to jerk my arm free from Jasper's grasp. He seemed stunned in the way that he held his hand up and stared at it.

Taking advantage of Jasper's hesitation, I scrambled backward, and it wasn't long until I felt a pair of hands pull me to my feet. Max and Deyo stood by my side while Juni still sat on the counter dangling her feet. Worry stood written across her face and I wondered how long I'd been out of it. *Was there still time to align the stones?* Without warning, Max pulled me into a hug and spoke close to my ear.

"Are you alright?" Not sure if my voice would work, I nodded my head against his shoulder.

"My lord Jasper," Danara said somewhere behind me and I recognized the uncertainty that had so often plagued me in his voice. Something must have happened while I was zoning out. Something that had Danara worried.

"Maximus, we have to hurry," Juni said. Max pushed me at arm's length and stared into my eyes.

"Are you ready for this?" he asked. It seemed a stupid question because it wasn't as if I had much choice. Still, for some reason, I didn't mind. Maybe it was because I had forgotten what touching the stones would do to me; maybe I just wanted this to be over with, or maybe I just didn't want Jasper to have the satisfaction of winning. Not after what he had put me through. Even if there was some distant alien race that needed his help, but if this was the way that he wanted to provide it, then he should probably get his priorities straight. One thing I knew for sure—I could do this.

Without giving it another thought, I grabbed Juni's hand, and a jolt of pain nearly brought me to my knees. I wasn't sure how but somehow managed to keep to my feet. It might have been because of Max's body pinned against mine for support, but I couldn't be sure. I couldn't be sure of anything anymore. Not of Danara's voice too close for comfort as he threatened us. He could either have been inside the kitchen or on the other side of the universe; I couldn't tell. The only thing I was aware of was the pain that ran through my body. My fingers felt as if they were the focal point as electricity ran from one arm through my shoulders down the other arm, and I tightened my grip.

The instant my fingers had touched Juni's skin, my eyes had slammed shut, and it seemed my senses had turned upside down. I couldn't tell what was left or right or if my grip was crushing Juni's hand. She didn't cry out, though. From somewhere far away, Max's voice penetrated my consciousness.

"You are too late."

Pain burst through my chest as I registered the words. *Had I failed? Had it all been for nothing?* It couldn't be. I needed to go home, to tell my mom that I was okay and make sure that she hadn't called the cops. *This couldn't be it, could it?*

Seconds later, the pain was gone. The turmoil inside my head was gone and everything seemed quiet. Max stood next to me with an arm around my waist and a big smile on his face. The arm around my waist turned out to be a good thing because my legs felt as if they weren't working anymore. Juni giggled as Max helped me sit next to her on the kitchen counter. As soon as I was seated, she threw her arms around me and gave me a big hug. Relieved to see she was okay, I didn't even hesitate to return the hug. It was but moments later that I realized that I couldn't feel her body give off the heat like it had before.

"You did it, Sam," Max said, padding my knee.

"So that was it," Deyo said with a note of excitement in his voice. "That was the alignment?"

"That was it," Max replied.

"I can't believe that I just witnessed the alignment," Deyo said. He threw his arms in the air and shouted, "Whoohoo!"

"And while you were holding hands, we were getting rid of the last of the Inanis," Cyril said as he entered the kitchen. Moira sheathed her sword as she followed. None of them seemed worried by either Jasper or Danara still being around. I couldn't say the same for myself.

"Where is he?" I said, sounding more frantic than I intended to. "Jasper, where is he?" I could feel my heart beating against my chest in a fast rhythm as my eyes roamed the room. Jasper wasn't where I had last seen him, but that didn't mean that he wasn't here anymore. I found Danara sitting on the ground in a corner with his legs pulled up to his chest and his head buried in his arms. Even with his massive arms hiding his face, he couldn't hide the fact that he was sobbing like a small child. There was certainly a thing or two the big man could learn from Juni. Danara's crying didn't ease my mind, though. Jasper was still out there and thinking what he had put me through made it hard to breathe.

"Ssh. It's okay, Sam," Max said, trying to calm me. "He's gone. The alignment has rebuilt the walls separating the realms. Jasper won't be able to breach them now. You're safe."

I knew Max wouldn't lie to me; I just had to convince my body that everything was okay. Fortunately, Max was there to guide me, and I focused on his soothing voice as he counted in a by now familiar rhythm to help me catch my breath.

CHAPTER TWENTY-ONE

I awoke, instantly aware of the comfortable mattress underneath me and the blankets keeping me warm. I snuggled my head into the plush cushion and buried deeper under the sheets. After a long sigh, memories came flooding back to me but without a notion of concern. I was in my bed, nice and comfortable, and it had all been a dream. An intense and elaborate crazy dream, but a dream just the same. It could not have been anything else.

Something snapped as if someone had stepped on a branch, and my eyes shot open. The sound wasn't something that belonged inside my bedroom, and I held my breath as I pushed the blankets away from my face. The smell of burning wood wafted up my nose, and I instantly recognized the snapping sound. I lifted my head and stared at the flames rising inside the small fireplace. I blinked, unsure of myself, although I was pretty sure that my apartment didn't have a fireplace in any of its rooms.

For the briefest of moments, I'd been so sure that it was all a dream, but as I gazed across the tiny room, it was clear that I wasn't home. A small rug covered the wooden floor, and a dresser stood next to the door. A rocking chair stood at the foot of the bed close to a window, and if it weren't for the drapes, I was sure I'd be staring at a sky without a sun.

This couldn't be Danara's castle, could it? This cozy room didn't resemble anything of the coldness within Danara's home, and the drawings that hung on the walls made me think of Juni. To my relief, these drawings didn't hold any of the scary creatures the young child had sketched before. These were drawings of green pastures and fluffy white animals.

The room reminded me of Oman's home, warm and cozy. I stretched my limbs, feeling oddly relaxed despite the unfamiliar surroundings. Pulling down the covers, I realized I was wearing an oversized garment that looked like a pajama dress. Staring at the nightclothes for a second, I found no recollection of how I'd gotten into them, but then I didn't even know how I got here or where I was, and I figured those were the more urgent questions. I swung my feet over the side of the bed and planted them on my sneakers. Picking up one of my shoes, I half expected to find a barrel of sand inside them, but they looked as if someone had cleaned them.

The rest of my clothes lay neatly folded on the top of the dresser. I hesitated, unsure if I wanted to get dressed as I felt reluctant to face reality. I tried to remember what had happened, but I could only come up with blacking out inside the kitchen with Danara's threatening voice in my ears.

Something must've happened, because how could I otherwise be here? I just hoped here was Oman's home, although I had a hard time believing that. The last I'd seen of Oman's house was the night the Inanis had come for us, and I vividly remembered the fires eating away at the structure.

Behind the closed door, I heard the sound of laughter, and I recognized Juni. My heart rate sped up at the joyous giggle coming from the little girl.

"I'll be right back." I heard her say before a door slammed shut. Back in Danara's kitchen, Max had told me that the alignment had fixed the walls separating the realms. By my understanding, the alignment had banished Jasper and would keep him from coming to Ora, so things must've gone all right. Besides Juni sounded happy, but I figured there was only one way to be sure and that was to get dressed and get out there.

My running pants and shirt were clean and smelled great as I pulled them on. Unfortunately, the tears over my knees would render the pants useless once I got home. I paused at the thought of home. *Could this be the day that Max finally took me back?* After some quick calculations inside my head, I counted three nights, and it had been Thursday when we left, so with any luck, it'd be Sunday today, and I would only have missed one day at work. I could probably figure out some excuse to tell Trish that wouldn't get me fired. I'd have to do some explaining to Mom, though.

A flood of excitement filled me as I thought of finally going home, but as I glanced into a small mirror that hung on the wall, what was revealed banished any thoughts of going or not going home. Staring at myself for the longest time, I moved closer to my reflection and blinked. It felt as if I were staring into the eyes of the stranger. Instead of the pale gray eyes that would've been familiar to me, a pair of deep blue eyes reflected back at me. The same color blue that I'd seen in Juni's and Max's eyes.

I squeezed my eyes shut and shook my head. Inhaling deeply, I blew out a long breath before I opened my eyes again. They were still the same deep blue. This wasn't good. *Was this the reason Danara had seemed so surprised and why Deyo had acted so nervous around me before?* I couldn't show up back home with different color eyes, and I didn't think explaining them away as contacts would work. *What would my mom say?*

The sound of Max's voice on the other side of the door made me think of the old Max. *His eyes weren't blue then, right? Or had they been?*

Taking a deep breath, I forced myself not to over-react. Besides, I shouldn't doubt myself. The old Max's eyes had never been blue, I knew that—back home Max had dark brown eyes. Eyes changing colors might just be a thing that came with being on this planet. I would just have to ask Max; he would know.

It wasn't as if Max had explained that much about this place, but perhaps now that the tides had changed and the alignment lay behind us, he'd be more forthcoming. I also needed to talk to Max about the things Jasper had shown me. *Was that really Max's home world and had he left his people there to die?* The idea that Max would deliberately do anything to hurt someone seemed ridiculous, but the more I thought about that place the more it felt as if something were off.

A shiver ran through me as the memory of being in that dark alley hit me by surprise. I had fought so hard to keep those memories at bay. Instead of facing what had happened, I wanted to run away from it—all of it. *I ran away from my home, my job, even my friends, and for what?* I wanted to hate Jasper for what he had put me through and even though I didn't feel much love for the menacing figure, I couldn't help but feel a strange sense of gratitude. At least I now knew that I had tried to fight. I hadn't let it happen like some lamb being dragged off to the slaughter. I had fought my attacker and I had survived. That must count for something.

I straightened in front of the mirror and made a decision. I wasn't going to wait for Max to explain. I was going to demand it. Determined, I headed for the door and eased it open. A hushed voice reached me from the other room.

"I don't understand. Is she like Juni?" I recognized Lana's voice, and even though she spoke in a whisper,

I had no trouble understanding the words. She could not have been far away from where I stood.

The determination I'd felt only moments before evaporated, and I couldn't decipher why. I hardly knew the woman, and considering how I'd just showed up on their doorstep with Max gave her more than enough reason to question me. Not to mention the fact that the Inanis had attacked their village soon after I'd appeared. Besides, I was glad to hear her voice, which meant that she had survived the Inanis attack.

"No, she's not like Juni," Max replied. "She's...different." A bit baffled and somewhat intrigued by his answer, I kept silent and listened.

"Don't play me for a fool, Maximus," Lana said. "She has the sapphire eyes, and if you need us to put her up, you know we'll help. She's already proven that we can trust her, but I'd still like to know a bit more about her."

My breath got stuck in my throat. *Had Lana said, "put her up?" As in, providing a place to live?* I couldn't stay here. I needed to go home.

My pulse started to race, and I was about to burst into the room when Max said, "No, she doesn't need a place to stay. I'm pretty sure I can get her home." Max chuckled before he added, "To be honest, Lana, I'm still trying to figure this one out myself."

I slowly blew out a long breath. The "pretty" part didn't sound that convincing, but at least Max didn't intend to leave me behind.

"What do you mean?" Lana asked.

"Well, for one, she wasn't supposed to be here,

although I'm grateful that she was because her being here kept Danara from aligning Jasper's stone with Juni. If that had happened..."

Max's voice broke a little at the end, and Lana finished his sentence for him. "The realms of existence would have fallen."

My face flushed, and I could feel the heat trail down my neck. *Did they really mean that? I hadn't done anything special, had I?* Memories of this crazy adventure raced across my mind, but all that really seemed to resonate was me freaking out most of the time.

"Secondly," Max continued, "I'm not sure why the stones connected with her. There are things I don't understand or know about her, but I have to find out. I mean..."

Max paused and as the moment stretched out, I wished that I could see their faces before he added, "Not just about her, but the how and what, so I can give her an explanation. I owe her at least that much."

I felt touched by the fact that Max seemed to think that he might owe me something, but nothing was further from the truth. He was right about one thing. Even though we had known each other for a little over a year and had shared this crazy adventure together, he didn't know that much about me. Not that there was much to know, and I didn't think my story would help pass the time if we were stuck here indefinitely. I shook my head, unable to allow that thought in just yet. I wanted to go home, and I hadn't lost hope on that.

Not wanting to eavesdrop on the conversation

any longer, I pulled the door open and stepped through. Even though I should've known it to be impossible, I half expected to step into Oman's spacious dining room with its long wooden table and a fire burning in the hearth. Instead, I walked into a space that wasn't even half the size of Oman's dining room.

A small counter stood next to a stove with a fire burning inside on one side of the room. A blanket lay spread before it on the ground. Stacks of papers and crayons lay scattered across the blanket, and I figured Juni must've used the spot for her coloring, although I couldn't detect the girl inside the tiny space, even though I'd heard her before.

Stairs lead up to the first floor, and through a window next to the front door, I could see activity on the square along with the makeshift platform where the people of the village had greeted us after we first showed up.

I spotted Lana and Max sitting at a table in the middle of the room. Lana had her hand wrapped around Max's as they sat across from each other. It felt as if I'd interrupted a personal moment, which from my eavesdropping, I knew I had. Feeling embarrassed about my intrusion, I looked away.

"Ah, look who's up," Max said in that warm voice of his.

Hesitantly, I returned my gaze to Lana and Max. Lana had pulled her hand from Max's, and both of them looked at me curiously.

"What?" I asked. Lana shook her head apologetically as she stood and held out her hand. She gestured at an empty chair.

"Please come join us," she said. "Are you hungry? Can I get you anything?"

I shook my head as I shuffled in the direction of the chair.

"No, thank you. I'm fine."

"How are you feeling?" Max asked. I paused a moment as if to take stock of my own body before I sat down. "Okay, I guess. What happened?"

Max smiled, but it didn't reach his eyes. Sadness lingered in his eyes, and it wasn't hard to guess why.

"The Sapphire Twins are aligned," he said. "Mission accomplished." His words might have stated the accomplishment, but his tone spoke of loss.

Voices came from outside as people milled about the small stalls trading produce, and it appeared to be business as usual. We definitely weren't in Oman's home, and even though Max's remark about aligning the stones should've lifted my spirit, I didn't feel like cheering.

Returning my attention to the table, I dug a fingertip into an indentation on the tabletop. I kept my eyes downcast as I opened my mouth. "Is that...I mean...can we go home now?" Before he could answer, the front door swung open, and Juni rushed inside.

"Sam!" she exclaimed the moment she saw me. Without hesitation, she ran toward me and clambered onto my lap. I froze as tiny fingers connected with the skin on my neck, expecting a sharp pain from her touch. Max was in the room, and I felt sure he had the sapphire tucked somewhere safe. Not eager to relive the experience of what had happened in Danara's kitchen, I braced myself, ready to push Juni away. Fortunately, nothing happened, and after a moment of realization, I returned Juni's hug.

Juni twisted in my lap until she faced the others sitting at the table. Her sheer presence lifted the awkward tension that had lingered inside the room ever since I'd entered, and it seemed Lana's mood lifted in Juni's presence.

"Good, you're still here," Cyril said from the open doorway. Moira followed him inside and closed the door behind her. Max stood and greeted Cyril with the familiar arm shake and a hug before he turned to Moira. The new arrivals greeted Lana and, to my surprise, turned their attention to me after.

Cyril offered me his arm, and, half standing, holding Juni in my arms, I awkwardly returned the gesture. Moira waved for me to sit before patting me on the shoulder and taking a seat next to me. Both her forearms were wrapped in bandages, and I figured they were the reason she'd skipped the usual way of greeting.

"You could have warned us that you changed the rules on us," Cyril said, sitting down at the table, "especially if it's with a gorgeous but strange creature like Sam over there."

Despite his weird choice of words, I felt a blush creep up my cheeks. Cyril noticed and winked with a mischievous glint in his eyes. Feeling a bit uncomfortable, I shifted in my seat and pretended my attention had been on Juni.

"I have a feeling Maximus wasn't completely aware of that either," Moira said. All eyes strayed to Max, but except for a warm smile and a look of satisfaction on his face, he didn't reveal anything. Well, not to the others anyway. Apparently, Lana and I were the only ones who knew that me being a conduit in performing the alignment had come completely out of the blue. Max hadn't even intended for me to be here, but in the end, it seemed to have worked out.

"Since we're all here, I think I'll start breakfast," Lana said as she stood. She turned to look at me as she added, "I know you've said you weren't hungry, but you must be. I'll fix something for all of us."

I was about to protest as my stomach rumbled, and Juni chuckled.

"I guess you're right," I muttered. "How long was I out for anyway?"

With a thoughtful expression, Max said, "Well, you missed breakfast yesterday, and lunch, and dinner for that matter." My mouth dropped open, unsure how to take that. It must've been around midnight when Max performed the alignment. It had to be because the alignment was supposed to happen before the end of the day so...in Earth terms that would count for what...over thirty hours. I didn't think I'd ever been asleep for that long.

"What the hell happened?" It wasn't as if I didn't remember, and although everything got a little fuzzy after Jasper had disappeared, I felt an urge to understand.

Max shrugged as if it hadn't been anything substantial. "Moira and Cyril kept the Inanis away long enough for us to align the stones," he said as nodded in Cyril's and Moira's direction. "Once the stones were aligned, Jasper couldn't cross over."

"You have to admit I displayed some excellent moves. I mean, did you see me take the head off that one Inanis that—" Cyril said as he mimicked holding a sword.

"You showed up late," Max chimed in before Cyril could finish his story.

Cyril shrugged and pointed a finger at Moira.

"You said, give me five minutes. She made me lose count." Moira raised an eyebrow and shot Cyril an incredulous look but didn't say anything.

I should have been amused by their banter, but instead, I shook my head. That couldn't be right.

"But...he was...he..." I said and hesitated. I could feel my heart rate pick up as I searched Max's face. "He took me...and he...he was right there." Words to describe what had happened in that kitchen failed me.

"What you witnessed was a manifestation of him. Not strong enough to fully cross over, but powerful enough to reach out and touch your mind," Max said without taking his eyes off me. "But he underestimated you, and you were able to fight him off." It wasn't hard to see that Max was sincere, but I doubted that even he knew of what apparently had happened inside my head.

"You were victorious, worthy of an Ora guard," Cyril said with a grin. I shot him a weak smile before my gaze returned to the tabletop. It shouldn't have come as a surprise that Jasper was messing with my head. I had already sort of guessed that we hadn't actually traveled to an alien planet. Still, he had used my own memories, my own fears against me. The idea of him doing that again terrified me, and I shivered.

"Sam," Juni said. Her voice pulled me out of my thoughts and I met her big blue eyes. I managed to smile at her and brushed a lock of curls away from her face. Clearing my throat, I ignored the worried glances around me and asked, "So, what happened after? I mean, the last thing I remember was that kitchen." As I thought of that kitchen, I suddenly realized that I was missing someone. "Where's Deyo? Is he alright?"

"You fell asleep," Juni said and turned her head to face me. "Maximus had to carry you all the way back, and then we laid you in my bed."

"Your encounter with Jasper along with everything else that had happened these past few days had left you exhausted," Max said. "You needed the rest."

"After we returned, Deyo went in search of his family. I'm sure we'll see him soon," Cyril added.

"I hope they're okay," I murmured as I looked at the girl sitting in my lap. I caught her beaming up at me, and I smiled at her. "Thank you for letting me sleep in your room."

"You're welcome."

"And I have to say it's a very pretty room."

A sense of pride fell over the young girl as she said, "Lana helped me decorate."

"Juni, can you come help me over here, please," Lana said from where she stood at the small counter next to the stove. "I can barely walk with all your drawings lying around."

From the look of it, Lana did not have any problems maneuvering around the blanket and the spread-out papers, but maybe she thought the grown-ups needed a moment in private. Juni obliged and, without a hitch, slid down from my lap, and I watched her skip toward Lana.

I raised an eyebrow and eyed Max thoughtfully.

"You carried me all the way back?"

"You would have liked that, wouldn't you?" Cyril said with a chuckle. My face turned red, and I averted my eyes back to the tabletop.

"It was more like a joint effort," Max replied.

"I'd say," Cyril chimed in. "You might look like a tiny thing, but you get heavy after a while."

"We used a stretcher," Max added to clarify. "Cyril was gracious enough to help, although we had to stop several times."

"It just seemed unfair that we had to do all the heavy lifting," Cyril said, "and Moira only came along for the stroll." He threw his hands up and waved. "That ought to teach you about playing around with the Inanis."

A thump underneath the table interrupted Cyril's laughter.

"Hey," he said and glared at Moira.

The warrior woman grinned, and her eyes held mischief before she shot me a smile. She seemed even more relaxed than she had at Oman's table. The fact that the alignment had been successful appeared to have taken years off her demeanor.

I shivered at Cyril's mention of the Inanis, and I shook my head as once again, my mind veered to what had happened after we had entered Danara's kitchen. I had no idea how much time had passed after Jasper had grabbed me, or what had happened while my mind was elsewhere. I wondered if Max would ever tell me. I could try to ask Moira or Cyril, but I doubted they'd be any more forthcoming than Max would be. These weren't the kind of people who boasted about their success, especially not when it had come with such a great loss. So many answers still eluded me. I didn't know where to start.

I glanced around the room before my attention shifted toward the window. Two men carrying a heavy load just passed by. They were moving planks, and I figured that the reconstruction of the village had started. The sight of them turned my thoughts to Cora and Oman. Their home had been destroyed, and both of them were gone, but it wasn't sorrow that washed over me.

For a few hours, they had shown me a glimpse of what it meant to be surrounded by friends and family. Without apparent blood relations, these people held a bond that I'd never witnessed. Even now, after they had suffered a great loss with Cora and Oman, they were all bound together.

I wasn't sure if I should bring up Oman or Cora. It seemed as if these people didn't mourn their dead as we did back home. Cyril's words came back to me from when that guard had died after standing up against the Anguis. "To the fallen," he'd said. "May they live in our memories—always." After that, it seemed to have been business as usual. That didn't mean that they didn't mourn in their own way, because I could see their loss written across their faces, but I didn't think it was something they'd share openly. It was probably best to ask Max after we got home.

"So now what?" I hadn't intended for my voice to sound so defeated, but for some reason it did.

"We'll go home after breakfast," Max said.

His words stirred some conflicting emotions. A moment ago, I'd been asking about going home, but now the notion felt somewhat alien to me. It wasn't that I didn't want to go home, but I couldn't shake this strange sensation that something was about to come to an end. As if leaving this place wouldn't just pull me away from here but something else, too, and it wouldn't be real anymore. I shook my head and pinched the bridge of my nose, hoping to clear my thoughts.

"Don't worry about them," Max said as he waved a hand at Cyril and Moira. His mouth morphed into a cheeky grin as he added, "With Juni in charge, they'll be okay." His comment was meant to be uplifting, but I could sense his sincerity.

I met Max's gaze, not sure if that were actually what I was worried about. *Did I worry about these people or the fact that this strange experience would become some distant memory never to be shared? How would this affect me after I got home?*

"Bye, Sam. Bye, Maximus," Juni said she stood in the doorway and waved. Lana, who stood behind her, also raised a hand as Max and I waved back before making our way across a small square. In an atmosphere that seemed so close to that of the previous meal we had shared, the six of us had enjoyed breakfast at Lana's tiny table. Juni had sat in my lap while she'd asked all sorts of questions, and this time, I didn't feel the need to withhold things of where I was from. She now knew that pizza was my favorite food in the whole wide world, and after explaining what it was, Juni had Lana promise her to make it for her. I'd also told her about this wicked witch named Trish who walked on stilts and tried to boss me around. Juni had suggested that I should chop down those stilts with an ax, and I'd told her that I'd take her suggestion into serious consideration. It appeared I'd earned their trust, and it had felt good.

Cyril and Moira had left before we had. Apparently, there was still lots to do as they, too, helped in rebuilding the village. Cyril had hinted about seeing me again soon, but I'd kept my reply evasive. Even though I'd enjoyed spending time with these people, I hadn't forgotten all that had transpired. Thinking about it sent a tremor through my body, and I had to force myself to keep the thoughts at bay.

From what I'd glimpsed through the window, I'd been partially right; only some of the stalls were open, but they weren't selling anything. The folks manning the stalls handed out food and drinks for the villagers who were hard at work. Several houses had been destroyed by the fires that had raged during the Inanis attack, and in a combined effort, the villagers had started rebuilding their homes.

Except for the small group of Max's closest friends, I hadn't actually met any of the villagers, and I didn't know of the losses they had suffered. *How many of them were taken by the Inanis? How many had died?*

However, the depressing thoughts didn't measure up to the determination I witnessed around me. The faces I came across as we walked to the other side of the square held a strength that told me this village would survive, no matter the cost.

Max lead me down the route that we had taken on the day we'd arrived. Well, at least we exited the square along the same narrow street that had led us there. Swift turns down narrow streets and alleys quickly followed, and it wasn't long after that I had no idea where I was.

The sound of a deep menacing voice made my blood run cold, and I froze on the spot. Max, who walked by my side, must have missed me, and a few steps later, he glanced back at me over his shoulder. He lifted an eyebrow, seemingly confused about my abrupt stop. He must have noticed the blood drain from my face as his confusion turned to worry.

"Sam?" he said as he stepped closer. Ignoring Max, I focused on the voice as I heard it say, "I think it's better if I hold the ladder for you."

I took a few steps back and turned my head to look down a narrow alleyway, and my mouth fell open.

"You're just afraid of heights," Deyo said as he hurried up the ladder. "Don't deny it."

Deyo carried a heavy load that he handed to another man hanging out of a second-story window.

It wasn't Deyo who had me staring in shock. It was the man standing on the ground holding the ladder who had caused fear to build inside me. Unable to speak, I pointed a finger at Danara as he patiently waited for Deyo to climb down the ladder. Following my gesture, Max turned to see.

"Ah, yes, that might need an explanation," he said as he scratched the back of his head. "It turned out Jasper did have some sort of a hold on Danara, and it broke once the stones were aligned again."

I managed to lower my arm and open my mouth, but nothing came out. Unconsciously, my fingers graced down my throat, and I swallowed hard as I remember the way Danara had held me down.

"And what, he said he was sorry and decided to help?" An edge of bitterness resonated in my voice that couldn't be denied. Max, not one to miss such things, placed a hand on my shoulder.

"No, he can't remember," Max said in a soothing tone. "It was actually Deyo's idea to bring them back."

As if he sensed us talking about him, Deyo turned and saw us standing at the mouth of the alley. With a smile on his face, he jogged to greet us. He offered a hand to Max and gave it a firm shake.

"Maximus, good to see you."

I was about to raise my hand to greet his, but it seemed Deyo had something else in mind. He threw his arms around my shoulders and pulled me in for a hug. "Hi, Sam, how are you?" He released me, and I nodded.

"Yeah, and I owe a lot of thanks to you," I said. "So thank you for helping me back there, I mean, helping us."

Deyo shook his head. "This is my home and you are the reason Maximus could align the stones..." Deyo must have said something else, but as he spoke, my gaze drifted over his shoulder. Deyo put a hand on my upper arm and squeezed it gently, shifting my attention back to him.

"He didn't know, Sam," Deyo said as if he needed to convince me. "He's a good man and he deserves another chance."

"Why didn't he stay at his castle?"

"We'll go back eventually, but for now, the village needs our help, so here we are," Deyo replied.

Taking a deep breath, I nodded. *If Deyo could get past Danara's indiscretion, then who was I to judge?*

"Oh," I said as a thought occurred to me. "Your family, are they..." I hesitated to finish the sentence, although the sparkle in Deyo's eyes provided an immediate answer.

"They're all fine," he said. "In fact, that's their home we're rebuilding." He half turned, with a pleased look on his face. "Would you like to come see?"

I was about to say yes, if only because of the pride Deyo exuded, but Max interjected. "How about next time?"

"You're going home?" Deyo asked with a hint of disappointment.

Even though Max had promised we were going home, a sudden fear of the answer caused me to leave the answer for Max.

"We are, and I'll see you next season, Deyo."

"You'll come too, right, Sam?" Deyo asked.

My throat felt dry at the unexpected question, and I could feel my heart rate pick up a notch.

"I...eh..." I started to say, but Max rescued me from having to answer.

"I'll see you then," Max said as he winked at the young man. A broad smile lifted on Deyo's face, and I feared Max had left him a message I wasn't ready to face. Before I could refute the gesture, Max tugged on my arm and headed us in the right direction again.

Only a couple yards later, Max stopped and glanced around while he took a deep breath and let his eyes fall on the people hard at work as they rebuilt their homes.

"What do you say? Should we go right now?" he asked as our eyes met.

"What do you mean?" I asked and felt a sudden urge to step closer to Max. The sensation felt like that magnetic pull thingy again that I'd experienced near the clearing right before all of this started. Even if I wanted to, I couldn't step away from him.

"Well the stones are aligned and there is nothing to hold us here anymore," Max said. He fiddled with the chain around his neck and pulled the sapphire stone from where it was hidden behind his breastplate. Wrapping his fingers around the gem, he took my hand with his free one and squeezed.

"Let's go home."

CHAPTER TWENTY-TWO

I kept my eyes closed as I held my head down until I couldn't feel the wind swirling around us, messing up my hair. That tugging feeling that had drawn me to this clearing in the first place relented, and as I sensed the calm settling around us, I opened my eyes.

The only light came from the pendant around Max's neck. The faint blue haze it projected seemed nothing like the bright light the sapphire stone had emitted earlier, but it was enough to recognize the bushes and trees surrounding the small clearing.

"That seemed a little too easy," I said while sneaking a sideways peek at the old stone bird feeder. It was still there, and so was the bench. The ride to Ora had felt so much rougher and had even caused me to blackout. Perhaps it had been the experience brought on by Jasper—transporting me so effortlessly from place to place that I felt reluctant to believe that I was home.

"The alignment makes the trip a lot smoother," Max said as he squeezed my hands, "I probably shouldn't cut it so close leaving next time."

"Ah," I said as I stared down at my hands. I seemed unable to redirect my gaze, and it wasn't because of my own hands. I couldn't stop looking at the hands holding mine. A scar in the form of a jagged diagonal line crossed the back of Max's hand, but it wasn't that either that kept my eyes downcast and unable to face Max. Worn and wrinkled hands that belonged to an old man held mine, and I couldn't help the sinking feeling that settled in my stomach.

It had only been a few days, but somehow it seemed I'd formed a connection with this younger version of Max, a connection I didn't feel sure would continue. The thought was stupid, and the sinking feeling in my stomach transformed into shame. *They were both one and the same person, so why would it matter? It wasn't as if this version of Max was a helpless little old man. He was an alien after all, and who knew how old he really was?*

I bit my lower lip as I forced myself to look up and meet Max's eyes. Dark, soulful eyes instead of the bright blue ones I'd come to be familiar with over the past few days gazed back at me. Deep creases revealed the years of hardship, of which I'd barely faced a glimpse. I would not have recognized him at all if it weren't for the brilliant smile that lit up his face.

"Don't look so worried," Max said.

I shook my head and had to swallow before I could answer. "It's not worrying..." I hesitated because maybe I did feel worried. Only moments ago, I'd been around a young Max, who, for all intents and purposes, resembled a god-like creature that could've stepped out of Greek myth. All my rationalizing didn't conceal the reality I faced.

"I might be an old man here," Max said, not waiting for me to finish my sentence, "but I'm not a fool." He squeezed my hand, and I looked down again before he released it.

"I can't help it, you know. It's weird."

"There is still much you don't understand," Max said, "and you'd be able to accept it better if you'd let me explain. Would you let me do that?" I raised my gaze to meet his but wasn't sure of my answer until I spoke the words aloud.

"I'd like that."

I hadn't thought it possible, but the smile on Max's face grew even wider as he lifted his head to stare up at the stars.

"It seems time is on our side."

Unsure of what he meant by that, I figured that would be one more question I had for him. Max gestured at the opening in the brush cover that would lead us back to what I could only imagine would be my normal kind of civilization.

I looked up at the streetlight that had acted up before and didn't notice anything off. As we stood underneath the now working light on the narrow path that would lead Max back to the retirement home and me in the opposite direction, it seemed as if nothing had changed.

The cool breeze of an early evening tugged at my hair as the stars gazed down upon us. I smiled as I looked up to meet the bright specks that dotted the night sky, relieved to lay my eyes on them once again. Until that moment, it hadn't occurred to me how much I'd missed them, and I couldn't wait for morning to greet the sun.

Glancing down, I expected to see my disheveled clothes, but to my surprise, they looked like they had after I'd put them on before my run. The tears in my running pants and shirt had disappeared.

"How am I going to explain where I've been all this time?" I said, more like a question for myself than for Max as I peered around. The path down to the lake looked deserted under the sporadically positioned streetlights.

"Not at all," Max replied. I stared at him unable to hide the doubt he must have been able to read on my face. "You don't have to look at me like that," he added. "Trust me when I say you have returned in the same moment as when we have left."

I glanced around, and even though everything looked the same as that night before we left, I knew that this path would have looked like that every night.

"Wait a minute," I said as something dawned on me. "Back in Ora before we reached the village, you told we that we hadn't traveled through space nor time, so how could we be back at the same moment we left after all that has happened?"

Slowly, a warm smile crept formed on Max's face,

and he eyed me expectantly as if he wanted me to figure it out for myself.

"Are you telling me this was all a dream?"

Max shook his head.

"It definitely wasn't a dream. What you experienced was very real."

I placed my hands on my hips and narrowed my eyes at him. "Then what?"

"There are no laws that say that something is less of an experience if it is born from your mind's eye. This is just a different real than what you are used to experiencing," Max said, sounding casual. I just glared at him as I tried to comprehend what he was telling me. *Had he just said from your mind's eye?*

"Are you saying that I made all of this up, that I imagined it..." I said as my mind started to trail off. "I'd never come up with a scenario like that...I mean, I've never felt so scared in my life, and you're telling me it was all...I...I..." Words failed me, and I threw up my hands.

Max shook his head as he took my hands in his.

"Like I said this will take some explaining, and you're right. The scenario was mine," Max said, "and I know this is a lot to take in, and I never intended to scare you, but you've fought through it pretty damn well."

"Your scenario!" I said. "How could that be? I mean, when Jasper...when he...he took me to an alien world, and then he put me through..." My voice left me, and I had to take a deep breath before I could continue. "Something that happened to me...something you couldn't have known."

Max's eyes grew wide as he stared at me. He looked unsure of himself, something that didn't suit with this version of Max nor would it have with the younger version.

"Your memories bled through?" he muttered questioningly as if he were talking to himself. He blinked and took a deep breath before he added, "Did he take you to Denuo?" I nodded vigorously at the mention of the planet.

"He did."

"Then you have seen my home world," he said.

"Well, I figured that because of the cream-cheese-on-toast landscape," I said, sounding more agitated than I wanted to feel at this moment. A hint of a smile emphasized the creases around Max's mouth, but vanished as soon as it had appeared after I added, "He said you had left them there to die."

Max's gaze traveled down to our joined hands, and he squeezed mine before he released them.

"Walk with me," he said. Before I could answer, he started walking in the direction of the retirement home, and I followed.

"My kind is not dying," he said as he gave me a sideways glance. "I suppose he took you to the repository."

"That sounds a bit morbid, but if you mean a football stadium filled with people lying around while being hooked up to machines then...yes," I replied.

Max looked up at the sky as the sounds that made

up my world penetrated my ears. The noise of distant traffic traveled on the wind, while that same wind rustled through the trees above my head. Along with the tread of our feet, the sounds were soothing, and I felt their calming effect on my nerves. Despite our current conversation and the weirdness of had happened, the knowledge that I had made it home overwhelmed any kind of tension.

"That is how my kind exists," Max finally said, and as his gaze returned to me, I could see a sense of longing behind his eyes. "Most of us choose to live like that. The machines provide us with an environment that is a lot more satisfying than what our planet can provide. Although it is nowhere near the wonders of what I found here."

"Was that the reason that you came here," I said and hesitated. At the lack of better words, I added, "For the entertainment? Wait...this was—"

"No, absolutely not," he said, cutting me off and sounding appalled. "This is part of our way of life. To sustain the environment, we have to align the stones."

"So, what just happened," I said, pointing a thumb over my shoulder in the direction of the clearing, "that's part of your...existence?"

"It is."

When he didn't add anything else, I considered to push him into telling me, but then he stopped walking. "I had to leave because there is something wrong with my brain and it interferes with...the environment we've created." The pause in his sentence made me think that he was looking for a simple explanation, one that even silly old me would be able to understand. But I had seen my fair share of sci-fi movies, and I felt like I knew what he was talking about.

"So...your brain messed up the programming for the virtual world that you build on your planet?"

Max grinned, and shook his head, although the shaking wasn't an all-out "no" gesture.

"Something like that."

"And that's why you came here," I continued, "to build your own."

"Well, that's one way of explaining it," Max said with a smile as I eyed him thoughtfully.

"So, what about Jasper?" I asked. "What does he want?"

"He just wants to go home."

This time, I shook my head. *So, if this hadn't been a dream and if the experience was real like Max had said, but none of it had happened in the real world, then...Where had I been all this time? Had all of this happened while we were stuck in some mainframe?*

"Wait," I said as something occurred to me and I glanced in the direction of the retirement home. "Back in your room...that was an Inanis. How could that have possibly ended up there? I mean if this is a virtual thing." Half turning, I stared down the path we had come with the clearing sitting somewhere in the dark. Before Max could answer my question, I quickly added, "Before we left...that black cloud...those red-gold flecks...I've seen that..." Managing to rearrange my thoughts, my eyes shot back to Max. "That was him, wasn't it? Trying to come here."

"I did tell you this would be hard to explain," Max said as he shook his head again. There was a note of playfulness in his voice, but his expression remained grim, and I had a feeling that I wasn't going to like what he was going to say next. "My presence here has made the Earth part of the realms. Jasper gets stronger the closer it gets to the alignment, giving him the ability to send in his Inanis or even to manifest himself. If Jasper succeeds in aligning the stones himself, then the realms of existence will fall, and he will be free to cross over to the real world." I read the pain behind his eyes and the regret in his voice as he added, "I am sorry, Sam."

"But Jasper is gone. We beat him," I said, but it sounded more like a plea than a statement. Max sighed as if he grew tired of explaining things. To his defense, I did feel like a five-year-old trying to get all of this.

"He'll be back," Max said. With a smile that I didn't think was entirely appropriate at this time, he added, "And we'll be ready."

"Huh..." I managed to utter before my mouth fell open and stayed like that. Max's smile grew until it reached his eyes before he padded my arm. "Go home, get some rest. We'll figure out the rest later."

As if the word triggered something inside me, I felt a sense of fatigue that was unfamiliar to me. I just nodded my head and kept on wondering if the experience had been real at all. Even though my heart had probably aged a few years and I'd suffered more panic attacks during this experience than I had over the past year, I sensed that I'd feel sad if all of this weren't as real as I'd thought it to be. Besides, deep down I knew it all to be true and not just the ramblings of an old man.

Despite the wonders that I had seen and the new friends I had made, I couldn't ignore the fear, which remained a big part of me, to play up. That part didn't want all of this to be real because I was afraid I wouldn't be able to handle the consequences.

My mind was running havoc, and I didn't think I'd be of much use absorbing any more information tonight. Max was right, I needed to get some rest and take some time to deal with all of this.

"So, I'll meet you here tomorrow at noon?"

"I'll be there, and bring one of those sandwiches from the kitchen," Max said with a grin. I nodded, knowing that I shouldn't bring anything with tuna.

"Will you be okay getting back?" I said and gestured toward the tall building behind Max. He patted my shoulder as he said, "I might be old, but I'm not senile. You go on ahead. Get home."

"Wait," I said in a moment of clarity as I turned back to Max. "Do you even have a place to sleep...I mean..." His room would still be trashed, and I didn't even want to think of the Inanis that was held up in there. Max grinned before he waved me off.

"Trish has assigned me a new room. Don't you worry about it."

I watched him walk up the path at a fast pace and shook my head. The how, the why, and the WTF of it all fought for my attention, but I was tired, and for a brief moment, I felt like getting under the covers to never leave my bedroom again. But as I headed toward the lake, it wasn't long before my step turned into a jog.

As my feet pounded on the gravel path along the water's edge, I felt a sense of freedom, and it wasn't just because my feet had been freed from the agony of sand between my toes. The feeling stayed with me as I bounded up the steps to my apartment building and slipped the key into the lock.

CHAPTER TWENTY-THREE

I found my phone on the coffee table and used it to check the date and time. Max had been right, only forty-five minutes had passed since I'd left the house to go on my initial run. I plopped down on the couch, my mind reeling with everything that had happened. *Had it even happened? It might as well have been a dream. But we both experienced the same thing, right? Or had we? Could Max have slipped me some sort of narcotic or something?* Not that I believed that Max would do that, but maybe it had something to do with pheromones or...*Why was I still doubting all of this?*

I shook my head at the nonsense rumbling inside my brain. Of course, it was real; I was just being my scared old self, preferring to hide from the world instead of living in it. Feeling frustrated, I stood and paced back and forth to the kitchen a few times. As I made another pass for the kitchen, I realized something and stopped. I lifted my hand and watched how a slight tremor affected my fingers. Despite this not being unusual at times that I had gotten myself worked up, somehow something was different. Instead of balling my fist or stuffing my hands into my pockets, I just watched.

The entire time spent in that strange place, I had felt afraid. Ending up in the desert with a younger version of Max looking like some ancient warrior, the Anguis, the attack on the village by the Inanis—all of it. Jasper had even forced me to revisit one of the worst moments of my life, but still, I had managed to get through it.

I turned the palm of my hand to face me, and in my mind, I pictured holding a brick. Closing my eyes, I forced myself to think about that moment a little over two years ago. For all that time, I had never allowed myself to think about what had happened, pushing the memories as far down as I could— blocking them out. Those memories of being dragged down that alley were terrifying and even now a cold shiver ran down my back as I remembered the taste of metal in my mouth, but there was also something else. The desperate need for survival, the will to live and not wanting to give up was also something that resided in those memories. *So, why had I stopped living?*

As I stood there in my kitchen with my eyes closed, I felt a need to talk to someone. Not that I'd be able to confide in someone about anything that had happened tonight. Anyone hearing a story like this might feel the need to call the loony bin to ask them to come pick me up and drag me off in a white jacket.

Heading back to the living room, I sat down on the couch again and found my phone on the coffee table. A small red icon on my phone indicated I had a voice mail message, and I pressed the app. It was a message from my mom from about five minutes ago, and I automatically sighed as I heard her voice. I wondered how one could love a person and be driven to the brink of insanity by them at the same time.

The message itself made me smile, though: "Samantha, I just got back, and I wondered if you might be interested in a meal or something. Call me."

Mom sounded uncharacteristically timid, and I wondered if something had happened on her shopping trip. Unable to sit still, I stood and paced the length of my small apartment from the couch to the kitchen and vice versa.

My body tingled with nervous energy, and I wondered if I should go on another run. The fatigue I felt in my bones halted any further consideration, but the restlessness and the stirring of thoughts stopped me from sitting or even lying down, which my body seemed to prefer.

Unable to shake the need to talk to someone, I glanced at my phone and remembered my conversation with Kay before any of this had happened. A brief flash of being in Danara's chambers crossed my mind. Trapped by the hand he'd wrapped around my throat, I'd thought about my mom and Kay. They were the two people who mattered most to me. At the time, I'd wondered why I wasn't a person who could accept a simple invitation from a friend. Kay had asked me to join her on a hiking trip. I knew it would be good for me to get away from everything and just hang out with a friend, but instead of accepting, I'd told her I'd think about it.

I might not be able to talk about what had happened tonight, but then that hadn't been what had plagued me for years. Maybe that therapist along with Kay had been right all along. With my phone still clutched in my hand, I took in my empty apartment. This shouldn't be all that my life had to offer, and I knew it didn't have to be. There were people in my life —people who cared about me.

On a whim, I switched my phone on and sent Kay a quick message, telling her that I'd go with her. After that, I made a brief phone call and headed for the bathroom.

Hot water pounding on my skin felt rejuvenating and reduced the urge to flop down on the couch even more. It also didn't decrease the nervous tension that kept running through my body. To my relief, my reflection in the mirror told me that my eyes had returned to normal. The deep blue had changed back to gray, and I felt glad I wouldn't have to explain that to anyone.

I pulled on a pair of sweatpants along with a hooded, long-sleeved shirt and ran a brush through my damp hair just as the bell rang.

The smell of molten cheese bread and mushrooms greeted me as I took the box from the pizza delivery guy and paid him. I didn't bother to venture back into my empty apartment, and I pulled the door closed behind me before I hurried up the stairs.

I paused in front of my mom's front door and took a deep breath. Before I could rethink what I was about to do, I knocked. A moment later she opened the door and smiled at the sight of the pizza box.

She was dressed in yoga pants and an oversized sweater, although her hair looked as immaculate as always.

"Hey, Mom," I said, feeling strangely self-conscious. It occurred to me that it had been quite a while since I'd last shown up at her door without being summoned. Sure, she'd called if I wanted to join her for dinner, but Mom hadn't been as adamant in her request like I'd gotten used to. Her coercive nature was one of the reasons of why I'd been avoiding her, and perhaps she'd realized that when I refused to show up.

"Have you...eaten yet?" I asked hesitantly.

Mom shook her head as she eyed the box. "Did you get mushroom?"

I nodded, and I watched the smile on her face grow. "Excellent. Come on in. I'll get napkins," she said as she opened the door for me. "Can I get you anything? A soda or something?"

She was already heading in the direction of the kitchen as I stood in her doorway. A jangle of nerves still ruled over my body, and I wondered if I'd be able to sit on her couch without fidgeting. My cheeks flushed as I imagined all the questions she'd be asking me about being so nervous. Mom was the kind of person that would home in on something like that like a hawk.

"You look tired," she called out from the kitchen. "Must have been a hell of a day. I've seen most of it on TV."

I blew out a breath, and some of the nerves inside me dissipated. I'd almost forgotten about what had happened at the retirement home, and I realized I could blame my aberrant behavior—which she would surely pick up on—on that.

"Now that you mention it, I could use a glass of wine if you have it," I said as I followed her inside and closed the door behind me.

The End.

AFTERWORD

Thank you for picking up this book and I hope you've enjoyed it.

As an independent author, getting a review or rating on any site is a pretty big deal. It helps us to keep the story going. So, if you had fun with this book, I would really appreciate it if you left a review on Amazon or Goodreads

Thanks again.

If you would like to find out more,
visit mvanauthor.com and join the mailing list.
*Don't worry I won't fill up your mailbox, just
keep you updated on new releases.*

ABOUT THE AUTHOR

It feels a bit awkward writing this page. I guess I prefer writing about characters having extraordinary adventures over telling you about little old me. Well, here goes nothing.

I live in the Netherlands, and most of the time, I'm a reader, writer, a sometimes slacker and a music junkie who is weirdly obsessed with Dr. Pepper and Vanilla. Unfortunately, I have no sane explanation for the latter two.

My love for stories originates from watching too many movies and TV series with the word Star in the title. From Wars to Trek, to Gate, I love them all, and one day I hope to reach for those stars.

SOCIAL MEDIA

You can find me on most of the social media platforms although it doesn't come naturally to me. On those places, I'm not that great at creating content, but notifications are on, and if you'd like to reach out, I'd love to hear from you.

facebook.com/mvanauthor

twitter.com/mvanauthor

instagram.com/mvanauthor

www.ingramcontent.com/pod-product-compliance
Lightning Source LLC
Chambersburg PA
CBHW050541260626
47157CB00002B/389